The Society

Larissa Willits

This book was originally published in hardcover by Larissa Willits in 2017.

ISBN-13: 978-1519480620

ISBN-10: 1519480628

For Mom, Dad, Luise, and Tete.

Introduction

We have no wars. We have no famine, no diseases, and no sickness of any kind. If fact, we don't even have arguments. At all.

If there is ever anyone who causes problems to the Society, they are taken to Society's Headquarters where they will talk to you, and make sure you don't do whatever you did again. If you do it again, they take you to the Institution. No one knows what happens at the Institution but everyone knows it can't be any good. If you cause problems a third time, you will be Erased.

This way, no one ever causes problems. Life goes on; the Society remains on top. It stays in order, and well, perfect.

The Society manages all we do. From the day we are born, to the day that we pass. Cameras are on every street corner, in every building, in every room.

Of course, we have our Handlers to make sure that we follow the rules and laws. We have many rules, many laws.

Here are some of them: You may not eat more than the portion given you. You may not participate in any activity that could be dangerous or harmful. You may not stay out past curfew. Nine o'clock. You may not cause harm to yourself or to others. Young ones must refer to older ones as Sir and Ma'am. In the presence of an older one, you may not speak unless spoken too.

Oh! And the critical laws: You may not talk to a boy or girl who is not your gender, that is the same age as you until you reach twenty-one years of age. You may not express interest in anyone not chosen for you in the year you turn eighteen. You may not kiss, hug, or hold hands with anyone that is outside of your family. (You may shake hands)

These rules are strictly enforced. These regulation keep us in line; these rules is our lives.

1

The Perfect Society

The alarm sounds at the same time that the sun peeks over the horizon. No later than seven a.m every morning.

I sit up in bed and look around in my illuminated room, everything is as it always is. My bed sits at the middle of the room, a table and chair are directly in front of the only window, a dresser rests against the back wall, to the right of my bed is the small closet that holds clothes that I wear at school and at home. Right on the top right corner of my room, sits a camera.

I swing my legs to the side of the bed and stand up. I immediately walk to the door and press my palm to the scanner on the wall next to it.

"Good Morning Larina Matthews." The scanner says right before it opens a compartment on the wall that holds two pills and a plastic cup filled with water.

I remove the two pills and take the cup into one hand. I quickly place the pills inside my mouth and swallow it down with the water in the cup. I place the cup back into the compartment and watch as it closes over, completely sealed like it was never there.

The pills are to keep everyone healthy. A healthy life is a better life.

I walk to my closet and throw open the door, I look inside, press my lips together and pull out a gray pair of pants and a gray long sleeved t-shirt. As I turn away from the closet it automatically closes. I leave my room and walk straight into the bathroom.

I can hear mom downstairs in the kitchen preparing breakfast for herself, dad and I. Even though I haven't seen my mother today I can picture her perfectly.

Her thick, black hair is wound up on top of her head in an official looking bun, her dark eyes are focused on the task ahead. She has on a white buttoned up shirt with a black skirt or pants. Her white lab coat is hanging on the hook next to the door so that she won't forget it when she leaves for the Institution. Mom is a Doctor there.

I open the door to the bathroom before stepping inside. It closes after me, I hop in the shower and let the cold water wake me up a bit more. Once I'm finished, I start changing. I slide the gray shirt over the gray tank top I've already put on and look in the mirror.

Today I'm eighteen years old. In the following weeks of my life, a lot will happen. As I look in the mirror I see that I still look the same as I have always looked. Long, messy, brown hair that I'll have to put up in a pony tail. The same light brown eyes and the same glum look that seems to invade everyone's face in the mornings. I try a smile but it looks fake and forced.

I pull my hair out of my face and tie it in a high pony tail above my head. After I've finished changing, I walk down the stairs and into the kitchen where mom is stirring something in a pan on top of the stove top.

"Good morning Larina," Mom says.

"Good morning Ma'am."

"Set the table." I nod my head and walk to the cabinets where I pull out three plates and like I do every morning, I feel like there's something missing as I stare at the lonely fourth plate left in the cabinet.

I set the plates on our designated seats before placing the forks and knifes next to it.

"Good morning Geo, morning Larina," Dad says walking in the kitchen. I look at him. Dad has dark hair and blue eyes. He's rather on the short side being under six feet. However my family is on the short side, so we all fit in pretty well with each other. Dad has on the same outfit he has every day. An all black uniform that is lined with body armor at the torso. Much like mom, he has his helmet hanging next to the door so he won't forget it. Dad is a Handler.

"Good morning Clef," Mom says as she brings the pan of eggs to the table. "Let's eat."

We sit at the table and mom serves us as she always does and we eat in silence.

Breakfast lasts for no more than fifteen minutes, then mom takes our plates to the sink, where they are automatically cleaned.

"Everyone took their medicines?" Mom asks throwing me a look. I nod and she smiles. "Very good, have a good day at school Larina, and you have a good day at work honey." Mom pats dad on the cheek before heading out the door.

"Stay out of trouble alright?" Dad says with a laugh before he walks out as well.

"Have a good day," I whisper even though I know they can't hear me.

I watch mom and dad both board the Monorail that will take mom to the Institution and dad to the Society's Headquarters.

The monorail passes all over the Society, every house is within a few feet of its tracks. It sure makes traveling easier. That is if you are a working adult because I'm under the age of twenty and don't have a job yet, I have to walk to school.

I walk on the sidewalk that runs alongside the monorail's tracks. The school is only a five-minute walk from my home. Across the monorail track from me I see two girls walking together but not talking or looking at each other.

I know that if I look behind me I'll see a group of people walking the same path they do every day to get to school. It's amazing we haven't worn a hole in the sidewalk yet.

Walking along in silence, I look up and around me. The sky is a gray color, matching the tall buildings that loom overhead. Even from where I am standing I can see the tallest building in our city, Society's Headquarters. Looking at it, all the other buildings are small in comparison. It stands in complete contrast of the gray sky behind it, the building is white. So white in fact that when the sun is out, its almost blinding to stare up at it for too long.

Exactly five minutes later I arrive at the school. I walk to the front door, press my hand to the scanner and the door opens. "Welcome to School, Larina Matthews." The scanner says. I walk forward and enter the classroom. Professor Cipher looks up from his monitor as I walk in.

"Morning Miss Larina."

"Good morning Professor Cipher."

"Have a seat." He says like he does every day. I sit down on the same seat I've been sitting in for the last thirteen years of my life. Every year we get a new teacher, we stay in our own classroom and the teachers comes to us.

Soon the classroom is filled with students all looking up at Professor Cipher, waiting for him to start our lessons for the day.

“Alright everyone good morning.” Professor Cipher says walking to the front of his desk before leaning his back against it and crossing his arms over his chest.

“Morning.” We all say.

“Very good, let’s start, shall we? Go ahead and turn on your monitors. Today you will read pages seventy-five through nine five. You may begin.” I press my index finger to my desk and the blue light of the monitor in front of me blinks itself to life. “As you read, I will ask a question to make sure you are truly reading. Make sure you are really reading.”

Every day in school we come in, sit down and read about twenty pages of content in every class. There are five classes in one day. A hundred pages to be read every day. The first class of the day is always Math followed by History, Writing, Science, and now that this group, including myself, is eighteen we’ll have a new class. One that prepares us for our Selection.

The Selection is a ceremony that takes place in our eighteenth year, it’s when we find out who we will marry once we turn twenty-one. What happens is that_.

“Miss Matthews.” I look up from my monitor and I’m caught completely off guard by Professor Cipher.

“Yes?”

“Solve the problem on your monitor.” My eyes go directly to my monitor. I read over the problem that he’s sent over and start to move shapes and numbers around the screen. As soon as I reach the solution, I send it to the front monitor, where everything I’ve just done is displayed for the class to see.

I watch as Professor Cipher checks over my work and looks over at me. “Very good Miss Larina, that was quite fast.” He moves his glasses up his nose as he stares at me. I nod my head and turn my attention back to the reading.

I've always been pretty good at solving problems. I guess my brain works faster when there's someone waiting for a response.

"And Miss Larina?"

"Yes?" I look up and feel everyone's eyes on me.

"You are to go to the Headquarters this afternoon, don't forget." I nod and return to my reading.

For the past two years, I've been going to the Society's Headquarters. I normally have to go once or twice a week, but for the past few months, I've had to go almost every day.

Whenever I go its always the same thing, I am asked questions about myself. I have to take tests about every subject. Many times I have to enter a simulation that will put me in many different scenarios, I've passed every time.

I always meet up with the Head Handler of our city, Sherrie Maxwell. She's always the one that is taking notes on my answers, or calculating what every action of mine means from the simulation. Which is odd, she's the Head Handler, her job is to make sure the other Handlers are enforcing the rules not to be focused on one person out of millions. I don't understand why she's so interested in me.

The class goes by like normal, as I'm packing up my things I see Handler Sean standing by the door, watching me. I avert my eyes and finish shoving my materials in my bag.

“Miss Larina?” Professor Cipher calls out. I look over at him and wait. “You are excused from your other classes, Mrs. Maxwell would like to see you now.”

I furrow my eyebrows and look back at Handler Sean, so he’s here for me?

“Yes, Sir,” I say. I walk to the door and Handler Sean looks down at me, he stands about six inches taller than I am.

“Ready to go?”

“Yes, sir.” He leads the way out of the school, as we pass a few girls they all start giggling to themselves and I know it has to do with Handler Sean. Handler Sean is twenty years old. He no longer goes to school, he has a job and soon he’ll be Selected to be someone’s spouse. I know that all the girls hope he will be selected for them. I can see why. He’s very handsome. He has Brown hair, gorgeous hazel eyes, and a strong jaw.

I watch as he turns to the girls and sends them a glare. “Shouldn’t you girls be getting to class?” He asks. Their eyes widen before they quickly nod their heads and dash off to their next class. I hold back a laugh as I walk behind him.

“Right this way Miss Larina.” He says as we leave the building and walk to the hovercraft. Handlers use hover crafts and hover boards to get around. Handlers are the only ones allowed to have them. I personally prefer the hovercraft, for a few simple reasons, it holds more than just one person, you can actually sit down inside of it and not be standing up and possibly fall. It's also bigger than the hover board. It’s much like what people used to call a car, only it’s always black, has very sharp edges with thin wings and it hovers.

Handler Sean opens up the door for me and I step in, I sit on the passenger side and he boards the craft and sits on the pilot's seat. I put on the seat belt and he turns the craft on, I feel the hovercraft leave the floor and hover ten feet above it.

"Alright." Handler Sean eases forward and soon we are on our way to Society's Headquarters. I can see the tall, white building from here and we are about fifteen minutes away from it.

As Handler Sean drives towards the Headquarters I look out the window at the passing scenery. All the buildings seem too close, and it feels like we are going to get stuck in between them. I think it'd be better if we flew over the buildings, but I'm not about to tell a Handler that his driving skills are less than perfect.

"I'm not really used to this thing yet." He comments looking over at me.

"Wow, I would never guess sir," I say.

"Yeah?" He smiles over at me and I feel my cheeks get warmer. I look away from him and at the window of the craft, only to see something I've never seen before. My cheeks are a dark shade of red.

I slowly touch them with`my hand and furrow my eyebrow. What's going on? "Alright, we're here." He lands on the roof of the building where there's a landing pad and cuts off the engine.

I undo my belt and watch as he gets out of the hovercraft and walks around to my side to open the door for me. "Thank you," I say.

"No problem, watch your step." He offers me his hand and I slowly place mine in his. Sure it's a bit like holding hands, but he's just helping me off the craft is all.

We walk across the roof to the door that leads into the Headquarters. Handler Sean opens the door, I walk in, and he follows after me.

I'm not very familiar with this part of the Headquarters, I normally just enter through the front door. Handler Sean leads the way and soon we are walking down the hallway towards Sherrie Maxwell's lab.

"So, big day next week huh?" He comments.

"Yeah." Next week is when my Selection will take place, meaning I find out who I will marry in three years when I turn twenty-one.

"Are you uh, nervous?" I look over at him as he runs his hand through his hair, messing it up a bit at the top.

"A little." I keep walking and get stopped when he takes my shoulder in his hand. My eyes widen, we are inside the Society's Headquarters, he's a Handler and he's taking a risk to break a rule? "Uh_."

"I'm sorry!" He removes his hand quickly. "You shouldn't be nervous, it'll be fine."

"Thanks." He nods and looks around before turning to look at me.

"I have to get back to work, so I'll see you later." He backs up and bumps into a small table and nearly sends a vase to the floor. He quickly catches it with his foot though and inhales deeply. I watch as he places the vase back on the table before rushing away, his cheeks a slight pink color.

As I walk forward towards the lab's door, I find myself smiling. I stand in front of the door and knock once, right away the door is swung open.

Sherrie Maxwell stands there watching me. She has her blonde hair tied back in a bun, much like my mother's. She has a white lab coat over her white shirt and black skirt. She always wears that while she's in the lab, once she's finished I know she changes into the required black uniforms for Handlers. I've seen her patrolling the streets in her hover board a few times, making sure that the other Handlers under her, are doing their jobs.

"Good morning Miss Larina."

"Good Morning Ma'am."

"Come right in," She steps aside so that I can enter the room. The minute I do, she closes the door and locks it. "Alright, why don't we get started? Go ahead and sit down please." I sit on the only chair in the room and watch as she walks over to the sink that stands in the middle of the room. She rolls up her sleeves to her elbows and washes her hands, dries them on a towel and opens one of the white cabinets that sits above the sink.

I watch her pull out a syringe from the cabinet, and place a long needle to its end. She then takes a small container filled with a blue liquid and adds it to the syringe. I know from coming here so much, that the liquid is the simulation serum. She thumps the needle twice, making sure it's secured and in its place before nodding her head and turning to me.

"Excited for next week?" She asks with a smile on her face.

"Yes," I say with a smile of my own.

"Very good! Ready?" I only nod. "Good girl." She walks over and injects the needle into my neck. My eyes widen as I feel a sharp pain, they slowly close as I fall asleep. "Good luck Miss Larina."

I inhale deeply and open my eyes a few minutes later. My eyes wonder from where I'm sitting on a chair, towards the three people standing across the room from me.

I know from living here for my entire life that I'm sitting in my room. Everything is black though, the lights are all turned off and the window is shut tightly. I slowly stand up and walk behind the chair to put as much distance between me and the three people in the room.

I know them very well. One of them is Handler Sean, the other is Sherrie Maxwell and the third person is me. She has to be, only she has a few differences in her that aren't in me. For one thing, her eyes are smaller, her mouth is bigger and she's taller than I am.

"Hello, Larina Matthews." I turn around sharply and stare at the man that has just appeared. He comes into my line of sight and I stare at him. I've never seen him before in my life. "There's no use in trying to figure out who I am Larina, we've never met. My name is Don O'Brien."

"Hello, sir." He gives me a toothy smile before placing a hand on my shoulder.

"Now turn around for me and look at the three people in the room in front of you." I do so. He keeps his hand on my shoulders, as he stands behind me. "Do you recognize any of them?"

"Yes."

"Okay starting from the left, name them."

"Handler Sean, Sherrie Maxwell and Larina Matthews," I say.

"Very good, now take this." He has a syringe in his hand that holds a black liquid inside of it. "They can't move, they are frozen in place. What I want you to do is take this needle, and inject it into one of those people."

I turn my head to look at him and furrow my eyebrow. "What will it do?" I ask.

"Excuse me?" He backs up but keeps his eyes on me the whole time.

"What will the serum do to them?"

"This is a death serum Larina, this will kill the person that you inject it into." My eyes widen and I step back from him.

"Why would I want to kill any of them?!" I look back at the three people, frozen in place in the dark room. "Who are you even?" I throw him a look and he laughs a little.

"I'm the Head Handler for Sector 50A, I have instructions from Emma Jones herself. Now pick one and carry out your task." I stare at him as I try to figure out if he's telling the truth. Why would Emma Jones, the Leader of the Society, want to kill Handler Sean, Sherrie or me?

"Take the needle Larina and inject it into one of them."

"But why do I have to do it? What did they do?!" I look into his dark eyes and he glares at me before stepping forward and taking my wrist in his hand.

"Are you loyal to the Society?" He demands.

"Yes, But_."

"There is no but! Do as you are told!" He shoves me forward and I stumble as I try to keep my balance. I turn back to face him and shake my head.

“I won't!” I throw the needle at his feet. “One of the rules says, ‘You are not to cause harm to yourself or others!’ This would be breaking that rule. I will not kill anyone.” I turn away from him and walk to the three, frozen people.

They all stare back at me, not moving. “Then I will have to kill you!” Don O’Brien shouts. I turn around quickly and see him running at me with the needle out like a sword.

“No!” I scream. I bring my legs up quickly and kick him in the stomach, he doubles over in pain and in the process, he drops the needle. “No one’s dying” I step on the needle and it breaks under my weight. I watch the black liquid ooze out and spread on the floor.

My eyes widen as it keeps spreading and spreading without end. I keep stepping back, trying to avoid contact with it. A scream comes out of my mouth as the black liquid encloses itself over Don, Handler Sean, Sherrie and the girl that looks like me.

I turn around and run, but there’s nowhere to run, the room is closed off and I’m stuck with my back pressed against the back wall.

The liquid is nearly touching my feet, ready to take me as well. Right as it does touch me, I squeeze my eyes shut and hold my head in my hands.

“Miss Larina?” I open my eyes and look around me. I realize that I’m sitting on the chair, in the lab. I’m finding it hard to breathe, and I hold the arms of the chair so tightly in my hands, that my knuckle starts to turn white.

I look over at Sherrie Maxwell and swallow down a breath I’ve been holding. “Miss Larina?” She repeats.

“Yeah?” I whisper.

"Are you okay?" She crouches down in front of me and peers into my face.

"What happened?" I release my hold on the chair's arms and rub my knuckles.

"That was the simulation Miss Larina, it wasn't real." I inhale deeply and nod. "Why don't you tell me what happened."

"I_." I look down and try to figure things out. "I was in a room with three people, a man came in and said his name was Don O'Brien."

"Right, the Head Handler of Sector 50A."

"He told me that I had to kill one of the three people in the room, and I wouldn't, so he was going to kill me."

"Then what happened?"

"Then he came running at me and I kicked him in the stomach." I bite my lower lip as I look over at her and try to measure if she's angry.

"Right..."

"He dropped the needle and I stepped on it. The death serum started to spread and it consumed him and the three other people. I ran away from it, but I didn't have anywhere to go. That's all."

"Hm." Sherrie stands up and stands at the desk that is next to the chair I'm sitting on. I watch her touch the monitor with her fingers and type things in.

Within seconds the simulation that I just lived plays itself on the large monitor. "What I get from all of this is that you wouldn't break a law and kill other people even though it was Emma Jones herself that asked you to do it."

I press my lips together and look at her. "Is that bad?"

"No. I mean I'm glad that you didn't choose me!" She laughs and I feel a weight being lifted off my shoulder. I let out a sigh and nod. "You broke a rule which is, you didn't listen to your superior, however, you kept true to the law that states you must not harm yourself or others. That's very interesting Miss Larina." She nods and turns the monitor off. "You may go now, just make sure you come back in a few days alright?"

"Yes Ma'am, thank you." I stand up and realize how wobbly my legs are.

"Have a good day Miss Larina." She calls out as I reach the door.

"You too Ma'am." I open the door and exit the room, after I exit I close the door behind me and press my back against it, inhaling deeply.

"Everything okay?" Handler Sean asks. I look at him, he's walking over.

"Um yes, sir!"

"You sure?"

"Yes, it was an intense simulation."

"I'm sure you did fine."

"I hope so." He smiles and looks around before looking back at me.

"Well uh, have a good day." He says, nodding his head and walking away. I press my lips together as I watch him leave, for a second it looked like he wanted to say something more.

I shake my head and walk down the hallway and out of the Headquarters.

2

The Selection

The school day goes by like usual, that is until the last class of the day comes. The one that prepares us for our Selection. There are only five students in that class, there are two girls,(Me and a girl named Sophie.) and three boys.

After the first few minutes, Professor Richards excuses himself and leaves the classroom. I sit there in the front roll and catch a glimpse of myself in the mirror across from me.

I don't talk, no one ever does. No one ever wants to break the rules. Or, that's what I thought anyways…

"Sophie." I hear one of the boys say from behind me. My eyes widen but I stay put, I don't turn around. "Sophie!" He calls out again.

"What is it, Trevor?" Sophie asks turning to look at him. I can see them from the mirror. The way she's looking at him and the way he's looking at her confuses me.

"I love you, Sophie, we can leave now. Before it's too late!" I watch as Trevor stands up and walks to Sophie, who happens to be sitting right next to me. He takes her hand in his and stands her up. "What do you say, Sophie?"

"Guys, you do know you're not supposed to be talking to each other right?" The blonde guy sitting behind me asks.

I shake my head and sigh. What is wrong with all of them?

"Yeah, if the teacher saw_." The red head guy gets cut off by Trevor.

"We don't care!" He pulls Sophie close and hugs her to him. I am pretty sure they are breaking every important law in front of my eyes. I don't breath out a word though, don't they know that about three different cameras are watching them?!

From the mirror, I can see that Sophie and Trevor are kissing. I quickly avert my eyes and slam my hands on the table as I stand up.

"Stop!" I shout, still not looking at them. Everyone's eyes fall on me, it doesn't last long though. We all turn to the door when it is slammed open against the wall.

Standing there are three Handlers. Two I don't know who they are, but the third is Handler Sean. His eyes meet mine and I don't look away as the four students are taken away by the other two Handlers.

The minute they leave, Handler Sean softly closes the door, after stepping inside the room.

I haven't realized it until know, but I'm shaking where I stand.

"Are you okay?" I slowly ease myself onto the chair and shake my head not meeting his eyes. "You did the right thing, Miss Larina." I look up at him and he smiles at me. He holds his finger up and walks back to the door where the Cameras are at. I watch as he touches his palm to the scanner next to the door and a keyboard appears. He types in something that I can't see, and the cameras turn off. He turned off the cameras, but why?

"You're the only one that didn't break a rule." He says.

“I did though.” I press my lips together and look down at my hand. I should have been taken away as well.

“I don’t understand.”

“I shouted at them to stop,” I explain looking him in the eye.

“You did well.” He reassures me. I only nod. “Your teacher should be back soon, I want you to hide this.”

“Hide what?” I ask as my eyebrows furrow. I watch him as he walks to me and places a single red rose on my desk. I stare at the flower feeling confused, I look up to ask him why he’s giving this to me, but when I do look up, I see that he’s already gone.

I take the rose into my hand and smile at it. It’s so beautiful.

The door starts to open and I quickly hide the rose in my backpack.

I lay in bed that night, holding the rose in my hand over my stomach. Why would a Handler of the Society, risk everything to give me this beautiful flower? Where did he even get it? Flowers don’t grow naturally nowadays. The last war in 2025 killed any nutrients left on the ground.

I sit up and look out of my window. It’s past my bedtime, I should have been asleep hours ago, hooked up to the Dream Catcher. The Dream Catcher is just a small device with a clip at the end of it, all I have to do is attach the device to my finger before going to sleep and it records all of my dreams. Dreams can be dangerous things, so the Society likes to go over them and see if any bad patterns can be found. In the morning all I have to do is plug it into the monitor in our hallway and it sends that night’s dreams to the Society’s Headquarters, where Sherrie Maxwell will then look it over.

I slowly lay back down and look up at the rose, I touch its soft pedal in my hands and smile to myself before slowly drifting off to sleep.

A week later

It has been a week since Handler Sean gave me that rose. Ever since then, I've been really careful. Tonight I'll find out who I will marry in three years, I can't help but wonder who Handler Sean will marry in a year when he turns twenty-one.

"Good Morning Miss Larina." Handler Sean says as I enter the Headquarters. I look over at him, he's reading something over on a monitor and not even looking at me.

"Good morning." I guess he doesn't really want anything to do with me today, I walk past him and head down the hall. "Nervous about tonight?" He asks suddenly walking next to me. I turn and look at him with a smile.

"Were you sir?"

"You could say that, but you know I ended up worrying for no reason."

"Why is that? if you don't mind me asking."

"The girl I am to be selected with wasn't in the database yet, so I don't know who I'm going to marry."

"That's a possibility? I didn't know that."

"Of course it is, I mean I could end up marrying someone a few years younger than me."

"Oh."

"Yeah. Well, see you later." I watch him walk back to the desk at the entrance of the Headquarter and start to move things in the monitor. Honestly, that didn't help me at all with my nerves. Now I'm more nervous than ever!

I reach out to knock on the lab's door, but before I get a chance to, the door opens and Sherrie smiles down at me.

"We are ready for you Miss Larina," Sherrie says stepping aside.

"Uh, yes Ma'am." I step inside and see Doctor Jamie Simmons, she's a specialist on the Selection, and anything to do with human behavior. Every person once they are eighteen, have to come to the Headquarters and talk to Doctor Simmons about how we're feeling, about what we have to do following our Selection and of course how we prepare for marriage.

"Hello, you are Larina Matthews right?" Doctor Simmons asks walking to me and extending her hand. I shake her hand and look up into her pale gray eyes, her hair is cropped and is a gray color. She has on the normal Doctor uniform.

"Yes I am, it's nice to meet you, Doctor Simmons."

"Very nice, why don't you sit down and we can begin yes?" I nod and follow her over to three chairs. I sit in the middle while Sherrie sits to my left and Doctor Simmons to my right.

"I'm just going to ask you a few question Miss Larina, just answer them as honestly as you can okay?" I nod and turn to look at her. "Very good." She gives me a warm smile and turns her attention to the clipboard in her hands.

"First question, how are you feeling?"

"Nervous honestly."

She smiles and pats my knee softly. "That's perfectly normal, it's a huge milestone in your life! Tell me what makes you nervous though?"

"I don't know, the whole thing. Especially having to be in front of thousands of people as they watch who I'm Selected for."

"Yes, that is quite nerve wracking isn't it?" I turn to look at Sherrie when she clears her throat at Doctor Simmons. "Oh sorry, any who let us continue!" Doctor Simmons jots something down before turning the page. "Next question! Do you believe that the Society will choose the right person for you?"

"I think so, there hasn't been any other way for hundreds of years right?"

"Very good Miss Larina." Doctor Simmons write some more before turning to look at me with a certain look on her face that has me anxiously waiting for the next question. "Question three! Is there anyone you would want to be Selected with?"

My cheeks start to burn against her gaze and I slowly drop my eyes to my hands and shake my head. "No, whoever the Society picks is fine." I nod and try to convince myself along with them of this.

"Okay, question four. Where would you like to live once you are Selected?"

"If at all possible, I'd like to live here in Sector 7B. I want to be close to my family."

"Your parents are wonderful people that have served the Society loyalty their whole lives! Geo and Clef must be very proud of you." Doctor Simmons says.

"Thank you, Doctor."

"Alright, one last question are you ready?" I simply nod my head. "Once you are Selected will you remain loyal to the Society and it's laws? No matter what happens."

"Yes, of course." I nod and smile.

"Good girl! You are going to make some young man very happy!" I feel myself flush again and try to hide it by laughing it off.

"Let's hope so," I say with a smile.

"Alright Miss Larina one last thing and you may go," Sherrie says. I turn to her and wait. "Come with me please." Doctor Simmons and I both follow Sherrie Maxwell to a large, white, cylinder machine that sits at the corner of the room. "This is The Selection Simulation machine, Miss Larina if you would please step inside it," Sherrie says.

I do so and look back at them. "You'll do just fine Miss Larina!" Doctor Simmons says smiling widely at me. I smile back and watch as the door slides shut. All around me is white, it's so bright. It gets worst when lights start to flash, making my vision a complete blur.

I squeeze my eyes shut hoping it will stop soon. When I open my eyes I see that I'm inside the city hall. Around me are girls and boys my age. Everyone is dressed up, I look down at myself and my eyes widen as I see what I'm wearing.

I'm wearing a white gown that goes all the way to my knees, everyone else is in black. Why am I in white? The dress code is black only. I catch a glimpse of myself in a mirror that is across the room. In my brown hair, which is up in a bun is the rose that Handler Sean gave to me. What's going on?! I start to panic as I sit there among all the other people that are actually following the rules.

My heart starts to ram itself against my rib cage, I wrap my arms around my midsection, willing myself to calm down.

I look up at Sherrie as she walks to the front of the room in the stage. My pulse quickens and my hands become clammy as I sit there watching her.

"Larina Matthews," Sherrie calls out my name. I stand up and in the sea of black, I walk forward. I'm the only one dressed differently, the only one breaking the rules. "You look lovely Miss Larina," Sherrie says as I reach the stage.

"Thank you, Ma'am."

"Are you ready?" She asks. I nod and look at the giant, blue monitor on top of the stage. As I stand there waiting, my heart picks up its pace even more. I watch in complete awe as Handler Sean's face shows up. My mouth parts and before I know what's happening, I'm running to Sean who is in the crowd.

"I always knew it was going to be you!" He says as he catches me in his arms.

"Me too," I say smiling up at him. I can't control what I'm saying, everything is just spilling out. He takes my face into his hands and leans down, I feel myself close my eyes and that's when I see bright lights flashing and I know that the simulation is over.

"Go ahead and step out Miss Larina," Sherrie says. I step out of the machine and stare at her and Doctor Simmons. Doctor Simmons is in complete shock, and Sherrie looks angry.

"Follow me." Sherrie turns and heads to the back door, she opens it and I look inside. Inside the room are many chairs and a giant monitor, much like the one in the simulation. "Sit down please." I sit on one of the chairs and Doctor Simmons stands next to me scribbling furiously into her clipboard. Sherrie walks over to the monitor and starts to drag things around until she's satisfied.

I watch the screen and see people my age entering the same simulation machine I had just entered. Every time it's the same, they are all in black like they are supposed to be. When Sherrie calls them up, they get up and walk to the stage. When she asks them if they are ready, they nod. Never, did a face appear on that screen. Sherrie then nods and tells them: "Good, wait until tonight."

Sherrie turns the monitor off and looks back at me. "Why are you so different?"

Why am I so different? That's the question I ask myself over and over as I walk home from the Headquarters.

The minute I walk inside the house mom rushes over. "Are you so excited?!" She asks grasping onto my shoulders. I only nod. "Let's get you ready okay?" I don't get much of a choice as I'm dragged up the stairs and told to get in the shower.

"Once you're done, I'll help you fix your hair."

"Thanks, mom."

"Language Larina!"

"Thanks, Ma'am." I correct myself.

"Better." I hear the door close after her and sigh loudly as the warm water washes away the events of the day. Once I'm done showering, I put on a robe and walk into my room where mom has laid out a black dress on top of my bed.

"What do you think? I thought maybe you could wear the dress I wore when I was Selected to your dad." Mom runs her hand over the fabric of the dress and smiles, most likely remembering the day.

"I think that will be great Ma'am, thank you." She nods and looks over at me. "Mom?"

"Larina_."

"Ma'am, were you nervous? On your Selection night?" She presses her lips together and sits down on my bed and pats the spot next to her. I walk over and sit down.

"I was a nervous wreck! I had no idea who he would be, or if he would be happy I was chosen for him or anything of the sort! My mother kept having to tell me to stop biting my lip and chewing on my nails the whole day." Mom lets out a laugh and hugs me around the shoulder.

"I worried for no reason, the Society chose the best man possible to be my husband."

"Did you love dad right away?"

"Love," Mom whispers and clasps her hands together. "Marriage is not about love Larina, it's about who will be the best for you. Marriage hasn't been about love for hundreds of year, you know that."

"But you and Dad love each other." I look into her eyes and she nods.

"We love each other very much, and I couldn't picture myself being married to anyone else but him." I smile and rest my head on her shoulder. "And one day soon, you'll know what that is like, now let's fix your hair!"

Mom stands up, as do I and we walk back to the bathroom where she helps me take out the knots on my hair and brush it so it's nice and smooth. Once she's done she dries it and smiles at my naturally curly style.

"You'll look so beautiful, Larina!" We walk back into my room and she instructs me to change into the dress. I carefully ease it on and find that it fits me like a glove. "So how did the simulation go?" Mom asks as she straightens out the front of the dress.

"Um fine?" Mom raises an eyebrow and looks me in the eye. "A face appeared on the screen," I whisper.

Her eyes widen and her hands go to her mouth. "Who was it?" She asks.

"A Handler."

"Larina why would a Handler's face appear on the screen?"

"I don't know!" I look away from her and my eyes quickly go to the rose that I hid behind the curtain of my window, unfortunately, mom follows my gaze and see's the shadow of the flower inside its plastic cup.

"Larina, what is that?" She asks as she walks over to it.

"Nothing!" I quickly dash to stop her, but she reaches out and takes the cup into her hands. Her eyes widen as she stares at the flower, she turns her attention back to me and I see her start to shake.

"Where_. Where did you get this?"

"Mom I_."

"Answer the question, Larina! Where did you get this flower?"

"A Handler gave it to me." Mom's left-hand goes to her forehead and she starts to pace.

"Is it the same Handler that appeared in your simulation?"

"Yes."

"Larina! You know that is not okay! This is not okay!" She walks to the trash chute and my eyes widen.

"Mom what are you_."

"This can't happen, Larina!" She throws the flower, cup and all into the trash chute and my mouth opens. The trash chute burns up everything that goes down into it.

"Mom!" I say.

"Mom nothing! You are lucky I'm not going to Sherrie Maxwell herself! Now finish getting ready!" Mom shakes her head at me and leaves the room, slamming the door shut after her. I cringe at the noise and look at the chute. It was such a beautiful gift. As I finish getting ready I can hear my parents talking about me.

"And you are sure that she said a Handler gave it to her?" Dad asks.

"Yes, Clef."

"Did she give a name?"

"It doesn't really matter now does it Clef? If he's not her Selected then it's wrong!"

"I know, I just thought I could talk to the boy that's all."

"Larina hurry up!" Mom calls up. I quickly put on some shoes and walk down the stairs, I stop when mom and dad both turn to look at me.

"Look at you, Larina! You're going to make some guy very happy tonight!" Dad says.

“He’s right Larina, you look beautiful,” Mom says tucking a piece of my hair behind my ear.

“Thank you.”

“Let’s get going, we don’t want to be late!” Dad ushers us out of the house and we stand at the station of the monorail. “Excited Larina?” Dad asks once the monorail arrives and stops for us to get in.

“Yes.” I lie. We board the monorail and sit down together, I sit next to the window staring at the black world outside.

It takes only a few minutes for us to arrive in front of the city hall which is normally a glum, gray building. Tonight, however, it's illuminated by tons of small lights that line the way to the door. I can see many people making their way inside the building, all lined up, one after the other.

Mom, dad and I exit the monorail and find our place in line, and take one step forward at a time until we reach the door, and isn’t it lucky that the Handler that is standing in front of the door to take our names, and make sure we showed up is Handler Sean himself?

“Good evening Doctor Matthews and Handler Matthews.” Handler Sean says nodding his head at them.

“Good evening son,” Dad says signing his name into the thin monitor in Handler Sean’s hands.

“Good evening Miss Larina.” Handler Sean says.

“Good evening,” I say. Mom elbows me and I look up at him. “Sir,” I add. As he looks down, I see a hint of a smile on his face.

“Alright go right in, good luck tonight Miss Larina.” As we walk forward, Handler Sean’s eyes and mine meet and I go back to the simulation where he held me in his arms and how he was my selected and I find myself hoping.

As we enter the city hall mom and dad turn to me. "We are so proud of you Larina," Dad says hugging me.

"Thanks, sir."

"You are a wonderful, loyal citizen to the Society," Mom says hugging me next. Her hug lasts a little longer though, not because she enjoys hugs but because she whispers something in my ear. "That was him wasn't it? The Handler that gave you the rose?" I only nod. She then says something that leaves me with my mouth hanging open. "He's a cutie." She pulls back, winks at me and walks with my father to where the parents are to wait.

I shake my head trying to get myself together before I walk forward and find my seat among the other people getting Selected. As I sit there, I catch a glimpse of myself in the mirror and inhale deeply feeling relieved that at least I'm wearing a black dress and not that gorgeous white one from my simulation.

As I look around I see that everyone is in black, the girls have their hair down and no matter who the person is, they are wearing the same nervous expression on their faces. We are called up by our names and based on who we are Selected too.

Many girls and guys are called up and selected, after which they meet each other on stage and shake hands. I inwardly sigh as I wait for my turn to come. I should have been right in the middle of the list my name being Larina Matthews, but for some reason, everyone's whose name starts with L goes and I'm left behind. The only conclusion I can come up with is that, whoever I'm being selected for, their names are at the end of the list.

My head starts running wild as I think about the name Sean being pretty down there.

I shake my head and look up at Sherrie Maxwell, who is up on the stage, still calling people up. Finally, she calls me up. I slowly stand up and make my way to the stage, this time I'm part of the black sea that surrounds me.

For some reason, I look behind me and I see Handler Sean at the door watching me as I make my way to the stage. He gives me a reassuring smile, which only makes my cheeks flush. My heart starts to beat at an unhealthy pace, and I feel a cold sweat run through me.

"Are you ready Miss Larina?" Sherrie asks. I only nod, everyone only nods. The truth is, I act like everyone else. Deep inside though, I know just like the Society knows, I'm different.

I wait for the name to appear on the screen and bite my lower lip. When something finally does appear I gasp and for some reason, I find it necessary to look back at Handler Sean. Gasps fill the room at city hall, Sherrie clears her throat and readies herself to speak at the microphone. "No match found." She repeats what the screen says.

That has never happened before, with Handler Sean it said his selected wasn't in the database, I am not selected for anyone.

"Take your seat, Miss Larina." Sherrie practically hisses at me. I return to my seat, no one looks over at me or talks, it's against the rules. I watch as Sherrie steps to the microphone, feeling sure that she's about to call out someone else.

She doesn't. "Miss Larina will be assigned as an Eraser." People applaud at the announcement but I just sit there squeezing my hands together and staring at my feet. I'm not to get my assignment until I'm twenty. "She will start as soon as possible, meaning her school days are over." I look up at Sherrie and her eyes meet mine. Never, on any of my tests that it say that I would match up as an Eraser. I keep silent though, what could I say?

I inhale deeply and deal with the fact that I have to do it, I have to Erase people.

3

The Old City

As soon as the ceremony is over, my parents and I stand up and leave the building like everyone else. We ride the monorail back to our house in silence, not until we arrive at home and we're sitting at the table that we actually start to talk.

"What does that mean? That I'm not selected for anyone?" I look at mom for the explanation.

"I don't know Larina, I never saw that happen before." I turn to dad then.

"I don't know what it means either." He whispers to himself. I hold my hands together and nod slowly. I'm just not a good Selection for anyone I guess.

"But an Eraser? That's an amazing privilege!" Mom says smiling at me.

"I'm going to have to erase people."

"Sweetie, you'll be doing the Society a great deal! That's a wonderful job, believe me. You're going to do fine at it." I shake my head and stand up. "Larina?"

"I'm tired, I'm going to bed. Goodnight." I turn to leave and hear mom say something to dad.

"I think it's a good thing that she wasn't selected, that way there won't be anything that will make her turn away."

As I walk up the stairs I wonder what mom meant by "Turn away." I sigh and enter my room before closing the door behind me. I thought I was going to be selected like everyone else, I thought I would finish school to prepare for marriage, not to erase people.

I change out of mom's dress and hang it next to the door of my room so that I can give it back to her in the morning.

After I put on some sleeping clothes I lay in bed, with the Dream Catcher device in my hands, but not clipped on. I stare at it as I think things over, I never do end up falling asleep worrying the way I am.

At two in the morning, I throw the covers off of me and place the Dream Catcher on the table next to the window. I quietly move to the closet and it opens for me, I pull out some black clothes and start to change into it. I do everything quickly before I change my mind.

I put on some boots and look out the window at the sleeping city, everyone's asleep. Everyone but me. I walk back to the closet and pull out a black sweater that has a hood on it, as I slide it over myself I make sure that the hood sits over my face. I grab my dark backpack from the corner of the room and tuck my hair inside the hood in a sloppy bun and walk to my window. I pull the window open and place my hand on its frame, trying to decide if I'm really going to do this. The last few times I was younger, if I had been caught I would probably just had gotten a talking too. Now, however, I'm eighteen and I could be erased for this. I shake my head and climb over the window and carefully scale down the house on the bricks that stick out every few feet or so.

When I'm three feet from the ground I jump down and land on both my feet before I run across my yard and into the dark street. I carefully run, avoiding any working cameras that are left on at night. During the night only a portion of the cameras in the city are left on, there's not much for the Handlers to check on. Tonight there is.

I leave the block that contains my house and start to walk alongside the monorail tracks that I know will lead me to the exit of our city. It takes nearly forty-five minutes before I'm standing on the street across from the Society's Headquarters. I keeping walking, making sure to look at the Headquarters every once in a while to make sure no one is around.

I nearly have a heart attack when one light inside, is switched on. My hand goes to my mouth and I quickly back up behind a tall garbage can. After five minutes I think it's okay to move so I do so, perhaps a minute too soon because right as I step from behind the garbage can, I'm yanked from behind and my back is pressed against a wall of a building in an alley

"What are you doing out past your curfew? State your identity!" The Handler yells at me. Wait, is that Handler Sean? I pull back my hood and stare up into his hazel eyes.

"Miss Larina?" He asks his eyes widening. He lets go of me and stumbles backward in shock. "What are you thinking?!" He snaps.

"I need time alone, everything is wrong. I was supposed to be selected for someone, I was never meant to be an Eraser!" I look down at the floor and feel something fall from my eyes. Huh? I touch my cheek with one hand and when I pull away I see that my cheeks are wet. My eyes narrow in confusion, I press my finger to my lips and pull back in surprise, the water coming from my eyes taste salty. "What's going on with me?!" I ask looking to Handler Sean for help.

He looks around, seeming worried that someone will find us.

"You're crying." He whispers.

"What does that mean?!"

"People did it all the time before the Society took over, it's to show sadness and sometimes happiness. Have you been taking your medicine in the morning?" I press my lips together and look into his eyes. "Miss Larina?"

"I forgot to, today." I lie. Mom and my biggest fights are about how I don't take the medicine every day, I take it once a week. I bite my lower lip and a small gasp escapes my lips when he softly wipes away the salty water pouring from my eyes. "It's okay Larina." My mouth widens as I stare at him, his eyes widen as well at the realization that he just called me by my first name. "Miss Larina, you need to go back to your house right now!" He turns away from me and starts walking off.

"I can't," I whisper. I form my hands into fists as I stare at the ground.

"And why not?" He stops walking but doesn't turn around to face me.

"Because I need time to straighten things out with myself, I'm so_." I let my words trail off as I stare at his back. I straighten my back and walk past him.

"What makes you so confident that I won't report you?" I stop cold in my tracks at hearing him say that.

"I don't know."

"Would you like me to tell you why?" I take that to mean that he won't report me.

"No." I start to walk away again.

"Larina!" He snaps coming after me. I stop right before I'm about to leave the alley and spin around to face him.

"Stop it already! You are a Handler! Aren't you supposed to follow every rule and law?" I look into his eyes and he stares down into mine.

"Calling someone by their first name, that bothers you?"

"With all due respect sir, but shouldn't all things against the law bother me?" For a split second, an angry look crosses his face. This takes me aback. I've never seen him angry before, as a matter of fact, I've never seen anyone angry besides Sherrie Maxwell.

"Stop calling me sir!" He says taking my shoulders into his hands.

I furrow my eyebrows at that. "What?!"

"I'm only two years older than you, call me Sean."

"Not happening! It's against the_."

"What you are doing right now is against the law! They try to program it into your head that it bothers you so much, but everything you say does otherwise. You break the laws more than everyone else!"

"I never break the law!"

"You are right now! You talk back, your simulations are different and_."

"That is way out of line!" I shout.

"You're way out of line Larina!" He shouts back. He takes my shoulders in his hands, and I stare up at him as he glares down into my eyes. "Look at you! Do you really think that you are like everyone else? Would anyone else leave their home after curfew to go only God knows where?!"

"No but_."

"You are different Larina, I don't know why, but you are. The Society will do anything to make sure they can control you."

"What are you_."

"Just be quiet and listen for once!" I clamp my mouth shut. "The worst thing they could have done is assign you as an Eraser. How could they think that you will be able to do? Everyone in that place will see how you are, how you're different and the ropes that they believe they have on you, will snap and they won't be able to tie them back." I look at him as he lowers his eyes to the floor, and thinks things through.

"Why are you telling me this?" He looks up at me and his hazel eyes have my heart leaping to my throat.

"Larina_." He runs his fingers through his dark hair and lets out a huge sigh. "If you go, they will erase you."

"Look, I appreciate your concern. Really I do, but this isn't the first time I am doing this and I was never caught before."

"You've_?" He stares at me in amazement before shaking his head. "I want to see it."

"See it, sir?"

"Stop calling me sir!"

I press my lips together to keep from laughing at him. "You want to come?"

"For research yes." Uh huh, sure that's why.

"Okay, I'll show you." I start walking but he takes my wrist in his hand and pulls me back into the alley.

"How far is it?"

"Two hours walk?"

"Two hours?! No, we're taking a hovercraft." He starts walking out of the alley and straight towards the Headquarters!

"What?!" I ask hurrying after him.

"Sh, keep your head low and follow me." I walk quietly behind him as we cross the street. The whole time I keep thinking someone is going to see us. Handler Sean must sense my nervousness from behind him because he stops, right at the door to the Headquarters and smiles at me.

"Don't worry, I know where to go so we're not caught." I nod and he turns around and sneaks to the side of the building. We walk alongside the wall in complete silence. The cameras that are normally on, taunt me every time I look up at them.

"Okay, hurry." Handler Sean takes my hand and we dash towards the back of the building, where there's a large garage that I have never seen before. "The hover crafts are under lock and key during the night, and if I try to get in by using the scanner, Sherrie Maxwell will be notified."

"So what do we do?" He grins and nods his head towards the side of the garage. We walk around the side of it, where I see an opened window.

"That's convenient," I say.

"That window has been broken for months now, someone should really fix it." He winks at me before stepping on top of some crates and pulling himself inside the garage.

As I stand there trying to figure out how I'm going to copy what he just did, I hear a sound coming from the Headquarters. When a light is switched on right on the side of the building where we just passed, my heart leaps to my throat. I then leap for the window, bruising my stomach in the process, and climb through it only to fall to the floor on my stomach. “Ow.” I murmur.

“You okay?” Handler Sean asks walking over to me. He offers me a hand and I take it, he pulls me upright and does a quick check over before looking into my eyes.

“A light came on outside!” I whisper.

“Where?”

“Right outside, on the side of the Headquarters.”

“Not good.” Handler Sean looks around and presses his lips together trying to figure out what to do. We both turn our heads to the main door of the garage when we hear it start to open. “Oh my_.” I take Handler Sean’s hand in mine and make a beeline behind the furthest hovercraft.

We crouch down behind it and I feel certain that the beat of my heart will definitely give away our position. I look at Handler Sean and see that he’s staring at me, he nods and I nod back. Someone walks into the garage and starts rummaging through some drawers and cabinets.

I keep catching myself holding my breath and turning a shade of blue. I poke my head from behind the hovercraft to try to see what the person is doing. From where I am, I can see the guy perfectly. He has a dark hood and some blue pants. His hair is messy and brown and when he turns around I know our eyes meet. He gives me a soft smile and I’m frozen in place.

I think my heart stops beating completely when he walks towards me, instead of calling me out or saying anything he just gets in the hovercraft that we are hiding behind. Handler Sean’s eyes widen into the size of golf balls as he shoves me out of the way, just in the time for the blast of the hovercraft nearly to miss me. I watch as the hovercraft hovers for several seconds before lifting off completely and flying through the opened roof.

In the process of knocking me over, Handler Sean fell too and now is over me. I look up at him and he quickly gets to his feet.

"Are you okay Miss Larina?" He asks helping me up.

"Yes, thank you." I look into his eyes and he smiles before frowning and looking up at the opened roof that the hovercraft just left through.

"Who do you think that was?" I ask.

"No idea. Let's hurry and get out of here." He starts for another hovercraft but I stop him with a hand to his shoulder.

"What are you doing?"

"Well, I want to see this place of yours. Come on." He smiles and we walk to the hovercraft where he opens the door for me and I get in first. My heart keeps ramming itself against my poor chest as I sit there, thinking someone else is going to just walk in. "What's weird is that whoever that was, was able to get in here without triggering the alarm that notifies Sherrie." He puts on his seat belt and looks at me.

"I don't think he works for the Society or is even part of it," I whisper. Handler Sean turns and stares at me. I go on: "His clothes were different, and he saw me." Handler Sean's eyes widen. "Our eyes met from across the room, he smiled at me but he didn't say anything. If he was part of the Society he would have immediately called me out."

"I think that you're right." Handler Sean eases us up and out of the garage, before taking off through the city, high above the buildings.

"So where to Miss Larina?" He asks not even looking at me.

"Leave the city, from there it's a pretty straight shot." As he pilots the hovercraft over and around buildings, depending on their heights, I look out the window and wonder who that guy back at the garage was. How did he get in without being detected, and why didn't he say anything when he clearly saw me?

"We're about to leave Sector 7B." Handler Sean says bringing me back to the present.

"Just keep going." He nods and turns to look ahead. I press my lips together as we pass over the large, iron fence that is the border between our city and the world beyond it. When I was younger and I'd sneak out, I would have to climb over the fence and I was never caught. Flying over it is a lot easier.

I watch as we pass over empty fields to get to where we are going, after only a few minutes I start to see the greenery that grows naturally outside of our city and I know that we are nearing our destination.

"I think you should land," I say. Handler Sean nods and I feel us being lowered into the ground. "Okay let's go," I say once the engines are cut and he opens the door for me.

We walk forward and I look up at the huge trees and vines that have infested this place that used to be a city. "Miss Larina, are you sure that it's safe to go in there?"

"Yeah, no one has been here in ages." I nod and we move forward and enter under the blanket of trees.

"I can't believe all this grew by itself, I guess that not all the nutrients were killed after all." I nod and duck under a low branch of a tree.

We keep walking further into the green infested place, the deeper we go, the darker it seems to get. I squint my eyes trying to find the building that I'm looking for, I look to my left and see the faded sign that used to welcome people to the city, years and years ago. I've named this place "The Old City" Of course no one lives here now, but many years ago some people did. There are signs everywhere that there used to be people living here.

There are houses, schools, hospitals and such things. Vines and weeds have taken over the buildings, so now the brick and concrete materials are hidden behind lush foliage.

"Wow!" Handler Sean exclaims as he stops to look around the place.

"It's pretty amazing isn't it sir?" I take a step forward and as I do, I find myself being hurled to the floor after tripping over something on the ground. Right before I land on the floor, face to the dirt, I feel Handler Sean grab me by the waist to keep me up. I look up at him and his eyes are filled with worry.

"Are you okay?"

"Yes I uh, tripped on_." I look down to locate what I tripped on and scream as I jump back pulling Handler Sean with me.

"What is_." He stops and stares at what I'm pointing at. Right at our feet is a skull. It's laying perfectly straight on the dirt, its eyes staring back at Handler Sean and myself. I watch Handler Sean take a step towards it and softly touch it with his foot.

I inhale as it rolls a few feet away and stops as it hits a tree trunk. My eyes go to where it had previously been and I see a neck bone sticking out of the floor, meaning the whole skeleton is buried down there. I take a step back and Handler Sean follows me.

"Is it a human skeleton?" I whisper.

"I think so." He says as we back up further.

"How do you think the person died?" I look over at the skull and its empty eyes.

"I'd have to assume that it was during the last World War."

"That's awful." He looks down at me and I can't seem to take my eyes away from the skull.

"Let's get going, Miss Larina." I nod as I tear my eyes away from it, before turning and heading deeper into the city. As we walk along I realize how tense I've become since encountering that skeleton.

My shoulders only ease up and relax when I step through some brush and see the familiar cracked road that at some point was paved with something black and yellow. "It's this way." I walk forward and look around for a little bit before locating the building that I'm looking for. "There!" I exclaim. I walk to the tall, white building that has a tree growing right in the middle of it, there is rubble surrounding the broken, concrete steps that lead to the front, wooden door. On top of the door are letters spelling out the word LIBRA Y."

"Can we go in?" Handler Sean asks stepping behind me.

"Yeah, I've gone in several times," I say only to receive an annoyed look from him. We walk up the broken, concrete steps and enter the building through the large hole on the side of the shut door. I pull out a flashlight from my backpack and switch it on, the light shines from it in a white, round, beam that covers a radius of a foot or so.

We walk deeper into the building and I see Handler Sean look around, trying to figure out what this place is. "They used to keep books here, there are still many but most of them are burned or ripped. It's really interesting how this building is still pretty well intact." I walk forward shining the light onto fallen bookcases and the scattered books that lay littered on the floor.

"I know exactly what this place is!" Handler Sean says from somewhere behind me. I turn around and look at him. He's standing behind a desk that holds a keyboard of some type and a broken monitor.

"You do?"

"Yes, they used to call it a library." I guess the letter missing from the sign on the top of the door is the letter "R" I feel my cheeks flush with color and feel really glad that I hadn't told Handler Sean that the building is called the "Libray." It's a good thing that it's pretty dark in here, that way Handler Sean can't see my cheeks and how red they are. "Yeah, people kept books here and borrowed them to read." Handler Sean walks around the desk and comes to stand next to me.

"I wish we still had that back in the Sectors." I murmur.

"Are there any books that are still readable?"

"Yeah, follow me." We walk past a few more fallen bookcases and past a large pillar that is attached to the roof of the building, before reaching the back of the library where there are books against the back wall.

I kneel down next to them and pick up several books into my arms. "Here are some." I stand up, but I don't realize how close to me Handler Sean is standing and I end up bumping him back a few feet. He tries hard not to fall, but as he stumbles backward he trips over a bookcase and is sent to the floor. I watch as he strikes the pillar with his shoulder and groan from the pain. I rush over to him, my eyes wide with worry. "Are you okay? I'm so_." My apology gets interrupted when I hear a low rumbling sound. Handler Sean's and my eyes meet.

"What was that?" He looks up to where the pillar is connected to the roof and I watch in horror, as it slides across the ceiling, making a horrible screeching sound before it's corner completely breaks off and starts to fall down on us. "Run!" I scream. I take his hands into mine and pull him to his feet. We take off to the other end of the library, right as we reach the wall of the building the ground shakes with the impact of the pillar crashing onto the floor. That's all that it takes for the building to start coming apart.

The walls start to crumble onto the floor, and I feel bits of rubble hit my legs as they fall down. The worst part is that with the walls coming down, the roof will be sure to follow them! Right as I finish the thought, I see one corner of the roof start to fall down.

"We have to get out of here!" I scream. Handler Sean and I make a beeline to the hole that we entered through. Right as we are about to exit the building the front wall shatters and falls down. Handler Sean pulls me out of the way just in time to avoid being crushed under its massive weight. I look around, trying to find another route out, but with all the noises around us, it's hard to think straight at all.

"There's no way out without us being crushed! What do we do?" I look into Handler Sean's eyes and he presses his lips together.

"Do you trust me?" I bite my lower lip before nodding my head. He takes that to mean that he can scoop me up into his arms and run to the other end of the library, where the roof is about to fall at any second.

"Oh my god!" I scream. As he runs towards the already fallen wall, the roof above us comes completely loose from the remaining foundation. I can tell, from being in Handler Sean's arms that he's holding his breath. I feel the rush of the wind coming from behind us as the roof nears the floor and is about to crush us flat.

When we are a few feet from being free I feel myself fly from Handler Sean's arms as he throws me away from him and to safety. I land on my back a couple of feet away from the building, the air is knocked out from my chest and I lay on the floor trying to breathe.

I slowly sit up and just as I do, the roof falls onto the floor crushing everything bellow it. A cloud of dust is shot out from all sides of the buildings. I turn my face away from it and feel glass and stone hit my cheek and neck. I bring my arms up to protect my face the best I can, once everything has calmed down I slowly get to my feet and look around.

Dust blocks my vision from the library. I take a step forward and start screaming Handler Sean's name. "Sean?! Sean!!!" I scream. I take off running towards where the building just collapsed and nearly have a heart attack when something grabs at my foot. Right as I'm about to kick at whatever it is, I see that it's Handler Sean.

"Oh my God!" I scream. I kneel next to him and he coughs a bit before sitting up. He's covered in dust and his hair is full of small pieces of rocks. "Sean?" He looks at me and smiles.

"We made it." He murmurs before laying on his back and staring up at the sky, breathing heavily.

"Are you hurt?"

“Just bruised from falling, but nothing broken.” I look down at him as he closes his eyes and tries to regain himself. He saved me, he threw me to save me and get me as far away from the building as possible. I look back at the building and see that he barely made it, had he been five feet back he would have died.

“Thank you,” I say. His eyes open and I stare at them, his iris are surrounded by a blue-green color, they are the most beautiful eyes I’ve ever seen and as I sit there looking down at him and him up at me, I realize that I have feelings for him that I shouldn’t have.

“It was nothing.” He says, slowly sitting up.

“You saved my life.” I smile softly and look down at the floor as I try to figure out these feelings building up in my chest, that I don’t quite understand yet.

“It’s a Handler’s job to protect the citizens of the Society.” He says.

“But you could have died.”

“I didn’t.”

“But you could have, I can never repay you.”

“You know what I just realized?” He asks smiling at me. I look into his eyes and wait. “You called me Sean.”

“I was worried! I don’t think rules apply in that situation, sir!”

“And there it is.” He chuckles and shakes his head. “We were lucky, we could have died.” He whispers looking down at the floor and letting a slow breath out.

“I’m sorry, it’s my fault.”

“It’s not, I was the one that hit that pillar.”

"I was the one that bumped you!"

"I was the one that flew us here."

"I was the one that wanted to come!"

"Okay you win, it's your fault." He teases as he stands up. He offers me his hand and I take it, he pulls me up to my feet and my eyes furrow as I look at him.

"Handler Sean?" I ask as we start to walk away from the fallen building.

"Yes?"

"Can I ask you something?"

"Depends." I inhale deeply and go to open my mouth when it happens. Something small, in the form of a liquid, starts to fall from the sky. My eyes widen in fear as I try to get away from it, no matter where I step though, it seems to follow me.

I don't know what this is, but I know what I fear that it is. Back during the last World War people used acid on their enemies…

"What is this?" I scream.

4

The Institution

"Miss Larina! It's just rain." I whirl around to look at him, he's pretty much a blur behind the blanket of the liquid falling down. I no longer think it's acid for the simple fact that I'm still alive and in one piece. "It's water, it falls from the sky naturally outside of the Sectors." Handler Sean explains to me. I hold my hand out and feel the water falling on my skin, I look out across the Old City and watch it being washed by this water from the sky. Rain, as Handler Sean called it.

Right as I'm starting to enjoy the rain, a loud sound clashes above us that has me jumping backwards and holding out my arms in front of my face for protection.

"What was that?! A bomb?" I look into his eyes and wait for his answer.

"Thunder." He says. I cock my head in confusion as I wait for the explanation of this new word, that I never heard of before. "It's just noise." He smiles down at me and reaches over and tucks a wet strand of my hair behind my ear.

I quickly avert my eyes and look up at the sky. "This is incredible!"

"This is nothing! There's this thing called 'Snow' and it's like rain only frozen. Outside of the Sectors, far from here, it gathers in the ground and piles up and up. The world turns white and it's really beautiful." I look back at him and smile.

"You've seen this before?"

“Yes, as a Handler I have to go out for training. I went outside of Sector 18Y and that's how it was, it was also freezing! We had to wear huge coats.”

“That’s so cool! I wish I could see that.”

“Maybe one day you will be able too.” I smile at him and he smiles back. “We should probably head back, we don’t want to miss the wake-up call.” He says.

“Good point.” We start walking towards the entrance of the city, we walk under the rain and I find myself smiling.

“What are you going to do once we get back? About being an Eraser?”

I stop walking and look at him. “What I have to do, I have to do my job. It’s my duty as a citizen of the Society.” He nods and I watch as his eyes flicker above me, I tense up immediately dreading what he’s looking at. “What is it?”

“Look.” Handler Sean walks past me and moves slowly towards a house that has been run down by weeds and vines. I follow after him and stop a few feet from him, my eyes wide as I stare at the back wall of the house. There’s a message written there in big, bold letters.

“If you have come from a Sector and escaped stay here, someone will come for you. We come every day, if you did not escape, then beat it! -The R”

“What do you think that means?” I ask looking up at Handler Sean. He has a troubled look on his face as he stares at the message written on the wall.

“I don’t know, but I don’t like it. Let’s get out of here.” He offers me his hand and I stare at it before placing mine to his. He leads me away from the house and walks quickly towards the hovercraft. I don’t know why he feels the need to hold my hand the whole time, but I know he's worried about the message so I don't bring it up.

Soon I see the hovercraft and feel Handler Sean relax a bit. "Let's hurry." He says looking down at me. I nod and we walk quickly to the hovercraft, where we get in and leave the Old City behind us.

We fly in silence, but neither of us has to say anything to know what the other is thinking. What does that message mean? Who is it meant for? Most importantly, Who wrote it?

After a few minutes of flying, we cross over the iron fence, entering Sector 7B. Handler Sean goes straight to the garage where we took the hovercraft from. As we hover above it, he softly brings it down and cuts off its engine.

"I'll walk you home." He says.

"It's okay I can_."

"You sure you want another Handler seeing you this morning?" He points at the side mirror of the hovercraft and I peer at it. My eyes widen as I look back at myself. My hair is a complete mess, it has rubble, rocks, and grass tangled into it, my face is covered in small cuts from the debris of the library and my sweater and pants are ripped in different areas. Honestly, I look like I just fought a war and lost pretty badly. "Let's get you home Miss Larina." We walk out of the garage through the front door, it's normal this time of day. Handlers are coming in to work right at dawn, to start their wake up call duties.

The wake-up call is where every family member has to be present when a Handler arrives at your door to check to see if everyone is up and ready to start the day because dad is a Handler we don't get one very often but you never know!

Soon we arrive at my front door and I turn to Handler Sean. "Have a good day Miss Larina, get yourself cleaned up alright?" He says in full Handler mode.

"Yes sir, have a good day." I walk inside the house and tip toe across the kitchen before walking up the stairs and into my room.

I grab a pair of clothes and quickly rush into the bathroom where I turn on the shower head and get in the shower. I watch as small pieces of rubble fall from my hair and the water turn a brown color from the dirt and dust.

After I finish, I get changed and stand in front of the mirror and no matter how clean I look, there's no hiding the cuts on my face. The ones on my neck I can cover with my shirt, but my face is a whole other story!

"Larina are you up?" I hear mom call from down the stairs.

"Yes! Getting ready." I call out.

"Take your medicines."

"Yes Ma'am."

I open the door to the bathroom and walk back to my room where I press my palm to the scanner and take out the pills and glass of water before swallowing them down.

"Hurry up Larina!" Mom shouts. I sigh loudly and walk down the stairs and into the kitchen. I avoid direct eye contact with my mother and keep my face turned away from her as I set the table.

"Good morning Geo, good morning Lari_." Dad stops talking and looks at me with a raised eyebrow. "What happened to your face?" He asks. That catches mom's attention right away.

"What do you mean? What's wrong with her face?" Mom turns me around and her eyes widen as she takes my face in her hands. "Larina, what happened?" Her dark eyes search my own for the answer that I'm not going to give.

"I fell." I lie.

"You fell? Where did you fall? Oh my God! Larina, your neck is like that too!" Mom says pulling on the collar of my shirt.

"Mom! I'm fine really! I just fell." I look into her eyes.

"When did you fall? We walked home together, we went to bed." Dad says.

"When I was getting ready for bed, I tripped over my backpack and hit my face on the wall. That's all. Really."

"Your wall did that?!"

"Yes?"

"Fine, look we'll talk about this later. We have to eat and get ready for work." Mom says clearly not believing my unbelievable story.

We sit at the table and eat without another word. After a few moments mom looks at dad and he stops chewing. "We have to go Clef." She says. He nods and wipes his mouth with the napkin before standing up. "Larina put the dishes in the sink, and get to your training. Have a good day." Mom says before she and dad walk out of the house. I sit there on the table staring at my plate for a few minutes before I actually do as mom instructed.

I leave the house and make my way to the Erasing Facility, which is right on the border of Sector 7B. As always I walk alongside the monorail and see people all around me, making their way to school. For the first time in years, I'm walking this path to get to somewhere other than school.

I look along and see the Erasing Facility still an hour away, standing tall and right beside the Headquarters. Only in complete contrast, it is a dark, almost black building. The building is also rather short, and there isn't one time that you look up at it, that you don't see smoke rising up from its many outlets.

The sky for once is blue, with big, puffy, white clouds floating across it from one end of the world to the other. It seems odd, the sky is so bright when I'm heading to the darkest place in our Sector. I step away from the monorail tracks when I hear the monorail coming, the rush of its speed, makes a strong wind that blows my hair back, making me lose my scrunchy.

"No!" I say out loud. I run after the scrunchy, which is drifting across the floor and past many people's feet. None of them stop to help. Finally, it gets stopped by a tall light post on the sidewalk. I bend down and pick it up, right as I'm pulling my hair out of my face to tie it back into a ponytail, I see a camera staring right at me. My heart stops for a split second thinking that whoever goes over the footage from this morning, when all cameras are turned back on, they are sure to see Handler Sean and myself making our way to my house. Then they will know that I left my home after curfew and got back minutes before the wake-up call. I find myself holding my breath as I stare at the camera, fear written in my eyes.

I don't have much time to dwell on it because I hear a distant clock strike from across the city and I quickly rush away from the light post and towards my destination. It takes me nearly an hour to walk to the building and by the time I make it there, I'm exhausted from walking. I press my palm to the scanner at the door and the door slides open for me.

"Good morning." A doctor says walking out of a room and into another right across the hall.

"Morning," I whisper. The first thing I notice as I walk deeper into the Erasing Facility is the smell. It smells of medicine and cleaning products, and the smell is so strong that I get an instant headache.

"Hello, how can I help you?" A lady at the front desk asks as I walk forward.

"My name is Larina Matthews, I'm supposed to meet Doctor Michael Webb?"

"Oh yes, he's waiting for you in the main lab. Go on in."

I press my lips together and she looks up at me. "What?"

"Where is the main lab?"

"Up the elevator one floor, last door on the right." She says going back to typing something into the monitor.

"Thank you, Ma'am."

"Uh huh, good luck." She calls out as I walk to the elevator. I inhale and press the button. The silver, steel door of the elevator slides open smoothly and reveals an equally silver interior. I step through and as I do, the door closes after me. I look at the button selection and press the 'Two' before the elevator slowly ascends a floor.

After a minute or so the elevator door opens and I stare at a hallway that is lined with doors on both sides. The doors are white against the beige walls. I walk down the hall, and with every step I take, my footsteps echoes down and up the hall. Soon I stand in front of the last door to the right, on top of it is a white sign with black letters, spelling out "Dr. Webb."

I knock once and I hear a loud noise coming from inside. "Do not come in! Give me a minute!" A man's voice shouts from inside.

"Okay, sir," I say.

After a few seconds, the door swings open and staring at me is a fifty or so year old man with dark blue eyes and grayish hair. He's nicely built and rather tall. "You are Larina Matthews?" He asks.

"I am, sir."

"Very well, you can come in." He steps aside and I enter the room and he shuts the door as soon as I clear the doorway. "I just finished Erasing my last one for the day, let me just_." He walks over to a dark gray machine, with a large, rectangle opening into it. My eyes go to the metal table that is directly in front of the opening. On the table, is something under a white blanket. I'm no expert, but judging from the shape of it, I'm pretty sure it's the person that Dr. Webb just erased. I watch as he pushes the table inside and then back out and the person is no longer on it. Dr. Webb closes a door over the opening in the machine and punches a code into the side of it. The machine comes alive and the smell of smoke surrounds the room. "Almost forgot!" He says pressing a button on the wall. I look up as a circular hole opens up on the ceiling right above the machine, where the smoke is coming out of.

“That is the cremator, you’ll learn how to use it eventually. Today I’m just going to take you through the steps of erasing. Are you ready?” I turn to look at him. No, I’m not ready, in fact, I may never be ready.

“Yes,” I say.

“Good, the first step is that the Erasers interview the people sent to be erased. They are kept in the Institution until they are to be erased.”

“Oh.”

“Yes, so let’s walk over to the Institution and interview one of the patients shall we?” Patients? How can he call them that? I simply nod and watch as he grabs a white lab coat that is hanging on the wall and hands it to me. “You are to wear only white when you come from now on, that is your uniform.”

“Okay.”

“And since you are now working, you are allowed to ride the monorail.”

“Really? Thank you, sir!” We walk down the hall and enter the elevator and ride it down to the main floor in complete silence.

“Judy, I’m going to the Institution.”

“Okay, Michael.” The lady at the front desk says. I press my lips wondering why they are calling each other by their first names when Dr. Webb speaks up. “Judy is my wife.” I nod and follow after him as we leave the dark building behind and head towards the building across from us.

Mom works as a Doctor at Institution. The building is nearly as tall as the Headquarters and just as white and bright. Especially today that the sun is out and there isn’t one cloud in the sky. I look up at the building, having to crane my neck to see the very top of it. Every floor has at least a roll of five large windows, indicating a room. There are easily over a hundred rooms in the Institution.

Dr. Webb and I walk inside the building and my eyes widen as my hands fly to my mouth. The smell in here is even stronger than at the Erasing Facility. It smells strongly of medications. As we walk deeper into the building, I find myself blinking several times because everything is so white. The only thing that isn't white in this building is the people's uniform. Their skirt or pants are black, their shirts and lab coat are white.

"Larina is that you?" I turn and see my mom walking over with a syringe in her hand that has a dark blue liquid in it.

"Hi, ma'am," I say.

"Hey sweetie, how's training going?"

"Fine." I nod and mom looks over at Dr. Webb.

"Hello, Doctor Webb." She says nodding her head at him.

"Doctor Matthews." He nods back and turns to me. "Shall we get going then, Miss Larina?" I nod and follow after him.

"Have fun sweetie!" Mom calls out, I turn back to look at her and see her entering a room and closing the door quickly after her.

"Alright this patient is here because this is his third offense, the next step as you know is to be erased." Dr. Webb says. We walk up the dark staircase, when I say dark I mean that it's poorly lit because the stairs itself is just as white as the rest of the building. "This patient's name is Matt Oscars." We walk down the hall that the stairs lead to and stop in front of a white door that is closed.

"Alright Miss Larina, here's the questions that we are to ask him. Once we've finished asking him questions, we will take him to be erased." He says showing me the questions in the thin pad in his hands.

"Okay," I whisper. Dr. Webb opens the door and inside is a young man in white clothing. He's sitting on a lone chair near the window.

"Hello, Mr. Oscars." Dr. Webb says. Matt doesn't answer, he continues staring out the window. "Say hello Miss Larina."

"Hello." I squeak. Matt shifts a little on his chair, but other than that he doesn't do much more.

"How are you today Mr. Oscars?" Dr. Webb asks following the questions very closely.

"How do you think I am?" Matt snarls, he turns to look at Dr. Webb and myself and my eyes search his face. He's angry, and as I've said before, I've never seen anyone angry besides Sherrie Maxwell. Matt has dark hair and equally dark eyes, his skin is very pale and he has dark circles under his eyes.

"Well, then why don't you tell us how you are feeling."

"Oh cut the bull crap Webb, I'm about to get killed. Let's just get this over with." Matt stands up and walks to us.

I take a step back as he starts for the door. Doctor Webb reaches his hand out and stops Matt from going anywhere. "We need to ask you a few more_."

“You can ask all the questions you want old man, doesn’t mean that I will answer any of them.” Matt stops near the door and turns to look at me.

“Lucky you, get to be an Eraser. Mommy and Daddy must be so proud.” My eyes drop to the floor and I press my lips together as I realize something. Erasers are hated. Why wouldn’t they be?

“Mr. Oscars you are way out of line.” Dr. Webb says rather calmly.

“Oh shove it, Webb, you know why I didn’t stop breaking the rules? Because I hate the Society, and I can’t wait for it to fall!” He shouts into Dr. Webb’s face. Dr. Webb straightens his back and glares back at Matt. “You are a despicable human being!” Matt shouts before spitting right into Dr. Webb’s face. He looks at me as Dr. Webb uses a handkerchief to wipe the saliva from his face. “And you just got stuck in all of this huh?”

“I_.”

“Miss Larina. You may go home now.” Dr. Webb says.

“Yes, sir!” I’m but too happy to be able to leave and get away from these people.

“Have a good day Miss Larina, there’s nothing better than to wake up in the morning and think ‘Who am I going to kill today?’” Matt says right as I open the door and leave.

I walk out of the Institution and don’t look back. I can’t believe I’ll have to do this every day. I have no choice though. As I leave the building I see clouds starting to move in and over the sun, and I think back to when Handler Sean and I were at the Old City and it started to rain. I know that it will never happen though, not in the Sector. I get aboard the monorail and ride it all the way home with dark thoughts crowding my mind.

I get home only a few minutes later and walk straight into the bathroom and slam the door shut as I press my back to it. I stare ahead at nothing in particular and feel water fall from my eyes. I'm crying, as Handler Sean had called it. The only place in the house that there isn't a camera is the bathroom, for obvious reasons. It's also very convenient for times like these where I start to cry and do things that we are no longer supposed to do. I don't know how I'm going to do this.

After a few hours, mom and dad arrive home and call me down. The tone in their voices, make me nervous. "Yes?" I ask once I'm down the stairs. I look at both of my parents sitting on the couch in the living room. Dad has a small monitor in his hands and is looking at me with a disappointed look stamped on his face. "Mom? Dad?"

"Come have a seat, Larina," Dad says. I slowly make my way to them, wondering what this could be about. I sit down on a chair across from them and wait. "Your mother and I know what happened to your face." He says.

My eyes widen as I stare at them, I quickly regain myself and straighten my back. "I told you, I tripped and_."

Dad shakes his head and types a few things in the monitor, I watch as the monitor sends a light into the middle of the room and a video starts to play in the form of a hologram. This video is much too familiar, it being of Handler Sean and I walking to my house this morning before dawn. Oh no.

"You were out with that Handler, and I want to know where you went and what you did there," Dad says. I look at mom who has her eyes trained on the floor in utter disbelief.

"Dad I_."

"Do not lie to me, Larina!" Dad shouts standing up and looming over me. I look up at him and slowly drop my head so that I'm staring at my feet.

"We've turned the cameras off in the living room Larina, you can tell us," Mom says.

I look up and take a deep breath before I tell them. "I needed time alone, I didn't want to be to an Eraser! So I sneaked out and Handler Sean caught me." I say.

"He caught you?" Dad asks.

"Yes, I was going to go outside of the Sector and_."

"Larina! You know very well how dangerous it is outside of the Sector!" Mom says.

"I know, but I needed time to myself without being watched."

"What happened after he caught you?" Dad asks looking at me.

"He escorted me home, he said he'd give me a warning but the next time he caught me out past my curfew, that he'd report it to Sherrie Maxwell," I say.

"I wonder why he didn't," Mom says winking at me. I feel myself flush red and look down at my feet.

"I guess it was because it was my first time?" I feel bad about lying to mom and dad, but there's no way I can tell them that a Handler helped me sneak out. He could be Erased.

"All I have to say about this is that this has better be the last time you do something like this, that and you are lucky I was the one who was in charge of looking the footage over," Dad says.

"It will be the last time," I promise.

“Good, get to bed. You have a busy day tomorrow.” I watch my parents leave the living room and walk into their room before slamming the door shut behind them. I sit there and close my eyes, feeling really glad that it was dad who saw the footage.

5

The New Eraser

In the morning, I take the monorail to the Erasing Facility. When I arrive at Dr. Webb's lab, he already has someone in the chair. My eyes go to the restraints on the girl's arms and legs, then they go to the metal cuff that Dr. Webb placed around her mouth so that she can't talk, or beg. Her dark eyes go to me and even though she can't speak, her eyes say a million words.

Oh God, I'm going to be sick. "Oh Miss Larina, you're here! Please get me the death serum from the cabinets will you?" Dr. Webb says. I nod and walk to the cabinet and throw the cabinet's glass door open. Inside it is many different things. There's the death serum which is inside a small, round and dark container with a silver lid. Right under the death serum is a container that looks exactly like it, only it doesn't contain the death serum, it contains sleep serum. "Miss Larina, are you having trouble finding it?" Dr. Webb walks over to me and I tense up as he reaches over my shoulder and takes the death serum into his hand.

I turn and watch him use the needle to suck the serum into the syringe. My eyes go to the girl as she starts to struggle in her chair.

"This step is pretty easy Miss Larina what you do is_." Dr. Webb stops talking when there's a knock on the door. I watch him walk over to it and open it, I can't hear what the person says but whatever they say makes him set the syringe down and turn to me. "I'll be right back, why don't you go ahead without me?" He nods and closes the door after him.

I turn to the girl and she looks at me and presses her back to the back of the chair as I approach her. She becomes a blur as tears start to appear in my eyes, I quickly blink back the tears and sigh loudly.

"I'm not going to kill you," I say. Her eyes widen and she stares at me as I undo the restraints and remove the metal cuff from her mouth. "I can't erase you, but if you stay here they will. I don't know what you did but I just can't do it."

"I_."

"Listen, go through that door, it leads down a hallway that they store some cremators, just keep going and you'll see a door that leads outside the building and you'll find yourself at the border of the Sector. You'll have to find a way to climb the fence or go under it, I don't know if you'll be able to do it during the day, maybe you should wait until night."

"Thank you so much!" She flings her arms around me and I hug her back.

"You're welcome. There's an abandoned city that is two hours walk from here. Stay there. That's all I can do for you."

"That's more than enough! Thank you!" Tears line her eyes and she leaves through the door that I had told her about and I quickly grab a few towels from the drawers and walk to the cremator and shove them inside before I slam the door shut and punch the code I saw Dr. Webb do the previous day. I then open the outlet on the ceiling and let the smoke from the burning towels leave through it.

I only remember about the syringe that Dr. Webb had left on the counter next to the door when I see the doorknob start to turn. I race to the syringe and then run to the sink and drain the serum behind my back, down the sink, right as Dr. Webb steps into the room.

"All done!" I say turning towards the sink and opening the faucet to let it wash the black liquid from the white surface. I pretend to wash my hands as he walks over.

"You did everything?" He asks raising an eyebrow at me.

"I erased her and uh, turned the cremator on."

"Very good Miss Larina! Now fill out the form and you're good to go! Tomorrow you should be able to start all by yourself." Oh dear God. I take the pad from his hands into my shaky ones and look down at the screen and the words written in it.

"Erase to occur 13:00 hours, Name of patient: Samantha Andrews." Right at the bottom of the page is a statement. "State of Being." On the empty line right next to it, I write in big, bold letters: "Erased."

"Very good Miss Larina. You may go home now, tomorrow you officially start being an Eraser! Well done." Dr. Webb smiles at me and opens the door to the room. I throw a glance at the door that I sent Samantha through, praying that she'll make it out alive for both of our sake. "And Miss Larina?" Dr. Webb says as I'm about to leave.

"Yes, sir?" I look at him, scared that he'll know something is off.

"It will only get easier." I nod and close the door after me. As I walk down the hall to get to the elevator, I shake my head. I hope I never find killing someone, easy.

A week later

I've been an "Official Eraser" for a week now, I got my own lab which happens to be right across from Dr. Webb's.

I sit on the chair that holds the restraints and think about how lucky I am that no erasing is ever recorded. In fact, I think that the only building that does not contain cameras inside it is the Erasing Facility. If I had to guess, I'd say that the Society doesn't want any evidence of any of the erasing.

I look up at the monitor as it flashes on with my new "Patient" for the day. I walk over to the monitor and press my finger to its screen. "DNA accepted." The computer says. I scroll over the screen and see that I have two patients that I have to go interview. A mother and her baby.

I feel my knees buckle under me, I take a deep breath before taking the thin pad in my hands and making my way out of the Erasing Facility and to the Institution.

"Good evening Miss Larina." I look behind me as I'm crossing the street and see Handler Sean on his hover board.

"Handler Sean, how are you, sir?" I ask.

"Fine, I'm on street patrol." He explains. "You?" He adds.

"Just going to get the new patient." I cast my eyes to the floor and sigh silently before looking back at him with a fake smile.

"And you're doing okay?" He asks studying me closely.

"Yes fine. I do have to go, I don't want to be late. It was good seeing you." I smile a less than fake smile before turning and walking across the street.

"Have a good night Miss Larina." Handler Sean says.

"You too sir," I say.

I walk inside the Institution and mom greets me at the door. "Hey, sweetie!"

"Good evening Ma'am."

"My little Eraser! Are you going to get a patient?"

"Yes Ma'am."

"I'll leave you to it." She nods and I nod back before heading up the staircase. I walk down the hall and enter a closed door. The woman who is in the room is sitting on the white carpet that matches perfectly with her white clothing. Her blue eyes fly to mine as I enter the room and I watch her tighten the hold on the bundle in her arms as if to protect it from me.

"Hello, Mrs. James," I say.

She watches me as I approach her. "Are you the Eraser?" She asks her eyes widening.

"Yes, I am."

"But you are but a babe!" Her eyes glimmer against the dim light of the room and the soft sunlight coming in through the window.

"I need you to come with me, Mrs. James," I say knowing very well that I'll release her like the previous three people I was supposed to erase. I watch her slowly get up to her feet and walk slowly to me.

"Where is my husband? Mr. James?" She asks.

“He’s next door to you, ma’am,” I whisper.

“Can I please see him? I need to say goodbye!” I watch her come close to tears, however, the water never drips down her cheeks and onto the floor.

“I_.”

“Please, Miss! I’ll never see him again!” I find myself nodding as I open the door.

“I’ll need you to keep quiet,” I say. She nods and follows me to the door next to her’s. I slowly open the door and the minute she see’s the man inside the door she runs to him and hugs him and at that point, the both of them start to cry.

“We’ll be strong until the end Ellie.” He says cupping her face in his hands. “Until the end, for Bailey.” He says stroking the baby’s head.

“Yes, my love,” Ellie says. “I love you, Jonathan.”

“I love you too.”

Not being able to bear it any longer I step into the room and they both turn to look at me. “I need you both to come with me,” I say.

“But my Eraser isn’t due for another_.” I hold my hand up and stop Jonathan.

“I’ve spoken with your Eraser, he’s not feeling well. Come with me.” I see the despair in the couple’s eyes, they don’t want to see each other or their baby being erased. “Now.”

They both quietly follow behind me as we walk down the stairs and out of the Institution, and finally into my erasing lab.

“I’ll go first,” Jonathan says.

"No! Please!" Ellie says tears staining her cheeks.

"Please don't worry, I'm not going to erase you," I say. They both look at me and their eyes widen before Jonathan asks:

"What do you mean? Is someone else going to do it?"

"No, I'm going to release you." I walk to the door with the cremators inside and open it. "Go through here, there's a door that leads you to the border of the Sector."

"You truly are letting us go?"

"Yes, I can't erase you. You're a lovely family, what could you have done wrong?"

"We had Bailey," Ellie says.

"What?"

"We had Bailey, we already had a daughter her name is Emily James, she's a Handler." I nod my head in understanding. You are only allowed to have one child in the Society, if you have more, you are erased. Of course, if you happen to have twins or triplets they let you keep one baby and they erase the others. It's all about keeping order. The parents don't even get to chose who they keep but again, how could they?

"I'm truly sorry," I say.

"It's okay, you are doing so much for us!" Ellie walks to me, after handing Bailey to Jonathan, and hugs me. "We will always remember you Miss_.?"

"Larina, my name is Larina. Please go. There's an abandoned city two hours from here. You can go there, anywhere. Stay safe and take these to keep Bailey warm, it's cold out there." I open a closet and pull out three white blankets that are used to cover the people erased.

“Thank you, Miss Larina,” Ellie says stepping towards her family.

“You’re welcome,” I say.

I watch them turn to go. “If you see Emily, tell her that we said goodbye,” Jonathan says. I nod my head. I will, I know Emily.

When Jonathan, Ellie and Bailey leave, I sit down on the chair with my hands on my face and try to slow down my breathing so that I won’t start crying. Once I’ve regained my composure, I stand up and walk to the cremator and turn it on, once I’ve done that I walk to the pad that sits next to the sink.

I type down “Erased” On Ellie’s and Bailey’s file. My eyes widen at the sudden realization that I don’t have Jonathan’s files.

That’s when someone throws my door open and I turn to face them. I exhale in relief as I see that it’s Donnie Meyers, the new Eraser.

“Hello Mr. Meyers, how can I help you?”

“I went to retrieve uh, Mr. James and he’s not in his room in the Institution.”

“I erased him,” I say.

“You did?”

“Yes, he was right next door to Mrs. James so I got it done.”

“Leave it to you to get twice your erasing in Miss Larina.” He says smiling at me.

“Thank you.” I nod

"No thank you, now I get to go home early! Have a good night!" He calls out as he leaves.

"Wait!" I shout. He pops his head back into the room and waits. "I need the files for Jonathan James."

"Oh right, here." He holds out his pad and I take it from him.

"Have a good night." He nods and then leaves. I close the door after he's gone and let out a breath before typing: "Erased" Onto Jonathan's file as well. That was a close one.

I walk over to the cremator and switch it off and find that I'm crying. All the people that the Society sends to be killed, it's not right. They aren't criminals. I slowly sit down on the floor with my back to the steel cabinet and just let the tears flow freely from my eyes, someone needs to do something.

I can only release the people I'm assigned to erase, the other people are all killed for no good reason. I look up at the clock as it strikes nine o' clock. It's past my curfew. I inhale deeply and bring my knees up to my chest and my head to my knees, I'm not ready to go home and face my parents yet. I don't want them to see my red and blotchy cheeks from the crying and think something is wrong. There's something wrong, I just don't want them to know about it.

I sit there thinking things over for about an hour before someone slowly opens the door to the room and calls out: "Hello? Anyone in here?" I look up from the floor when I realize that it's Handler Sean's voice.

"I'm here," I call out.

"Larina?" I don't cringe at hearing him calling me by just my first name. The Society's laws and rules don't make sense to me anymore, I don't care if someone breaks them. Sean looks around for a bit before locating me.

"Hi," I say slowly getting up to my feet.

"What's going on Larina? I saw the light on and came to check."

"I was just thinking."

"About what?" He looks into my eyes and I inhale before turning my eyes away from his.

"You were right, I can see it now. How wrong the Society is." I look up at him and his eyes are wide. "Do you know how many people they send to die for no good reason?"

"I_."

"These people_." I lose my voice as tears build themselves up and I feel a lump in my throat. I start crying and making strange sounds as I cover my face with my hands. "How can you work for them? Knowing this for so long?" I whisper.

"I patrol the city, I make sure people are safe." He says.

"You report people and send them to get erased," I say glaring at him.

"I've never sent anyone to be erased Larina, and let me ask you this? How do you do it? Knowing?"

"Me? Are you kidding? I don't do it." He stares at me with a confused look on his face. "I can't do it, Sean, I can't kill." I feel my heart thump against my chest, at being angry.

"Erase." He whispers.

"KILL!" I scream. He backs up from surprise. "They are killing them, Sean! They send babies in here, what wrong can they possibly do?!" Thick tears slide down my cheeks as I look at him.

"They_." Sean turns pale as he stares at me.

I look down at the floor and see the tears hit the ground with small splashes. "They kill infants." I look back at him and sigh before wiping at the tears. "Even though it's awful and I have to deal with it every day, I'm glad I got to be an Eraser. I see how things truly are! I know what they do and I let these people escape the control of the Society. I saved a lot of people Sean and that makes me happy!" I smile for the first time in the week.

"You stopped didn't you?" He takes my shoulders in his hands and I find that it no longer feels wrong. Before the Society took over, people were touched by other people all the time.

"Stopped what?"

"Taking the medications, you're really not under their control anymore." I press my lips together as I look at him. It's true, I haven't taken the medication for the last week and to be honest, I do feel different. A lot different.

"I feel different now, I still pretend when there are people around but at least here, I'm never watched."

"Larina, it's true. You're not watched but you have to be careful." He lets his hands drop from my shoulders.

"I will be." He studies me for a minute and then nods.

"You need to go home before someone catches you."

"I am."

"I mean right now Larina, don't go sneaking off to that city. I don't want you getting hurt!" My heart does a flip inside my chest at hearing him say this. He must sense that he said too much because his cheek colors before he turns away.

"Have a good night Larina."

"Good night." I nod my head and walk past him, as I'm walking down the hallway I hear his footsteps as he tries to catch up to me.

"I'll uh, walk you home." He says quietly.

"You don't have too, I can get there by myself."

"The monorail already past and it's an hour walk from here. I'll be happy to walk you home."

"Sean_."

"I want to walk you home." He doesn't look at me as he says it. I smile to myself and look at my feet as we walk out of the building.

We walk in silence for about thirty minutes or so then Sean places a hand on my shoulder. "Larina." He whispers. I look back at him and wait, he just stares into my eyes for the longest time and I can see that he's trying to decide if he'll tell me or not.

"What is it?"

He closes his eyes and I hear him sigh. "Nothing, never mind." He starts walking again, leaving me behind.

"Sean?!" I call out. He runs to me and gently covers my mouth with his hand. "You can't call me that! Not out here!" The fear is clear in his eyes. Not for himself but for me. I see it. I get a strong urge to ask him if he loves me like I love him. I don't though and we just sit there staring at each other, I feel his hand leave my lips and they move down towards my chin. He takes my chin softly between his fingers and tilts my head up so I'm looking at him.

My mouth parts in surprise and he brings his lips to mine and kisses me. I close my eyes and feel my heart start to beat faster and ram itself against my rib cage.

"Larina?" He whispers when he pulls away. I open my eyes slowly and look up at him, he's looking down at me with a sad look in his eyes.

"Yeah?" I whisper back.

"We can't_."

I sigh loudly and nod. "I know." I step aside and start walking by myself. I wrap my arms around my torso and frown deeply. It was dark when we kissed, it'll take a little while for the Society to pinpoint who it was.

6

Medal of Service

I get off the Monorail and my parents follow after me. It's been nearly a month since Handler Sean and I uh, kissed. Today my family and I were asked to go to the Headquarters.

Mom, dad and I didn't speak for the whole way over but I know what both of them are thinking. "What did she do?" While I know exactly what I did, and I don't know how they'll take it, finding out that their daughter is going to be erased. How ironic, the Eraser getting erased.

We walk to the entrance of the Headquarters and the first person I see is Handler Sean. My eyes goes to his and he lets a small smile play on his lips before he sees my parents and a serious look crosses his face.

"Good morning Matthews family." He says.

"Good morning Handler Clarkson," Dad says nodding his head. We pass him and he throws me a look and I only shrug.

"Larina!" Mom shouts. I stop walking and jump backward at her scream.

"What is it, ma'am?" I ask.

"You almost ran into that vase!" Mom says pointing to the vase that I'm standing in front of. Oops. My cheeks turn red and I bow my head.

"Sorry, I was lost in thought."

"That's okay, just pay attention okay?" I nod and we continue on. I look back at Sean as my parents knock on Sherrie Maxwell's door and let a smile cross my lips as he starts to quietly laugh. As I turn away from him, I wonder if this is the last time I'll see him.

Sherrie opens the door and smiles at the three of us. "Good morning Matthews!" She says motioning us in. We step inside the room and she shuts the door. "How are you today?"

"We're just fine Head Handler, what is this all about?" Dad asks. It's incredible how tall he seems to be even though Sherrie is easily six inches taller than him. He just has this air of authority I guess.

"Yes, I'm sure you must be wondering why I've called you all here. Please have a seat and I'll explain everything." We sit down on three seats set up for us and Sherrie sits directly in front of me. She smiles softly at me before turning to my parents. Here it goes…

"Your family is an excellent example of what a family truly loyal to the Society should be. You have very important roles, With you being a Handler Mr. Matthews and you being a very known Doctor Mrs. Matthews and then there's your daughter_." She pauses as she looks at me. I press my lips together, feeling my stomach twist in a knot. "She's an excellent Eraser, she's a fast learner and excels at doing her assignment. I heard from Doctor Webb that many times she even takes the assignment of other Erasers and does them herself. She's a very hard worker." Wait_. "The Society is truly happy to have you be part of her unit." So I'm not getting erased?

"That means a lot, Head Handler!" Mom says squeezing my hands. I see it in her eyes, how proud she is of me.

"And with such hard work comes rewards."

“We ask for nothing but to serve the Society,” Dad says straightening his back.

“Yes, Handler Matthews I know. However, we see it fit for the three of you to receive the Medal of Service.” My mouth drops open as I stare at Sherrie. As my parents thank her tremendously, I sit there thinking how funny this all is. I even find myself smiling at the irony of it all. Sure my parents deserve the Medal of Service, but all I deserve is to be erased. "So if you’ll come with me, we can get it done.” Sherrie smiles and leads us to the back room where a machine that makes the Medal of Service is at.

I guess now is a good time to tell you what the Medal of Service is. Basically, it’s a tattoo on your left wrist with the mark of the Society. Flames surrounded by a thin black circle. They mark you as a Society worker, very few people receive such a “Privilege” Handler Sean has one, I’ve seen it before.

“Handler Matthews, why don’t you go first?” Sherrie asks. Dad nods and sits down in front of the machine and extends his arm out across its flat surface. “Ready?” Dad nods and I watch from where I’m standing next to mom, a needle lower itself into dad’s arm and start marking his wrist.

He doesn’t flinch, which is really reassuring. He finishes after five minutes and mom steps up next and it’s the same thing, she doesn’t flinch either. Not as the needle lowers itself into her wrist or as it glides over it making the Society’s mark. Mom stands up once it’s done and looks down at it with a smile on her face.

“Your turn Miss Larina,” Sherrie says. I inhale deeply and sit down on the chair in front of the machine. From up close, the needle seems a lot bigger. I press my lips together as I watch it lower itself into my wrist.

The pain that I feel is incredible. It hurts so much, but I don't scream or thrash around or even say anything. I clench my teeth together and bare it, realizing that the reason it's hurting so much is that I haven't been taking my medication. Mom and dad didn't feel anything because one thing the medication does is ensure that the people taking it, don't feel pain. The five minutes seem to last hours, but eventually, it's finished. The needle lifts up and hides away inside the machine, and I slowly stand up. "All done."

I walk over to my parents and as I stand there I feel my entire body tremble from the pain, where the Medal of Service lies on my wrist, is burning. I press my palm to it and look up at Sherrie as she comes to stand in front of us.

"As you know Mr. And Mrs. Matthews, Emma Jones wants all citizens with the Medal of Service to work at the Center." My eyes fly to hers. The Center? That's the main place of the Society, it's like the Sectors only twice as big and only Handlers, Doctors and the Leader of the Society live there. That's also where they train their best Handlers, and they become Head Handlers of the Sectors once the current ones die. "So the both of you are being transferred there, you may have a week to pack any of your things that you wish to take. As you know a house is provided for you at the Center and because Miss Larina is not yet twenty-one years of age she is too young to work at the Center, so she will remain here until she turns twenty-one."

"That's three years away," Mom says.

"Indeed, think of it as a good experience for her. She'll be a wonderful Eraser for the Center after her three years of working as one here." I see that mom is about to say something more but dad places a hand on her shoulder.

"Thank you, Head Handler." He says.

So they are really going to the Center and leaving me behind? I look at my parents and mom turns to look at me with a fake smile on her face.

"Good job mom and dad," I say.

"Sir and Ma'am, Larina." Sherrie corrects me.

"Sir and Ma'am," I repeat after her.

"Well, you may all go. Have a good day and congratulation on being such loyal citizens of the Society." As she says this, she looks at me with a smirk on her face that sends a chill down my spine. The three of us nod at her before we walk towards the door. "Oh and Miss Larina?" Sherrie calls out. I stop in my tracks and turn to look at her. "Don't worry, we'll look out for you. So you'll never have to feel alone."

I stare into her blue eyes and she raises her eyebrow at me, daring me to say anything besides thank you. "Thank you," I whisper, and with that, we leave for home.

As we board the monorail to go to our jobs for the day, mom takes a hold of my hand and smiles at me.

"Sherrie is right, this will be a good experience for you." I only nod, knowing that mom is trying to convince herself of the same thing.

The monorail ride seems to take forever, but finally, we all go our separate ways. Mom to the Institution, dad to the Headquarters and I go to the Erasing Facility. The minute I step inside my lab room, the monitor flashes my new assignment.

I sigh loudly and ready myself for another day of breaking the laws and hopefully getting away with it for just another day.

That night as I arrive at home, exhausted and depressed, I see boxes on the floor of the kitchen with different things. From mom's books to dad's monitors.

"We won't need a week, Geo." I hear dad say from their room. I slowly tiptoe down the hallway and stop a few feet from their opened door.

"I don't want to go Clef!" I can hear the emotion in mom's voice and my heart starts aching at the thought of losing my parents.

"We have too." I hear loud noises. "Stop taking the stuff from the boxes! We're going!" Dad shouts. I step back and press my lips together. I've never seen my parents fight before.

"I don't want to leave Larina! She's not ready to be by herself Clef."

"It's you who's not ready to let her go." I press my forehead to the wall and close my eyes.

"I already lost_." Mom's words get muffled out by the sound of crying. Wait, mom is crying?

"Take your medication," Dad says. I back away and hurry to my bedroom where I close the door behind me and hide my face behind my hands. She already lost what?

I slide down the wall and sit on the floor, with my knees to my chest. I come to the realization that there's nothing we can do about being separated. Emma Jones ordered it, there's no disobeying the Leader of the Society. I sit in my room listening to my parents argue and talk for hours after our curfews and hours after we were supposed to be plugged into the Dream Catcher.

By the time I get up from the floor and change into some pajamas, I'm exhausted and I end up hooking myself up to the Dream Catcher, something I haven't done for months now.

Once you hook yourself up, you can't remove it from your finger until morning. Not without causing suspicion. So I lay there in bed, fearing the dreams I might have and trying to stay awake. Before I know it, I fall asleep and dream.

For several seconds after I open my eyes, everything is black. Then slowly my eyes adjust and I see that I'm in a nearly empty room, with a single light bulb dangling from the ceiling just overhead. I take a step forward and the light of the light bulb shines on the only thing in the room. A mirror.

I walk towards the mirror and where I assumed would be my reflection, isn't. In the mirror is a girl, looking down at the floor. Her hair covers her face, so I can't tell who she is. She has a plain black shirt and black pants on. "Are you okay?" I hear myself say. The girl slowly looks up and I jump backward as I see the girl's face. She looks almost exactly like me, that's when I realize that this is the same girl from that simulation almost two months ago.

"Get me out!" She screams pressing her palms to the glass. I look around the room for anything that I can use to break her free. Out of nowhere, a steel table appears with a bat on top of it. I take it into my hands and turn to run towards the girl, but where the mirror stood now stands a monitor.

I slowly make my way to the monitor and watch the scene unfold before me. There's Doctor Webb, he's walking around his lab room back in the Erasing Facility. I watch as he walks to the chair and I see the person he just erased. It's the girl, only now she has on a white, hospital gown. My eyes brim with tears as I stare at her, limp and not moving as he carries her from the chair to the steel table in front of the cremator. "NO!" I hear myself scream as he lies her down and covers her with the white blanket.

One of her arms slides from over her stomach and hangs from the side of the table. "Let her go!" I shout and before I know what I'm doing, I'm slamming the bat against the monitor over and over again until there's a hole large enough for me to step through.

Just as I do, I find the floor is gone and I fall down, screaming as I go. I try to grab a hold of the walls, but they seem to widen and my arms won't reach.

I prepare for the worst as I come closer to the floor, but where I would expect a hard floor to be is a soft bed. I land with a single bounce and quickly shoot up out of the bed. I recognize this place at once, it's the Institution. My eyes go straight to the door where the girl is at. She looks at me as I look at her and the both of us start to walk towards each other.

We are dressed in identical hospital gowns, with our hair down and our eyes wide with fear. "Who are you?" We both say at the same time.

"I'm Larina," I whisper. She doesn't tell me her name, she just reaches out for my hand and I do the same. The minute our hands touch each other, she screams from pain and disappears and she appears to fuse with me.

"It's your fault!" I hear mom scream. I whirl around and see her there, crying and holding a syringe with the death serum in it.

"Mom?"

"She's gone because of you!" With that my own mother runs to me and right when I think she's going to inject me with the serum, she runs past me and injects it into Emma Jones. I see Emma's eyes widen as the needle enters her skin and she falls to the floor, stomach down. That's when Handlers storm the room and take mom by the arms and take her away.

"MOM!" I hear myself scream and feel myself squeeze my eyes shut. When I open them again I'm back in my room, gasping for air, with tears flowing down my cheeks. I unhook the Dream Catcher from my finger and throw it across the room and watch as it hits the wall with a thud, before falling to the floor. I squeeze myself, trying to calm down.

"It was just a dream!" I tell myself. I slowly ease myself off the bed and walk to the bathroom where I go straight to the sink and splash my face with water. I hear noise from the kitchen and quickly dash down the stairs before entering the kitchen and hugging mom.

"Larina what's_." She stops talking as she hugs me back and holds me to her as I start crying. "It's going to be okay sweetie, you'll be fine." She whispers. I nod and hold on to her, not wanting to lose her like I did in my dream.

A week later

I walk with my parents to the monorail station, knowing that I won't be boarding it with them this time. They are off to their assignment in the Center.

"You be good," Dad says taking my shoulders into his hand. I only nod, knowing that if I talk I'll become a mess of tears outside where everyone can see.

"And take your medication," Mom says looking at me out of the corner of her eye.

“Okay.” I muster.

“We’ll be together again before you know it, Larina.” Dad messes my hair up and I let out a laugh as I look at them.

“I love you guys.” I hug my parents and they hug me back.

“We love you too Larina.” Mom whispers against my hair. She strokes my cheek and smiles softly at me before she turns to dad.

“Should we go then?” Dad asks. Mom only nods and they hold hands as they board the monorail.

“Bye!” I shout as the monorail starts to move.

“Stay out of trouble!” Dad screams back. I stay there watching the monorail until it’s nothing but a speck in the distance. “I’ll miss you guys,” I whisper to myself. I inhale deeply and make my way back home, as I enter I immediately feel lonely. The house seems darker. Darker and empty.

7

Erased

It's been nearly three months since mom and dad left for the Center. I'm finally starting to get used to living, eating and being alone in general.

I slowly sit up in bed as the sun peeks into my room, telling me that it's time to get up and live another day filled with lies and hatred. I hurry around my room getting the white outfit I'm supposed to wear to work and then go into the bathroom to shower and get changed.

Once I've finished, I walk down the stairs and stand at the bottom of the stairs looking into the empty kitchen. I got so used to seeing mom cooking and preparing breakfast every day since I was a kid that now, it just feels so sad. I skip breakfast and walk out the door getting my lab coat on the way out. Right as I'm about to leave the door, my small monitor starts to blink. I pull it out of my bag and press my finger to its screen and wait. "Go to the Headquarters, before going into work, -Sherrie." I sigh loudly wondering what she could possibly want with me this time.

I walk to the monorail station and wait there along with a couple, for the monorail to arrive.

"Don't." The husband says. I look towards them and press my lips together as I discreetly watch them.

"They took our baby." The wife says. She covers her face with her hands. "He's going to be erased, Jack!" She adds. I inhale deeply and thankfully the monorail arrives and I board it and sit at the very back where I don't hear their exchange.

The ride to the Headquarters isn't long at all and soon I'm stepping out of the monorail and walking towards the Headquarters entrance. I find myself smiling as I think that maybe I'll get to see Sean today. I haven't seen him at all lately.

All happiness flee me as I step inside the building and the Handler that is there to greet me is just some other Handler I don't know.

"Good morning Miss Larina." She says.

"Morning," I whisper. I press my lips together and stare ahead at the hallway. I make my way to Sherrie's room and soon I arrive in front of it and knock on the door.

Sherrie Maxwell opens the door and smiles at me, I smile back and look inside the room. The first thing I see or rather I should say the first person I see is, Doctor Jamie Simmons. Uh oh.

"Come in Miss Larina," Sherrie says and I do, what choice do I have?

"Good morning Miss Larina!" Doctor Simmons says waving at me.

"Good morning Doctor," I say nodding my head. I turn to Sherrie who is watching me carefully. "What's going on?" I ask.

"Why don't you have a seat dear?" Doctor Simmons says patting the chair opposite to her. I nod and sit down, Sherrie sits beside Doctor Simmons. "So, Sherrie here told me that you've been on your own for three months now? Because your parents moved to the Center."

"Yes."

"How are you feeling, Miss Larina?" I look at Sherrie who seems rather impatient at the Doctor. She's tapping her fingers on the arm of the chair, obviously wanting to move things along.

"Fine, when my parents first left I felt lonely but I'm okay now."

"That's great to hear I_."

"Miss Larina as you know as Head Handler of Sector 7B, it is my job to look into the Dream Catchers as it is Doctor Simmons," Sherrie says interrupting the Doctor.

"Yes, I know that." What could she possibly be getting at? Does she know that I haven't been hooking up to the Dream Catcher? Why bring it up now? I haven't done it for five months.

"Good, as you know we search everyone's dream for any signs of problems." Sherrie clasps her hands together and smiles at me. "It takes some time to review everyone's dream but soon we do and we found one of yours that is quite concerning." I bite my lower lip and stare at her.

"Oh?"

"Yes, let us see it shall we?" Sherrie stands up and walks to a monitor and types somethings in. I look at Doctor Simmons and she smiles at me.

"We just want to go through the dream with you that's all sweetie." I nod and Sherrie clears her throat to get our attention. "Impatient as always." I hear Doctor Simmons murmur.

"I heard that, thank you." Sherrie snaps. I suppress a laugh as I watch the exchange between the two. They seem very close.

"This was your dream from the night you found out that your parents were moving to the Center," Sherrie says. As the dream begins to play on the monitor my eyes drift to the floor as I recognize the dream all too well. "Don't you think it's strange Doctor, that she keeps seeing herself in her dreams?" Sherrie asks looking at Doctor Simmons. I look at the Doctor and watch her reaction go from understanding to simply agreeing.

"Yes."

"So, this girl that I keep seeing is myself?" I ask pointing to the girl that is clearly not me, just looks like me.

"Yes," Sherrie says. Sherrie scrolls forward into the dream to the part where mom kills Emma Jones. "This whole dream is how you felt about your parents going off to the Center, you seeing yourself being erased, I assume is you thinking you lost a piece of yourself when your parents left." I only nod, what can I say? That's not me? Plus if she's not me, then who is this girl?

"Nothing strange here Sherrie, just her subconsciousness is all." Doctor Simmons says.

"Hm." Sherrie nods and looks at me. "What do you think Miss Larina?" She asks.

"I don't think that girl is me." I blurt out. Sherrie raises her eyebrow and waits for me to continue. "There are differences in the two of us, I mean look at her. She looks like me, but she's obviously not me."

Doctor Simmons looks at Sherrie quickly before turning to me. "Sometimes in our dreams, we portray ourselves as what we would like to be. Maybe the differences in this girl is that for you."

"No, it's not. I've seen her in a simulation months ago."

"Why don't you tell us who you think this girl is then Miss Larina?" Sherrie asks resting her chin on her hands and giving me a mocking smile.

"I_. I don't know who she is, I just have a feeling that she's not me. I don't know what she's supposed to signify but I know she's not me."

"I'm sure it's just you trying to figure things out Miss Larina, now go on and get to work. Thank you for coming." Sherrie says.

"Okay, thank you, ma'am." I nod my head at her and Doctor Simmons before walking to the door.

As I'm about to leave I hear Sherrie talk to Doctor Simmons. "She can't know, double her dosage." My eyes widen as I close the door after me. So they know what this girl is supposed to mean?

I quietly walk to the Erasing Facility, a few minutes walk from the Headquarters and enter it without as much as a glance at Judy, Doctor Webb's wife. "Morning Miss Larina." She calls out.

"Good morning Ma'am."

"Doctor Webb is running late today. Do you mind taking this assignment for him please?" Judy asks holding a pad in her hands.

"Oh, sure thing Ma'am." She smiles sweetly at me and watches as I walk back out of the Erasing Facility and towards the Institution. The sky is clouded over and almost completely covered by clouds beside the small cracks of blue and sunlight pouring in and over the city. I walk into the Institution and a few Doctors nod their heads towards me as I make my way to the staircase that leads me to the patient's room. Before I start ascending the stairs, I look down at the pad and read the number of the room the person is in. "Main floor, room A," It says.

I press my lips together, knowing that the patients on the main floor are Handlers or Doctors. I turn around and walk back to the room that sits directly in front of the entrance to the Institution. My hand goes to the knob and when I open the door and see the person inside it, I nearly fall to the ground. This explains why I haven't seen him, he's been here getting ready to be erased.

"Sean," I whisper.

"Hey." He actually smiles at me. My mouth parts as I stare at him. "Close the door will you?" I do so and turn to look at him.

"What happened?" I ask as I walk to him. He's hurt, his lip is cut and he has bruises on his jaw. I slowly approach him and he scoffs at me.

"I'm not a wounded animal Larina, I'm not going to run you know."

"What happened?" I repeat staring into his hazel eyes. Who did this to him?

"This is courtesy of my fellow Handlers, Sherrie Maxwell wanted to find out a few things, when I didn't answer her questions, she had them beat me." My eyes start to water and he quickly approaches me and wipes away at the tears that haven't yet left my eyes. "Don't cry, they're watching." He whispers. I feel his breath against my cheek and my heart throbs for a second before calming down to its normal pace. He looks down at me and as I look up at him, all I want to do is hug him and help him get cleaned up. "Stop looking at me like that Larina, I've been trying to protect you." I lower my eyes to the floor and focus on a random point. It's my fault. He's hurt and getting erased because of_. "It's not your fault, I was the one that_." He looks around and then back at me. "You know." I nod slowly and inhale ready to act my part.

"Mr. Clarkson, I'm going to have to ask you to come with me."

He simply nods and follows me as I make my way out of the room. We walk in complete silence and towards the Erasing Facility. We look like an Eraser and a Patient, nothing more, but deep inside in my heart where no one can see, it hurts. Seeing him this way hurts me.

Soon we enter my room in the Facility and I close the door and throw the bolt. That's when I turn to face Sean and hug him around the waist. "I'm sorry," I say when I've regained myself and pulled back.

He stares at me in shock and then he smiles. "It's okay, what does it matter anyway if we break the rules."

"Laws." I correct him. He glares at me.

"Let's get you cleaned up." I murmur.

"Why? Aren't you just going to erase me anyway?"

"I'm not erasing you," I say.

"But_." Just as he's talking there's a knock on the door.

"Sit down quick!" I say. He does so and I quickly restrain him like I'm supposed too. "I'm sorry," I whisper. He only nods and watches me as I walk to the door and open it.

"Doctor Webb?" I ask when I see him standing there with a girl.

"You are about to erase Sean Clarkson is that correct?"

"Yes, sir."

"Great!" He smiles and lets him and the girl into my room. Oh dear God. "She's new, I think this is a great opportunity for her to watch a great Eraser do her job.

Miss Larina is a wonderful Eraser, she has the Medal of Service." Doctor Webb says turning to the girl. I see Sean's eyes widen at the fact that I have the Medal of Service.

"Wow." The girl says. "That means you'll go to the Center when you're old enough right?"

"Uh yeah." Sean throws me a look and I press my lips together.

"Doctor Webb, are you sure that's a good idea for more than just the Eraser to be in the room with the patient?" I ask.

"Of course Miss Larina, now go on." Doctor Webb nods and sits down on the table across from where Sean is at. The girl sits beside him and as I stand there in complete fear, I realize that I'm going to have to erase Sean.

I slowly walk to the cabinet containing the serums in it, as I open the doors I stare at the serum and the solution is right there in front of me. The sleep serum. I take it into my hands like it's a lifeline and slowly turn to face Sean as I suck the serum into the syringe.

He doesn't know that this is sleep serum, and as much as I want to tell him that I'm not going to kill him, I can't. Not without Doctor Webb and the girl hearing it.

"Miss Larina, why don't you explain what you are doing?" Doctor Webb suggests. I sigh and nod my head.

"I'm just putting the death serum into the syringe, the next part is really easy. All you do is walk to the patient and inject it into their necks." I take a step towards Sean and our eyes meet. Right then and there I see that he trusts me because he turns his head the other way, making it easier for me to inject him with the needle. "Like so," I whisper. I inject the needle into Sean's neck and watch as the liquid disappears from the syringe and enter him. “They don’t feel a thing, and soon they're erased.” I watch as Sean’s head becomes limp and drops down as he falls asleep.

“Just like that,” I say.

“Wow, look at that.” The girl says.

“Next you put them in the cremator and that’s it,” I say.

“Demonstrate.” Doctor Webb says.

“Hm?”

“Demonstrate how to do it.” He repeats. Seriously?! How am I going to fake this?!

“Of course!” I unstrap Sean from the chair and bring the metal table over to where he’s at. With a lot of effort and grunting, I get him up on the table. “So you put them on the table and cover them with the blanket, like so.” I cover Sean with the blanket and nearly start panicking when I cover his face.

“Next you just place them in the cremator, punch in the code and never forget to open the outlet so the smoke can escape through it,” I say.

“Very nice Miss Larina, now place him in the cremator and turn it on.” I clench my jaw tightly as I stare at Doctor Webb, silently wishing that some sort of miracle will happen. Funny enough, it does. Right as I’m wheeling the table in front of the cremator, my monitor starts flashing indicating my next assignment. “Oh, well we’ll let you go, Miss Larina, thank you so much for showing us.” Doctor Webb says standing up.

“Of course! Anytime.” I want to punch myself after that one, but I only smile.

"Thank you, Miss Larina, have a good day." The girl nods her head and leaves after Doctor Webb. I let out a huge sigh and throw my head back in utter relief. I quickly uncover Sean's face and then bolt to the door and lock it.

"Okay Sean, let's hide you until you wake up," I whisper as I wheel him towards the cremator closet. "Sorry." I murmur as I close the door and leave him in there, in the dark.

Once I know he's hidden away I go on with my day, releasing people and asking them to please not bump Sean as they leave through the closet.

Right as the last light of the Facility are turned off and I'm filling the last files for the day, the door to the closet is thrown open. "Good evening sleeping beauty." I tease as I type "Erased' onto the pad.

"Funny, how did you do that?" He asks walking over to me.

"Sleep serum." I turn to look at him and smile. "Are you okay?" I take one of his hand into mine and look into his eyes.

"Yes, never slept so well before." I burst out laughing and quickly place a hand to my mouth. "I can't believe you're laughing!" He says with a mock glare.

"I'm sorry Sean, I'm just relieved is all."

"Me too, if I'm being honest." He pulls me to him and we stand there hugging.

"I was so scared," I whisper before closing my eyes.

"I knew you'd think of something Larina, even if it was to erase me."

"I would never_."

"I know." He cups my face in his hands and makes me look up at him. "But you could have gotten caught, then the both of us would have been erased."

"I wasn't caught though." I step back and he drops his hand from my face. "And I would do it again if I had too." I walk to the sink and get a small towel wet before returning to him. "Sit down, so I can clean you up."

He does so, and I slowly dab at his cuts and wounds. "I can't believe they beat you like this," I whisper as I softly clean his lip.

"They went easy on me." I look into his eyes and frown. "It was worth it Larina, I got to kiss you." I start blushing red but immediately cover it with a snap.

"It wasn't worth it! What if I hadn't been the one that had to erase you? If it had been_."

"It was worth it."

"You're an idiot." I murmur.

"I guess I deserve that." I look into his eyes and let a smile form on my face. "Now what do we do Larina?" He asks taking my hands into his.

"Now you have to leave, go to that city I showed you. Stay there and stay alive." I feel tears start to pool around my eyes and I quickly try to blink them away, only they fall down my cheeks instead. "I'll miss you." Sean stands up and holds me to him.

"What about you? What are you going to do here?"

"I have to stay and release as many people as I can, and when I have too, I'll run." I step back and look up at him.

"There might not be a chance to run Larina, you should come with me."

"Sean I can't! I have my parents to think about and all these people_."

"Your parents are at the Center Larina, you're going to stay here doing this for the next three years and then what? Move to the Center and become a real Eraser? It won't be like here."

"I have to stay, you don't understand. If I go these people are going to die."

"And if you stay, you'll die!" He takes my shoulder into his hands and I lower my eyes to the ground.

"You have to hurry Sean before someone comes and checks to see why the lights are still on." I hear him sigh loudly as he lets go of my shoulders and walks to the closet door.

I press my lips together and hear him open the door. "Sean wait!" I look up at him and he walks back to me. "Please be careful and stay alive." I let my tears go now and he softly wipes them away.

"Let's do this, I'll stay alive if you stay safe. Deal?"

"Deal," I say with a laugh.

"Goodbye Larina." He leans in and plants a small kiss on my lips.

"Bye Sean," I whisper with my eyes closed as he pulls back. He leaves then and I stand there in that room, praying for his safety.

8

Raphael Minkus

I look up from the book I'm reading in my living room, when the monitor across the room start to blink, indicating that I have a message. I set the book down and walk over to the monitor and press my palm to it so I can read the message. The minute the screen turns on I see that the message is from Sherrie Maxwell. I start to read it and worry floods my mind.

"Miss Larina Matthews, your presence is required at tonight's Selection Ceremony. As you are well aware, a year ago when you attended your own ceremony, your results were less than satisfactory. We believe that this year you will find that you will be selected for someone. The Selection Ceremony takes place at eight p.m. Thank you - Head Handler, Sherrie Maxwell."

My eyes widen to the size of golf balls as I read and reread the message over and over again, willing it to be a mistake. However there is no mistake, I'm going to have to go to the ceremony and be selected for someone. I shake my head as I back up from the monitor, I don't want to be selected for anyone. The only person I'd want to be selected for was supposed to have been erased six months ago!

Not having any other choice, I begrudgingly get ready for the Selection Ceremony. I put on the same black dress I wore a year ago and let my hair down and as I leave my home and board the monorail with the eighteen-year-old's, I pray that the same result will show up on the screen. I pray that it will say: "No Match found."

The monorail ride seems to fly tonight, and soon I'm standing in front of the town hall where people are walking in and taking their seats. The feeling as I enter the hall is all too familiar, a feeling of nervousness and almost dread. There's no way that I'll be selected for someone, the data is never wrong. I have no one that is a good match for me. After I realize this, I take my seat and calm down at once.

The ceremony is started right away, with Sherrie Maxwell taking her place on the stage and calling up names one after the other. Finally, she arrives on the names that start with L. I'm the fifth person called up, unlike last time. I stand up and make my way to the stage where Sherrie smiles at me.

"You look lovely Miss Larina, are you having a sense of Deja vu as well?" She jokes. I smile and face the crowd of people staring up at me. "Ready?" Sherrie asks. I only nod, like everyone else. A year ago, everything was so different, I was so different.

I look back at the screen expecting it to say "No match found" once more. However, no one gasps and Sherrie looks almost too happy as a name indeed does appear on that screen. I don't recognize the name though.

"Raphael Minkus," Sherrie calls out.

I watch as the young man that is now to be my husband makes his way to the stage to meet me and shake hands. As he climbs up the steps to get to the stage my eyes widen as I recognize him. He's the same guy that stole that hovercraft from the garage a year ago. He's_. He's my selection?!

"Shake hands, Miss Larina," Sherrie instructs as I totally zone out. I snap out of my trance and extend my hand out to him. He takes it firmly into his and smiles at me, when Sherrie isn't looking he winks and my mouth flies opens. He recognizes me too. I can't believe I'm selected for someone, let alone this guy!

"Thank you, Miss Larina and Raphael Minkus, you may go with Doctor Simmons now." I take a step towards Doctor Simmons, who is at the left side of the stage. Raphael finds it fit to place a hand on my back and lead me off stage.

"You guys do make such a lovely pair!" Doctor Simmons says smiling. I look over at Raphael and he smirks at me. Given he's very handsome. He has brown hair and the deepest Caribbean blue eyes I've ever seen, he's tall and very stocky. Any girl would be ecstatic to be selected for him, only I know that he's not part of the Society. So what is he doing here? Most importantly, what does he want?

"You guys can step inside there and talk! Get to know each other, I have to go assist the other couples." Doctor Simmons says opening a door to a small room with two chairs inside it. Raphael and I step inside and she closes the door after us.

I turn to look at him and go to say something when he holds a finger up and moves one of the chairs up to the corner of the room and stands on top of it. I watch as he reaches up and turns off the camera that was pointed directly at us. "Now you may talk." He says.

"You're the guy that stole the hovercraft!" I say and I honestly can't believe that's what comes out of my mouth. He laughs and brings the chair back and sits on it backward.

"And you're the girl who releases people instead of erasing them. Now that we both know we are clearly law breakers, how about we sit down and talk?" He points to the other chair and I ease myself down onto it.

"What do you want? Who are you?" I ask.

“Sean was right, you are a persistent one.” Wait_. He knows Sean?!

“I_.”

“My name is Raphael Minkus and I’m the leader of the Rebellion.” My mouth widens as does my eyes as I stare at him.

“You’re joking right?” I ask laughing.

“No I’m not, Sean told me about you when we got him out of that abandoned city. He said that you release people and send them there. My numbers have increased significantly since you turned into an Eraser, Larina.” I sit there staring at him, with my mouth wide. “Close your mouth, you’ll catch flies.” He winks at me and I shake my head.

“What do you want from me though? I mean_.”

“Look, Larina, you’re cute and sweet and I do like that in a girl. However, I’m not really who you are selected with. I hacked into their database and put my name in there so that I’d have a chance to talk to you without getting caught.”

“So who is supposed to selected for me?”

“No one, it said ‘no match found’" Oh thank God!

“So, why do you want to talk to me?”

“You helped me a lot, you never knew it but you did. My numbers as I’ve said, have increased a lot and I thought that I’d return the favor. I’m preparing my soldiers to attack the Society and once that happens, everything will be chaos and_.”

“Attack here?”

"Not here directly in your city. Your city is one of many Sectors run by the Society, it's like this_." He starts gesturing with his hands to explain how it all works. "The Center, where everything happens and all the control is at, is dead in the middle of everything. Protected by all the Sectors that surround it. Once one of your cities get hit, everything will go crazy all over the Society."

I take all of this in slowly. "So_."

"So, before that happens you need to get out. Preferably before they find out who Sean kissed." He stands up.

"Wait, you know about that?!" I flush red and stare at him.

"I know lots of things. I gotta go, chose quickly doll face." He winks at me before climbing back onto the chair and turning the camera on. "So my dream is to get to work at the Center." He says acting like he's really a Society member. "How about yours?"

"Me too, I already have a Medal of Service," I say.

"No kidding? I can see why we were selected for each other. How about kids? How many do you want?" I glare at him with a "Don't push it" look on my face.

"One of course," I say.

He nods at me and we go on talking nonsense until Doctor Simmons opens the door and tells us our time is up.

"You guys come to the Headquarters tomorrow and we'll go on to decide when your wedding date will be and all of that!" Doctor Simmons says waving at us.

“Of course Doc, can’t wait!” Raphael leads me out of the town hall. We don’t get on the monorail, we walk towards my house. “Sean really misses you, he talks about you non-stop,” Raphael whispers as he walks along side me with his hands shoved into his pockets.

“Really?”

“Yup, he’s a good guy.”

“I know.” He chuckles as he stares at me.

“And you’re a great young lady Larina, why didn’t you run with him?”

“It didn’t feel right, running and leaving the others here to be erased.”

“Hm.” We walk in silence for a while and then he stops walking once we are five minutes from my house. “Unfortunately I can’t walk you the rest of the way.”

“It’s okay.” I nod and he smiles.

“I’m also going to have to ditch you at the alter.” I laugh softly and shake my head.

“That’s fine.”

“Hurtful! Hopefully, I’ll see you here soon Larina.”

“Yeah, maybe.” He smiles and I watch as he takes off running, blending in with the dark buildings. “Have a goodnight!” He screams when he’s a bit away.

“You too,” I call back. I hear him laugh and then he disappears behind the buildings.

I walk the rest of the way home, wondering about Raphael and how he’s planning to attack the Society. I also feel grateful that he came to warn me. I hope to soon be able to run and escape this place as well and never look back. Until then though, I'll have to stay here and release as many people as I can.

I get home and change out of the dress and put on some comfy pants and a shirt and crawl into bed. With the Dream Catcher far from me, I don't have to worry about hooking it on by mistake. I thought I'd have a really hard time falling asleep, with everything that unfolded today. However, the minute I close my eyes I find that I completely lose myself to sleep.

When I open my eyes, I have to squint as I stare at the bright, white room that I'm in. Everything is white, even what I'm wearing is white. I look towards the door when it opens.

The person that walks in is Sherrie Maxwell. I can't help but notice the very large syringe that she is holding in her hand. The black liquid that it contains, is a complete contrast to the room. "Well, well. It's about time." I hear her say. I try to say something, but I find that my words come out as nothing but a muffled sound. Why can't I talk? I reach up with my hand and touch my mouth, my hands touch cold metal. The realization that I'm getting erased is so strong that I start feeling faint. I quickly bolt out of the chair that I'm sitting in and hear Sherrie chuckle. It's a sound so cold that I feel a shiver run down my spine. "I always knew that it was only a matter of time before you were erased Miss Larina, you were always different."

I back away from her, she has a crazy look in her eyes, like she knows soon I'll be gone and that makes her happy. "We were never able to control you, and we could never do anything because you followed the rules so closely even if you were able to break them. You see Miss Larina, the Society is very fragile. That is why we have to get rid of the people that cause it to weaken, now it's your turn."

“You monster!” I try to scream, but nothing comes out. I start to feel sick to my stomach as I watch her get closer and closer to where I stand. With every step she takes forward, I take one back but soon there’s nowhere for me to go and my back is pressed up against the wall.

What do I do now?! I look up and past her when I see the door thrown open and Raphael Minkus standing there completely in black.

I watch him run to Sherrie and steal the syringe from her hand. Before she knows what’s happening, she’s in a state of shock, collapsing to the floor and soon dies. The needle lying next to her motionless body.

“Let’s get out of here,” Raphael says. He takes my hand in his and leads me out of the bright room. Sirens start yelling out at us, I try to block out the noise by covering my ears but it keeps coming through.

I open my eyes and sit up gasping and looking around like a crazy person. The back of my head is wet with sweat and I find myself swallowing a few times. I place my hand on my forehead and try to calm down, it’s still pitch black outside. I slowly lay back down and cover my face with my pillow as I think back to the dream. I know that it’s only a matter of time before someone finds out that it was me who Sean kissed, and then I will be erased.

“It’s only a matter of time,” I whisper before slowly drifting back to sleep. Only I had no idea, how soon that would actually be.

9

Hideout

Today there was very few people to erase, so Doctor Webb told me to go home earlier than usual. I place the pad into it's cabinet and fire up the cremator one last time, it sure does get dirty with all that blanket dust.

I take my bag into my hand and leave the room and lock the door after me. I walk down the hallway towards the elevator, when I see a door open, that has never been opened before.

Out of curiosity, I stop and peer inside it. At once I realize this is Doctor Webb's office, where he files all the paper work and sends it to the Headquarters to Sherrie. I press my lips together as I take a step forward and into the room and close the door behind me.

It's odd how Doctor Webb just left this door unlocked, no one is supposed to go in the room besides him and yet here I am. I look around the room that is scattered with papers in the main desk, and cabinets have been thrown open. It appears that Doctor Webb was looking for something in a hurry, but what? I look towards the back of the room where there is a huge monitor.

My eyes narrow as I stare at it, on the screen is a loading screen, it takes a few seconds for it to completely load. When it does I furrow my eyebrows. The picture that is displayed upon it is of my face, dead center of the monitor. What is that? I slowly walk closer to the screen and start messing around with it, trying to figure out why my picture is up there.

I end up figuring out that the picture has been zoomed in, and when I zoom out of it I see that it's a picture of me and Sean, that night when we kissed.

"Holy cow!" I say taking a step back, my hands fly to my head and I look around trying to figure out what to do. I look back at the screen and realize that I'm going to have to delete that data. Now.

I walk back to the monitor and go to press the delete button when I hear the door start to open. "Well? What were the results?" My eyes widen and my stomach ties itself into a knot. It's Sherrie!

I look around the room and quickly dive under the long desk. My heart starts ramming itself against my rib cage and I'm scared that they'll see me.

"Let's find out shall we?" Doctor Webb says. I see his brown shoes, followed by Sherrie's black ones move closer to the desk. To my horror, he sits at his desk and I find myself backing further into it. His knees are right in front of my face, if they find me… I'm done for! "Well look at that, it is Miss Larina. Just like you thought Sherrie." He spins his chair around to face her.

"Yes, I'm usually right when it comes to these things. All things really." I roll my eyes at her words. "Is she still here?" She adds. A breath catches itself inside my throat.

"No, I send her home early. It's been a slow day."

"Get her, I want her erased. Today Webb." I try to control my breathing, I'm worried that my heart is beating so loud that they will be able to hear it. I quietly tell it to shut up before it gives away my position.

"Of course Ma'am." Doctor Webb says standing up from the chair and heading for the door.

“Finally, I shall be rid of you Larina.” I hear Sherrie says right as she shuts the lights off and leaves the room.

I let out a slow breath and quickly dash out from under the desk. I have to get out of here! I make a beeline for the door, only to find that it’s locked. I look around, trying to find another way out when I see the window. I race to it and just as I get to it, Doctor Webb walks back inside the room.

“Miss Larina?” He asks. It takes him only a second to realize that I’ve been here during his conversation with Sherrie. He reaches for a gun that is sitting up on a shelf, I don’t know if that gun is meant to kill, but I’m not waiting around to find out. I throw the window open and hear the bullet hit the wall next to my head. I gasp and look at the bullet, only it’s not a normal bullet. It’s a tranquilizer bullet meant to put people to sleep. I fling my leg out of the window and right as I am outside of it, holding on for dear life, a bullet enters me right on the shoulder.

“Ah.” I let out a small scream and slowly lower myself down the building by grabbing a hold of the bricks. Immediately, my vision starts to blur as the bullet takes its effect. Sirens start to blare out across the entire Sector as I drop down to the floor.

“You’ll never get away Larina! Give up!” I hear Doctor Webb scream. I feel a sharp pain on my back as another bullet enters me. No! I start to run, I have to get out of this place before I pass out and the Handlers catch me. I take off towards the iron fence, seeing two of everything as I make my way to it.

I place my arms out in front of me, so I don’t bump into the fence. I can’t really tell if I’m closer to it than it appears or not. My eyelids become heavy as I find the same place in the fence that I would climb through, when I was younger.

“Where did she go?!” I hear several people scream. I take off running towards the Old City, leaving Sector 7B behind me. I’m scared that they’ll look out past the border and see me running off, it’s a field out here with nothing to hide behind. I have to get far_.

“Whoa!!!” I scream as I trip over my own feet and am sent crashing down towards the floor. I scrape my entire left arm on the ground trying to protect my head. I moan as I slowly get back up to my feet and feel the medicine that is in the bullet start to take its full effect. There’s no way I’ll make it to the Old City. I have to try though.

I’m amazed that no one has caught up to me, I guess no one would think that anyone would attempt to go out of the Sector. I’m sure they are still looking within the border.

Soon they’ll realize it though, and I’m out here in plain sight. I look behind me and I can still see the Sector, it’s a blurry mess, but I can see it.

At some point of running, I fall to my knees and find that I can’t open my eyes. I’m half awake and half asleep as I crawl onward, I can’t give up, I can’t get caught!

I can only fight the medicine for so long before it all starts to spread and I fall onto the ground on my face. I lay there on the dirt and slowly give away to sleep.

When I open my eyes some hours later, I know it's been hours because the sun is starting to set, I see that I’m being carried. My eyes widen as I realize that someone found me. Without a second of hesitation, I punch whoever is carrying me right on the face.

I scream as they drop me to take a hold of their face, I take the chance and run. I look around as my eyes try to adjust to the new scenery. Where’s the Old City?

"Larina!" I hear the person scream. I stop cold in my tracks as I recognize the voice. Oh my_. I turn around and bump straight into Sean's chest. "You can punch!" He says holding his jaw in his hands.

I start to laugh and cry all at once as I hug him around the waist. "I thought you were a Handler!" I say.

"I was once, I guess." I look up at him and smile as he wipes away the tears. "I'm so glad to see you again, Larina I've missed you." He cups my cheeks in his hands and I look at the floor.

"They found out that we kissed and they wanted me erased. I ran away with them after me." I explain.

"And are you okay?"

"I was shot twice with a tranquilizer bullet. One on the shoulder, the other on my back." I say placing a hand on my shoulder where I can still feel the dull pain from the bullet.

"Seriously?!" His eyes widen as he starts to fuss over me.

"Yes, let's get out of the open," I say.

"Do you see those mountains?" He asks, pointing further down the horizon.

"Yeah." I nod.

"In between those mountains there's a small valley, do you think you can make it that far?"

"Yes." He offers me his hand and we start to walk towards the mountains.

"How did you find me?" I ask looking up at him.

"Raph asked me to go check in the Old City, to see if there was anyone there. When I climbed up one of those trees, I saw you laying on the floor a few feet away from the entrance of it."

"Oh."

"I was both happy and sad when I realized it was you. I thought you were dead, but then I saw you breathing." He says smiling.

"Thank you, Sean," I whisper.

"Of course."

"Sean, where are we going?" I ask after a few minutes of walking.

"To the Rebel's Hideout, it's just ten minutes from here or so." I nod and stop walking so I can pull my hair back into a ponytail and out of my face.

"Oh, crap," Sean whispers as he stares at my arm.

"What is it?" I ask.

"I completely forgot about your Medal of Service!" He says.

"I_." What's wrong with it? Is there a rule against it at the Rebel's Hideout or something? "What about it?"

"Um," He looks into my eyes and runs his hand through his hair, trying to figure something out. "Larina, you can't come in the Hideout just yet. I don't want to leave you alone but_." He sighs loudly and hugs me to him. "I'm going to run there real quick and I'll be right back okay?"

"Okay," I whisper.

He lets me go and presses his lips together. "I'll be right back." He nods and jogs off.

I only nod as I watch him run off towards the mountains, I can see his shadow as he goes into the valley and disappears behind the mountains' large shape. I look around at the darkening world and sit down on a large stone.

As I sit there staring at the tattoo on my wrist, I think back to the Society. I ran away from it, I can never go back. My eyes widen as I think about mom and dad. I'll never see them again!

A few minutes later I look up when someone calls my name, the voice is really familiar. I look up and see Raphael Minkus walking towards me, with a scary looking knife in his hand. Oh, God. "Hey, there doll face." He says, only to receive a hand to the back of the head by Sean.

"What's with the knife?" I ask slowly standing up.

"That tattoo consists a tracking device, that means that the Society can track you down. If they haven't already." My eyes widen as I stare at the two of them. They're tracking me?

"So, what do we do?" I whisper.

"We have to remove it from your arm." Raphael takes a step closer to me and Sean places a hand on his shoulder. "What is it, Sean?"

"Can't we wait for Doc?" He asks.

"He's out Sean, we either have to do it now or she has to leave. She's too close to the Hideout as is!" Raphael snaps. I look from Sean to Raphael.

"I'll take her far and when Doc gets back_." Raphael shakes his head and Sean stops talking.

"You don't understand Sean, if you don't remove that tracking device now, they will find her and you."

"If they do, I'll protect her. This is too dangerous."

"Look, Sean, love isn't the answer to every problem. So hurry up and decide, stay or go."

"Just do it," I say. Raphael and Sean both look at me. "Let's get it over with." I nod and hold out my arm.

"Brave girl, it's going to hurt Larina. I'm not going to lie to you." Raphael says. I hold in a breath as I nod my head, I'm not the biggest fan of pain but who is? Raphael takes a hold of my wrist and looks over at Sean. "You might want to hold her or something, she can't struggle. If she moves at the wrong moment, I don't know if she'll make it." My heart stops beating as I stare at him. Is he saying, that I could possibly die?!

"Raph_." Sean starts.

"Just do it, man! The sun is going down, I'm sure the Handlers are on their way now." Sean gives in and holds me to him.

"It'll be over soon." He whispers against my hair. I turn my face away from Raphael and bury it against Sean's chest. I squeeze my eyes shut and wait for the pain to come, once it does it's unbearable. I bite down on my tongue so I don't scream, I start feeling dizzy and I feel like I'm going to fall over from the pain when Sean hugs me closer to him.

At some point, I let a loud scream escape my lips and hear Raphael murmur something that sounds like encouragement. "Almost done Larina, you're doing great." He adds. Tears slide down my cheeks as I wait for the pain to stop, only when Raphael announces that it's done, the pain doesn't go away. My wrist is throbbing and my legs feel like jelly under my weight.

"Here." I turn, still in Sean's arms, slowly to look at Raphael and see him remove his shirt and wrap it around my bloody and damaged wrist. I look down at the once white shirt that soon turns red in different spots. That's a lot of blood. I feel myself start to shake as I take a step away from Sean. "I'm going to go place this somewhere else, they'll follow the tracking device and it'll lead them off our trail," Raphael says.

I nod slowly and feel myself start to lean forward. Sean catches me in his arms as I lose my footing. He looks down at me with a worried expression on his face. "God Sean, take her to the hideout and have Doc stitch her up before she bleeds to death." Raphael takes off running in the direction we came from and he is soon nothing but a speck against the setting sun.

"Let's get you to Doc." Sean scoops me up in his arms and takes off running towards the mountains. I feel nauseous at the bouncing motion of him running. "Almost there Larina." He whispers as I close my eyes. "Stay awake." He says placing his lips to my forehead. I open my eyes and look at the valley that we have just entered. It's just a normal valley that sits between two mountains, until Sean takes a left and enters a tunnel in the mountain.

I straighten myself up so I can see where we are going, but everything is very hazy to me. I don't think I'm doing too well, the blood hasn't stopped seeping through Raphael's shirt. I hold my wrist with my hand and watch as Sean walks straight towards some vines, he ducks under them and my eyes widen as I see a huge metal door that is attached to a large building within the mountain. The building is made out of concrete, it looks super sturdy and appears to be etched into the walls of the mountain.

“What_.” I start.

“This is the Rebel’s Hideout,” Sean explains. Sean steps forward and presses his palm to a scanner on the wall. I hear the metal door give a low rumbling sound before it splits down the middle, opening up to a metal hallway that is brightly lit.

“How did they make this?” I ask.

“Lots of help, I assure you. It’s pretty amazing isn’t it?”

“It’s unbelievable!” I say forgetting about the pain on my wrist. He walks down the hall and stumbles into another, equally massive metal door. I look behind us and see that the door that we entered through is now closed. When I look forward again, the door is opened and I stare at the scene in front of me. It’s bubbling with people walking around and doing many different things. Everyone seems to be talking all at once.

“I’ll give you a tour, later on, let's get you to Doc,” Sean says. He walks further into the building and enters a door that leads to a staircase that goes down. He quickly bounds down the stairs and goes down another hallway with many doors on both sides. “This is the hospital wing.” He says.

“Wow.” They have a whole hospital wing?! Sean knocks on a door and less than a second later the door opens and standing there is a man that is bald, with kind eyes that are behind a pair of thick, oval glasses and has a five o’clock shadow. He’s probably around five feet eight inches and is pretty fit for being in his fifties.

“What is it, Clarkson? I’m very busy and_. The man looks at me and his eyes widen. “What happened to her?!” He demands before ushering Sean and me inside the room, that turns out to look a lot like a normal hospital room. “Set her down Clarkson.” Sean sets me down on the medical table and the man undoes the shirt around my wrist.

“Hi there, I’m Doctor Finn. You can call me Doc though.” Doc says.

“Hi, my name is Larina Matthews.”

“Larina Matthews?” Doc looks over at Sean. “The Larina Matthews?”

“The one and only,” Sean says smiling.

“Well Miss Larina Matthews, I’m glad you made it out of the Society. I heard a lot about you from this one over here.” Doc says. I watch as he accesses the damage in my wrist. “What exactly happened here?”

“There was a tracking device in her, Raphael removed it.” Sean murmurs. Doc stiffens and slowly turns to look at Sean.

“Are you telling me that Raphael Minkus removed a tracking device out of this girl’s wrist without being medically qualified to do it?” I can see his face turning a slight red color as he becomes mad.

“Yes, they could have found her Doc.”

“Clarkson you’re an idiot! She could have died.” Doc walks away from me and towards a cabinet at the back of the room. He rummages through it for a few seconds before coming back with some medicine and sharp tools that look really painful.

“Alright, sweetheart lets get you stitched up okay?” I nod. “Clarkson you can go.”

“But_.”

“I said go!” Doc throws a glare at Sean and Sean nods before taking a step back.

“I’ll be right outside Larina.” He says. I smile and watch as he leaves.

The minute the door closes, Doc turns to smile at me. “He’s a good kid, but those two are idiots. They should have called me to remove that tracking device from your arm. They know nothing about arteries.” I bite my lower lip as I stare down at my hands. I don’t point out that I let them do it to me, I don’t want to be placed in the “Idiot” category. “Alright, these are pain medicines.” Doc hands me two small, white pills with a glass of water that I drink. “And what I’m putting in your wrist here, is to numb the pain so that I can stitch it okay?”

“Thank you, Doc.”

“Of course.” I watch as he stitches me, Even though I can’t feel the pain, it’s still a bit alarming to see a needle going inside and out of my skin over and over again. However, Doc is a professional and he has me stitched up in no time. I look down at the stitch and smile.

“In a few weeks, we’ll get those removed alright?” I nod. “Anything else I can help you with Miss Larina Matthews?”

“Um, yes. I got shot with tranquilizer bullets back at the Sector. One on the shoulder, the other on my back. Can you remove them please?”

“Of course, it looks like you went through hell and back huh?”

“Yes.”

“Well, at least you got out. A lot of people don’t.” A sad look crosses his face as he says this.

"Doc, do you mind if I ask you a question?"

"No, go ahead."

"How did you start to work for the Rebels?"

Doc smiles at me as he starts to remove the bullets from my shoulder. "I used to be a Doctor at one of the Sectors. My wife and I realized that the Society was wrong so we stopped taking the medication and everything seemed so clear." I listen closely as he tells me his story. "My wife was pregnant at the time, and her due date came and we went to the hospital that I worked at. While I waited in the hallway, Handlers came and took me to be Erased. I guess they found out about our plan to leave the Society. I uh, somehow managed to inject the death serum into the Eraser and escaped. I ran back to get my wife, but they had already killed her and the baby." Tears slide down his cheek. "I ran away then and Raphael's parents found me and asked me to join them."

"I'm so sorry Doc," I whisper.

"I know you are, alright all done. You're going to have to stay here the night I'm afraid, I need to make sure you don't get an infection on your wrist alright?"

"Okay, Doc."

"Alright let's get you in a room." I hop off of the table and follow him out of the room we are in. I see Sean before he sees us, he's leaning against the wall with his head tilted up and his eyes closed.

"Clarkson," Doc says. Sean looks over at us and smiles as he pushes off the wall and walks towards me.

"All good?" He asks worry in his eyes.

"Yeah, I have to stay here the night so Doc can make sure I don't get an infection," I explain.

"That's a good idea."

"When you see Raphael, you tell him to come see me," Doc says to Sean. He turns his back to us and walks down a few doors before stopping on the last one to the left.

"You can stay in here Larina, I'll come check up on you later alright?" Doc says.

"Thank you, Doc."

"Anytime." He winks at me and starts walking back to his room. "Oh and Larina?" He says turning back to me. I look into his eyes and wait for him to continue. "Welcome to the Rebellion." He smirks before walking inside his room.

Sean and I walk inside the room and I look around in it. It's a normal hospital room that reminds me a lot of the rooms back in the Institution. I inhale deeply and sit down on the lone bed, dead center of the room.

"You should get some sleep," Sean says shoving his hands into his pockets.

"I'm not all that tired."

"Then we can sit here and talk until you are, lay down." He nods towards the pillow and I smile as I lay down on the bed feeling like a little kid. "Want me to tell you a bedtime story?" He teases.

"No need thanks." I laugh and look down at my hands. "Thank you, Sean, for finding me and bringing me here." He reaches over and takes my hand in his.

"I've missed you Larina, a lot. Every day I thought you would get erased. I'm so glad that you're here now."

“I’m glad to be here,” I whisper. I look up into his eyes and our eyes lock with each other. He starts leaning down and my mouth parts in surprise when the door is opened and Sean jumps to his feet.

“Let’s go Clarkson.” Raphael murmurs. He looks like he just had a good talk with Doc, and got chewed out.

“You’ll be okay here right Larina?” Sean asks turning to look at me.

“Yes of course.” I smile and he smiles back.

“Romeo, we are late let's go!” Raphael grabs Sean by the arms and I watch them go.

“Thanks, Raphael!” I call out.

He pokes his head back in the room and grins. “You’re welcome, kid. Welcome to the Rebellion by the way.”

I smile and the door closes after them, I lay there in the bed and look down at the stitches in my arm where the tracking device used to be.

There’s something eerie about how they were keeping track of me from the inside. I find myself thinking back to mom and dad, they are being watched too. That’s all the Medal of Service is, I wonder if they know.

I lay there in the bed until I eventually fall asleep, and this is the first time in the year that I don’t dream about anything.

10

Claire

"Rise and shine sleeping beauty!" I jump up from the bed at the loud voice coming from directly above me. I look at the person in my room and take my pillow in my hands to use as a weapon. Given it's not the best weapon, however, it's the only thing I have at the moment.

"Who are you?!" I demand, staring at the person standing a few feet from the bed. He's wearing black clothing and a mask over his face.

"I'm Raph's second in command, they want you down at the shooting range." He says in a low, rumbling voice. "Careful not to hurt yourself with that pillow Larina." He lets out a loud laugh that seems unnatural before walking out the door.

"Wait!" I call out throwing the covers away from me and running after him. I open the door and look down the hallway, but he's gone.

"Morning Larina," Doc says walking out of his office.

"Morning Doc!" I smile and start walking with him. "Could you point me to the shooting range?" Whatever that is…

"Just up those stairs, just pass the main lobby and take the elevator to the second floor. That whole floor is the shooting range." He says not taking his eyes from the files in his hands.

"Thank you." I nod and start to run off.

"Hold it." I stop and turn around to face him. "Let me see the stitches." I walk back to him and hold out my arm. “Hm very nice, no infection. Alright, you can go, have a good day Larina.”

“Thanks, you too!” I call out as I run up the stairs and step into the main lobby. Much like last night when I arrived here in Sean’s arms, there are people everywhere. Running up and down the stairs, going from one room to the other and just talking in general.

“Hey, it’s the newbie!” A woman says waving at me as I pass her.

“Good morning,” I say.

“Good morning!” She says. I smile and walk to the elevator that sits at the very back of the lobby. I press the button on the side of the door and wait for the elevator to arrive and open its door.

“Let me come with you.” The same woman says walking over to me. “You’re going up to the shooting range right?”

“Yes.” I nod and we both step inside the elevator.

“In those clothes?” She looks at me with a raised eyebrow. I suppose she has a point, I still have on my uniform as an Eraser. White shirt, pants and a lab coat over the whole thing. “Let’s go up to my room and I’ll let you borrow some clothes until you get yours situated alright?”

“Oh, thank you.”

“Sure thing kid.” She smiles and presses a button on the elevator’s control panel and the doors close and we start to move up. “So my name is Sally Gibbs, what’s yours?”

“I’m Larina Matthews.” Her eyes widen as she stares at me.

"Matthews? As in Geo and Clef Matthews?"

"Yes… They are my parents."

"What a small world! Your mother and I used to be best friends in school, and then, of course, I had to run off and I never saw her again. So, how is she doing? Still at the Society huh?"

"Yeah, her and dad moved to the Center."

"The Center? Yikes." She bites her lower lip and the elevator door opens. "I'm glad you got out Larina."

"Thank you." I nod and follow her out of the elevator and down a hallway and finally, into a room.

It's a simple room. A bed sits up against the wall, a dresser, and a small closet is to the left of it.

"This is it, it's not much but it suits its purpose." She says rummaging through her closet and throwing me a pair of black pants and a maroon colored t-shirt. "Alright you can go ahead and get changed, I'll head to the shooting range, see you there newbie!" She winks at me and leaves her room.

I quickly change out of the Eraser outfit and throw it down a trash chute that is attached to the wall, much like the ones back in the Sectors. Once I'm changed I make a simple braid down my back and walk out of Sally's room and enter the elevator. I press the number two button and soon the elevator door is opened and what stands in this level is unbelievable!

For starters, it's huge. There are people everywhere, all on a roll as they aim at white and red targets with guns and many different weapons I don't recognize. I'm at once drawn to where people are throwing knives.

“Hey kid, want to try it out?” Sally asks walking to me from the guns.

“Sure.”

“Alright, it’s simple. Watch me.” She faces the target, holding the knife at its blade and sends the knife twirling towards the target. The knife edges itself a little bit off from the center.

“Wow,” I say.

“Give it a try.” She hands me a sharp knife and nods towards the target. I take it into my hands and face the target. I bite my lower lip as I throw the knife and watch as it twirls across the air. My eyes widen in surprise as the knife sticks to the center of the target. “Would you look at that!” Sally says.

“I_.” I look at her and smile sheepishly. “Beginners luck,” I say.

“Try it again, let’s see.” She hands me another knife and I turn to face the target. This knife actually hits the knife that I just threw and makes it fall to the floor before the second knife hits dead center once more. “Gee kid! Here.” She hands me a third and fourth and fifth and every time it hits the target dead center. “Stay here, I’m going to go get Raph to see this!” She smiles and jogs off.

“Hey, Larina!” I look away from where Sally went and towards Sean’s voice. I see Sean standing near the Guns’ shooting range. He waves me over and I find myself smiling as I walk over to him. “Did you sleep okay?” He asks as I get to him.

“Yeah.”

“How’s your wrist?” He takes my wrist in his hands and nods. “Looks good.”

“Yeah, Doc said there wasn’t any infection. So that’s good.”

“It is.” He smiles at me and I smile back and sad to say we stand there just staring at each other and smiling until Raphael walks over.

“Hey, lovebirds focus.” Raphael hands me a gun and leads me to a spot beside Sean’s. “Sally Gibbs told me you’re good with the knives?”

“I’m okay.” I look back to the target I was just at, there stands five knives stuck to the middle of the target.

“You look better then okay, let’s see if you’re as good with guns.”

“Why are we practicing shooting these targets?” I ask looking up into Raphael’s eyes.

“That would normally be a person.”

My eyes widen as I stare at the gun in my hand, I guess that makes sense. “Um okay, can you show me?” I hold out the gun to Raphael and he shakes his head.

“Rule one with guns Larina, never point it at a person unless you are going to pull the trigger.” I quickly lower the gun and he sighs. “Or at your foot!” I feel my cheeks become hot with embarrassment.

“Sorry.” I murmur.

“Raph, I’ll show her,” Sean says.

“Good. See you later Larina.” Raphael nods at me and walks off, checking all the other people’s performance.

“I’m not shooting anyone.” I point out as I look at Sean.

"I know, but it can't hurt to learn something new right?" I only nod. "Okay, so the first thing you want to do is know how to hold a gun." I stare at the gun that I'm 'holding' and look back at him with a raised eyebrow. "You have to hold it tightly."

"Oh." I tighten my grip on the gun and look back at him. "Like this?"

"Almost, here try it like this okay?" He moves closer and places my hands where they are supposed to go. "Right there, see how it feels secure now?"

"Yes."

"Now for your stance, spread your legs shoulder width apart." I do so. "Good, now face the target." I turn to the target and point the gun at it. "So right, um… You're slouching."

"I am?!" I look up at him and he smiles softly.

"Yes, straighten up a little." He places his hand on my back and I tense up at once. I look up at him and he stares down into my eyes.

"Am I'm straight now?" I whisper.

"Yes." He starts to lean towards me and I feel my breath catch in my throat when I hear someone calling out to Sean.

I turn away from him and see a girl walking over to us. "Sean, do you mind helping me out?" I bite my lower lip as a new emotion starts to take over me. I'm confused if it's anger or jealousy.

"Larina, this is Claire. She's a friend."

"Hi," I say.

“Hey.” She smiles the fakest smile I’ve ever seen and turns back to Sean. “Wait, did you say that’s Larina Matthews?!” She asks her blue eyes widening to the size of golf balls.

“That’s her,” Sean says smiling at me.

“Wow! Sean talks so much about you.” She says.

I get the urge to say: “Funny, he’s never mentioned you before.” However, I hold back and say. “That’s me!”

“Sean, the way you talk about her I’d think she’d be like at least our age, I mean what are you sweetie fifteen?”

“Nineteen,” I say coolly.

“Really?!” Her eyebrows raise up and she laughs loudly. “Someone forgot to grow up!” I glare at her and she turns to Sean. “Anyway, so can you help me?”

“He’s actually helping_.” I start to say.

“I’ll be right there.” Sean murmurs. I find myself with my mouth opened a bit.

“Great!” She winks at me before walking away. I clench my jaw as I watch her stroll away. What does she think she is? A model?!

“Larina, I’ll get Raph to help you alright? Then we can_.”

“I got it.” I snap. I face the target, point the gun and press the trigger three times. I watch in amazement as the bullet hits the target dead center every time. I smile with satisfaction and hand him the gun. “I think I’ve had enough of training for today, I’m going to rest for a bit.” I turn and walk away. I stare at the floor as I head for the exit. I guess it never crossed my mind that Sean might find someone else when he left Sector 7B. It seems that way, I guess I've been misreading things. Before I get to leave the range, Raphael catches up to me.

"Let's see you with the bow." He says handing me a new weapon that is made out of steel and has a strong cord running across it, he also hands me a small bag filled with arrows.

"This is a quiver, you place it around your hip. It makes it easier for you to be able to load the bow." He explains.

"Oh, sounds fun," I say smiling.

"You're great with the knives and gun, let's see you with this baby!" He grins and leads me towards three people who are practicing with the bow. I find myself looking back to where Sean and Claire are at. She's shooting with guns, she's pretty decent at it.

"Focus Larina," Raphael says. I turn my attention back to him and he smiles. "Just pretend the target is Claire." He teases.

My eyes widen and I shake my head. "That's awful Raphael!"

"Call me Raph will you?"

"Fine, Raph it is." I smile and face the target.

"Just hook the arrow right there." He points to the middle of the bow, I do so. "Then pull back." I find that it's hard to pull back on the string. It's heavy, believe it or not. "And release." Just as I'm about to release my first arrow I hear a loud scream coming from right beside me. My eyes widen and my hands fly to my mouth and the bow drops to the ground.

On the floor with an arrow sticking out of her thigh is a girl my age. "Oh my God!" I scream. I hurry to her side and Raph places a hand on my shoulder.

“Go tell Doc, I’ll bring her in,” Raph says. I nod and race ahead of him as he picks the girl up in his arms and hurries to the elevator.

I hold the door open for him and I try not to stare at the blood that is dripping out of her thigh and down onto Raph’s dark green shirt. The girl has tears in her eyes, but I have to admire her bravery. She’s not screaming, I think I would be bawling if it would have been me.

The door to the elevator opens and I run through the lobby with Raph behind me, leaving a trail of blood behind him.

“Move out of the way!” I scream as I run through. It works, people move to the sides and stand there watching as Raph and I run through the lobby and finally down the stairs that lead to the hospital wing.

Doc is leaving his office when we make it there. He takes one look at her and nods. “Get her inside.” He says. I walk in after Raph and stand at the door as he lays the girl on the bed. I hear her moan out a thank you, before resting her head on the pillow.

“You’ll be okay Bea.” He says nodding his head. He steps back and stands beside me.

“Thank you, Minkus, you may leave now,” Doc says.

“Will she be okay?” I ask Doc when he walks over to us.

“I think so.” He nods and looks back at the girl, I turn to face her. She’s holding her thigh in her hands and holding back a scream at the same time.

“Come on Larina,” Raph whispers tugging on my hand. I follow him out of the room and stare at the ground as we make our way back up to the lobby.

I'm surprised to see that all the blood is cleaned up. I look straight ahead as Sean runs over to us, Claire following close behind him.

"What happened?" Sean asks. I realize that as he asks this, he's looking me over to make sure that I'm okay. To be honest, I have to swallow down my heart as I watch him. Raph starts to explain but Sean cuts him off. "Are you okay?" Sean takes my hand in his and looks into my eyes.

"I'm fine, it wasn't me," I whisper looking down at the floor as my cheeks flush.

"Oh." He lets out a sigh of relief and nods. "Good, that's good."

"Bea isn't so good." Raph murmurs.

"Poor Bea," Sean says.

"Look I'm going to get a new shirt, Claire can you go stay at the hospital wing and check on Bea in a few minutes_."

"But_!"

"Now Claire!" Raph throws her a look, and she'd be crazy to disobey him.

"Of course Raphael." She nods and starts walking towards the stairs. Half way there she stops like she's forgotten something and walks back to us. "Bye Sean." She leans forward and is about to kiss him when he turns his head and looks at me.

"Let's go find you a room." He says offering me his hand. I slowly place my hand in his and look up into his eyes. Maybe, he doesn't like her after all? My blush returns when I realize how happy that thought makes me.

Sean pulls me after him as he makes his way to the elevator.

"I hope Bea will be okay," I whisper as I stare at the white floor of the elevator.

"She will be, Doc is the best doctor there is," Sean says.

I look up at him and smile. "I'm glad to hear that." I look towards the door as it opens. "This place is amazing isn't it Sean?" I ask. I let out a small gasp when he takes me by the shoulders and looks down at me with a serious look on his face. "What's wrong?"

"I was so worried when I saw that you were gone, all I saw was a pool of blood on the floor."

"You thought it was me?" I look into his hazel eyes as they close and he nods his head. "I'm fine Sean."

"I'm glad you are." He lets out a sigh and hugs me quickly before pulling back just as quick. "This is the quarters, there are three floors that are just rooms for the residents. This is the floor my room is in, you can have the room across from mine if you want." I see his cheeks start to turn a pink color.

"Sounds good," I say.

We walk down the hall and he opens a door on the right side of the hallway. I look inside and see a room that looks just like Sally Gibbs'. "Looks great," I say.

"I have to go do some more training now, but maybe tonight we can_."

"Sean!!!" I hear Claire scream as she runs down the hallway.

"Oh boy." Sean and I say at the same time. We look at each other and laugh right as she stops in front of us.

“How’s Bea?” Sean asks.

“Fine, Raphael told us to go to that dumb city to check for new recruits.”

“Both of us?” He asks.

“Yes.”

“Can’t you go alone? I was going to show Larina_.”

“She’s a smart girl, she can find her way, Sean.” She says it like I’m not standing right in front of her. “Plus, I don’t know how to get to it by myself. What if I get lost?”

“That would be good for everyone.” I think to myself. “It’s fine Sean, I’ll have Raph show me the ropes.” I nod and turn to my room.

“Thanks for showing me to my room though.” I smile widely and go to enter but stop. “Be careful okay?” I look into his eyes and he nods before turning to Claire.

“Yay! Let’s go!” She grabs his hand and drags him off. I roll my eyes as I enter my room, I don’t know what to think anymore. I need to stop worrying about Sean and Claire and focus on what’s really going on. What exactly do they do here at the Hideout? Raph told me that he’ll attack the Society with his soldiers, is that what he’s preparing for? I guess I’ll find out soon enough.

A week later

I’m practicing my shooting with a gun when I overhear Raph talking to Claire a few stations away. “All you have to do is take aim and shoot!” Raph snaps.

"I've tried Raphael, there's something wrong with this gun!" She points at the target and shoots three bullets, they miss every time hitting the outer rim of the target. "See?!"

"Let me see." Raph takes the gun from her and shoots three times just like she just did. Every time it hits the red circle. "It's you," Raph says. Claire glares at him and shoves past him as she walks off.

Raph looks up and catches me staring at him and walks over. "How about you Peaches, you still got it?" I burst out laughing and double over holding my sides. "What?"

"Did you just call me Peaches?"

"Yes. Now let's see what you got." He backs up and sits down on a large bench right behind me.

"It's been a week Raph, I don't think that I lost my sense of shooting."

"Let's see it then." He nods at the target. I hold the gun in both my hands and inhale deeply, I fix my stance and shoot. Bull's eye every time. "Huh, you are good, great actually." He jumps up to his feet and smiles at me. "You ready for a promotion Peaches?"

"A promotion? Yeah!" I nod feeling really excited.

"You're taking night watch with Claire tonight." My eyes widen and I look around to make sure no one is watching us.

I take a step closer to him and say: "That's not a promotion Raph! That's a punishment."

"Come on Peaches, play nice."

"She can't even shoot!" I point out.

"She can, she's just a pain in my a_."

“Raph! We got a situation.” Mike, one of the day spies yells running over to Raph.

Raph simply nods and takes the gun from Mike’s hand. “Cole, Jackson and Smith you’re with me!” Raph orders.

“Yes, sir!” They scream. I stand there watching as they leave.

“Alright wimps! Get back to training!” The guy that is Raph’s second in command snaps. I look over at him and see that he has on the same mask from the first time I saw him. What is he hiding? “What are you looking at noob?” He asks looking over at me.

“Nothing.” I quickly look down at the floor.

“I think you were, are you any good at shooting?”

“Yes.”

“Oh aren’t we confident?” He lets out a loud chuckle and points at the target with his gun. I sigh loudly and point the gun and shoot. Bull’s eye. “Not at that one, that one.” He holds out his gun in one hand and shoots a single bullet at a target standing three stations away. My eyes widen as it hits the bull’s eye all the way from here.

“Wow,” I say.

“I’ve been here since I was born, I’ve had a lot of practice.” He says. I watch him walk off and take on the bows, and then the knives. He’s amazing at them all. I turn away from him and go back to shooting. I stop when Sean walks over.

“Hey, Larina.” He says smiling.

My heart drops to the pit of my stomach before launching itself into my throat and sliding down to rest on my chest again.

"Hi," I say, with a huge smile on my face.

"Just practicing?" He asks.

"Yup, how about you?"

"I have free time right now. Want to take a tour with me?" He smiles one of those smiles of his and I find myself nodding. "Let's go." He offers me his hand and I place mine in his and we walk out of the shooting range with people whistling at us.

"Ignore them." He says.

"Ignore what?" I say with a smile.

"Very nice, so you've been to the shooting range, the cafeteria, the quarters and the hospital wing right?"

"Yes."

"Have you seen the library?" My mouth parts as I stare at him.

"They have a library here?!"

"Yes come on." He grins and pulls me behind him, as we enter the elevator I see Claire rounding the corner. Oh no. She see's us and starts running to us. Just in time, the elevator door closes and I sigh loudly. "Aren't you a bit too happy that she missed the elevator?" Sean teases.

"She doesn't like me much."

"I think you don't like her much either." He says.

"I don't care either way." I look down at the floor as my cheeks flush from my lie.

"Really?" I look up quickly as the elevator stops moving.

"What happened?"

"Looks like we are stuck," Sean says looking around.

"Seriously?"

"Yes, do you not liking Claire have anything to do with me?"

"What? N…No!" I can't believe he's asking this when we are stuck in an elevator!

"Larina_."

"Sean_." I copy his patronizing tone and he glares at me.

"Tell me the truth." He says stepping closer to me.

"I don't care either way, Sean Clarkson!" I look at the elevator door and see a button that stops and starts the elevator. "Did you push the button?!" I demand. I move to push it again and he blocks my way. "Move!" I say with a laugh in my voice.

"No." He mocks glares at me and I roll my eyes.

"Seriously Sean, I have to be somewhere in a few hours. I want to see the library."

"Where do you have to be?"

"Old City, Raph is sending Claire and me out."

"You and Claire alone? Oh boy." He runs his hand through his hair.

"You obviously don't like her Sean," I say.

"I don't?"

"No, you don't."

"And who do I like then?" He cocks his head and dares me to answer.

"Me of course," I say. Of course, I mean it as a joke but he smiles and pulls me to him. "What?" I ask.

"You are right."

I let out a soft laugh and feel relief building up in me. "Can we get moving now?" I ask looking up into his eyes.

"Yes." He pushes the button and looks back at me as the elevator starts moving.

"Do you still_." He doesn't get to ask the question before the door opens. "This way." He leads me down the hallway and towards double wooden doors.

"I'm so excited!" I say feeling all giddy.

He throws open the two doors and I stand there staring inside the non-ruined library. "Come on!" I pull him inside with me.

Sean and I spend hours at the library, reading and talking. The more I spend time with him, the more I realize how happy I am to be where he is at. We walk into the cafeteria for dinner and that's when Raph returns. He and the three other guys that went with him, have their rifles slung over their shoulders.

"Well?" Claire asks from across the room. She's glaring daggers at me.

"False alarm, they were just dumping again," Raph says.

"Dumping?" I ask looking to Sean for the answer.

"Everyone erased." He whispers. I stare up at him, still confused. "They throw all the dust out Larina." I shudder at that and stare down at the floor. So that's what the Society does with all the dust.

"It's truly awful!" Claire says sneaking her way over to us and grabbing onto Sean's arms. This girl is seriously getting on my nerves.

I clench my jaw at that and see Sean discreetly remove his arm from her hands. "Peaches, can we talk a second?" Raph calls out. Sean smiles at me as I walk over to Raph.

"Yeah?" I stop at the entrance of the cafeteria where he is waiting.

"Let me see your wrist."

"Raph_." He takes my left arm in his hand and pulls the sleeve up. The stitches stare back at me, like a constant reminder that I was being watched from the inside.

"Medal of Service, ironic isn't it? The Eraser released and was to be erased but ran away."

"Uh huh."

"Peaches, let me ask you something."

I snicker and shake my head at him. "You're not going to stop are you?"

"Stop what?" He crosses his arm over his chest and narrows his eyes at me.

"Calling me Peaches."

"Oh, that?" He chuckles. "No" he runs his hand through his hair and looks towards Sean and Claire. She's back to grabbing his arm again. That girl is worst than a leech. "You really like him don't you?"

"Sean?" I ask. Raph only nods. "I_. I do, I've known him since I was sixteen."

"Wow."

"Yeah." I look back to Raph and smile.

"I don't trust Claire." He whispers.

"You don't trust her?" My eyes widen as I stare back into his eyes.

"No, you see, most people here are from the Sectors. Lots from your Sector. Not Claire, she came from the Center."

"The Center?" My eyes widen even more.

"Yeah, but I don't have any reason to doubt her loyalty to the Rebellion. Just a feeling, you know?"

"I know."

"Well, I'll let you go eat. Just be careful out there tonight alright?" I nod. I head back to where Sean is at and he smiles at me, looking glad that I'm back.

"Want to eat?" He asks.

"Yeah," I say nodding. He leads me to the line and Claire, much to my annoyance, follows us.

We stay in line and get our lunch, all in complete silence. When we are about to sit down Claire takes a hold of Sean's wrist and pulls him to the side and pretends to whisper: "I don't trust Larina, I think she's a spy." She did not just say that!

"She's not." I hear Sean say. I watch him shrug her hand from his arm and start to walk towards where I'm standing next to the table.

“Sean, just because you knew her back when she was part of the Society doesn’t mean she’s the same person!” Claire says running up to him. She throws me a glare and I set my food down on the table and turn to face her, head on.

I really want to snap at her that I’m not a spy and that if anyone is it’d be her, but I don’t. I stay quiet and look at Sean as he shakes his head.

“I’m going to go get ready for going out tonight,” I say.

“Wear something bright,” Claire says. I roll my eyes and turn to Sean and nod at him.

“Larina, be careful out there alright?”

“I will be.” I smile and leave the cafeteria.

11

Recruits

Claire and I walk in complete silence towards the Old City. "Watch your back, you never know what a jealous girl might do," Raph told me as I got myself ready to leave.

"Her jealous? Difficult to imagine Raph."

"Peaches, she needs a whole lot to help her look like that. You are yourself and you are ten times the person she will ever be." I flushed red when he said that, actually I'm still pretty red.

"What are you gushing at?" Claire murmurs as she pulls out her gun and dusts it off with the hem of her shirt.

"Nothing." We go back to walking in silence when I see a dull light in the distance. "Look!" I say to her. She looks towards where I'm pointing and nods.

"Hide!" She instructs. We are in a large, empty field that extends to the valley that the Hidcout is at. There's not much to hide behind, but there are a few large boulders if we keep walking forward.

I take off running towards the boulder and reluctantly Claire follows. We dodge behind the boulders and I peek my head out from the side of it. My eyes widen as I see that the source of the light is a hovercraft. "False alarm, that's our craft," Claire says standing up.

I sigh loudly and stand up, we start to walk again. After a few hours of walking, we see the outskirts of the Old City. "Okay, you go to the front end, and I'll stay here at the back. We'll meet up in a few hours got it?" She says loading her gun with the magazine.

"Got it."

"Good, go!" She waves me away and I walk forward and enter the deep foliage that is the Old City. My walk leads me through the ruins of the library. I stop there and stare at the pile of rubble that used to be a building, and remember when Sean and I came here. He saved my life then. I shake my head and focus back on the mission, to see if there are any recruits in the City.

I walk onward and once I arrive at the welcome sign of the city, I climb up a tall tree. This way, I can get a better view of the plains that sits ahead of the city. From up here, I can see the dim lights of Sector 7B and wonder if the Handlers have stopped looking for me.

I feel safe up here in the tree knowing that no one can come in or out of the City without me seeing them first, of course, there is always the chance that there could be someone inside the city already.

An hour goes by and I sigh loudly as I ease myself to a sitting position on the thick branch of the tree. A few seconds later I tense up when I hear a soft giggle coming from… My pocket?! I pull out the machine that Raph called a "Walkie-talkie."

"What happened? Are you guys okay?" I hear Sean ask. I at once jump to my feet and stand there. Did someone sneak up on Claire?!

"No, we're fine. Just wanted to say hi, nothing is going on. Can you believe that I'm doing all the work while Larina sits around?!" My mouth hangs open as I stare at the small machine. I can't believe she's lying! Well, I guess it's not all that far fetched. I shove the walkie-talkie back into my pocket and start to climb the tree to get a view of where Claire is at. I look around once I've cleared the blanket of leaves and see Claire's flashlight in the distance. I can see her silhouette perfectly fine, she's laying down.

"That's hard to believe," Sean says making me smile.

"It's true Sean, the girl is lazy. Or maybe it's worse than that. Maybe she doesn't want to find anyone because she's a Society spy!"

That's it! "Can we have a little silence on the line please? I need to focus if we want to find someone!" I snap, pulling out the walkie-talkie. I hear Claire gasp and I lower myself to the branch I had been previously been on.

"Hi, Larina," Sean says.

"Hey Sean, how are you?"

"Worried about you. Everything okay?"

"Yeah, I'm on top of a_." I hear a swooshing sound right next to my ear and stop talking as I try to locate the source of the sound.

"Larina?"

"Sh!" I say into the walkie-talkie before shoving it into my back pocket. I press my back to the tree's trunk and stay still. I hear the noise again, this time, it's followed by a loud "Whack" sound. I look to my left and see a hole on the trunk of the tree that is next to the tree I'm on. Holy cow, I'm being shot at!

I pull out the walkie-talkie and flip it back on, before placing it back into my pocket. "I'm being shot at!" I shout.

"What?!" Sean voice screams.

“Someone’s shooting at me!” I climb down the tree quickly as the bullets keep coming closer and closer to my head. I take out my gun and start running deeper into the city.

“Over here! Over here!” I hear a man say from somewhere behind me. Oh no. “We got her now!” I stop as I’m surrounded by three guys, two look my age, the other looks like he is in his thirty’s.

“Lari_.” I turn off the walkie-talkie before Sean can give away who I am.

“Hey sweetheart, what are you doing in these part of the woods eh?” A tall and muscular guy with dark hair asks.

“I’d ask you the same thing!” I say taking a step back as I see the gun in his hands. I feel my walkie-talkie start to vibrate, indicating someone is trying to talk to me.

“That’s a big gun for such a small girl.” The guy behind me says. I whirl around to face him and glare into his eyes, all three have guns pointed at me.

“I like it.” I snap.

“Who are you with?” The one who seems like the leader asks.

“Myself!”

“Are you from Sector 7B?”

“I was once.”

“And now?”

“It’s none of your business!” It’s dark, I’m one girl facing three large guys with guns and I can’t see their clothing, they could be Handlers for all I know. If they are and they find out who I am, I’m done for.

"Get her." The leader says. I back up and run straight into a fourth guy that I hadn't noticed before. "Take her in." The fourth guy picks me up like I weigh nothing at all and throws me over his shoulder. I struggle against his hold as I try to free myself.

"HELP!" I scream. I start to punch at the guy's back but he doesn't even flinch. All I can do is scream and hope that Claire is running this way, but again she does hate me. They start to walk towards one of the buildings and enter the side of it where it's covered in vines that I'm sure they placed there to hide the entrance. They walk down a tunnel, I can't see anything because it's so dark. I'm carried down the tunnel for a few minutes, before the leader takes down a huge painting from the wall that leads into a room.

The guy carrying me sets me down on a chair that is sitting in the middle of the room. I look around the room as they flip on a light switch, how did they get it to work?! As I look up at the four of them and they look down at me, I cock my head. They all look very familiar.

"Miss Larina?!" The leader asks his mouth dropping open.

"How do you know who I_." I squeal when three of them close in on me and gives me a huge hug. The older one, is just watching me with his arms crossed over his chest. "I can't breath!" I gasp out.

"Let her go!" The leader orders. "Larina, you were our Eraser, you released us."

"I did." I nod, suddenly realizing why they look familiar.

"We had no clue that it was you! Here's your small device back." He hands me my walkie-talkie.

"Thank you." I slowly stand up and smile at them, feeling relieved that I don't seem to be in any danger anymore.

"I'm Jake, this is Steve and the big guy over there is Silv, and this ginger here is Kyle."

"Don't call me a ginger," Kyle says running his hand through his straight, red hair.

"It's nice seeing you all again," I say.

"We found this place all in different days, we've been looking out for one another and_."

I cut Jake off with a question that has been eating at me. "How did you get the guns?"

"Huh?" Jake asks.

"The guns?"

"Oh, some girl came here last week I think, and gave it to us," Steve says. I look up into his green eyes and bite my lower lip.

"A girl?"

"Yeah, she said there was going to be a spy coming here from the Center," Silv says. He glares at me a bit, trying to figure out if I'm the spy or not. His eyes never leave mine as he says it, he has gray eyes and dark hair.

"What did she look like?" I ask looking back to Jake.

"Long dark hair, very pretty," Kyle answers.

"Did she tell you her name?"

"Claire?" He says looking at the other guys for a confirmation. My eyes widen as I stare at the four of them. It was Claire, meaning she's been trying to get rid of me since day one. My eyebrows furrow as I look down at the floor.

"Are you okay La_." The five of us look towards the entrance when someone barges in. My eyes widen when I see that it's Sean, however, the four guys don't know that he's a friend. They all surround me and point their guns at Sean.

"Let her go!" Sean shouts glaring at the four of them. My heart melts a little as I watch him, logically he'd never be able to take the four of them by himself. However, I know he's not thinking logically, he's thinking about how to get me out of here alive.

"Stop guys!" I shout at the four of them. Jake, Kyle, Steve and Silv turn to me. "He's a friend," I say. I watch the four of them lower their guns, much to my relief.

"Larina are you okay?!" Sean runs to me and takes my shoulder in his hands and I just look up at him.

"I'm fine," I say nodding. He sighs and hugs me to him, I look up at him and see that he has his eyes closed. "How did you get here so fast?" I ask.

"Hovercraft."

"Raph let you take the hovercraft?"

"Who said anything about Raph letting me?" He grins and I let out a laugh. "You sure that you're okay, did they hurt you?"

"No, they are all from Sector 7B. I was their Eraser." I explain.

"Oh." Sean turns to the four guys and smiles. "Sorry about the misunderstanding." He says.

"Us too," Jake says extending his hand out to Sean. Sean takes it and they nod at each other.

"You guys hate the Society?" I ask turning to face them.

"Of course," Silv says looking annoyed.

"Good you can join us then," Sean says placing an arm around my shoulders.

"Who are you with?" Kyle asks raising an eyebrow.

"The Rebellion," I say with a smile.

"Let's get out of here," Sean says leading me out of the building. I walk out first, and the first thing I do is stop cold in my tracks. This is the worst scenario possible, standing a few feet away are three Handlers holding guns and pointing them at me.

"End of the line Larina Matthews." One of them says. That's when Sean and the four boys walk out. "Crap." I hear Sean say. I take a step back and the Handlers move in.

Sean and Jake take their stand in front of me and the three other boys follow suit. "Get to the hovercraft, it's at the entrance of the city," Sean says looking back at me.

"But what about_."

"Go, Larina!" He snaps. He turns back to the Handlers and I see that he has his gun back out and pointed at them.

"Get out of here," Silv says shoving me inside the building. So I do, I go through the secret tunnel and find myself easing my way towards the entrance of the city where Sean said the hovercraft is at. From behind me, I can hear shots being fired.

I run through the dense city and soon stumble out of it and see the hovercraft a few feet away from me.

"I have to help them," I tell myself as I get inside the hovercraft and sit in the driver's seat. I stare at the control panel and try to figure out how I would even start to fly this thing. I press my lips together and press the on button and the hovercraft lifts off the ground. "Okay, good," I say. I take the lever into my hand and pull it towards me, I scream as the hovercraft is thrown to the left side and rams against a building. "Ow," I whisper as my head hits the window.

After a few more tries and failed attempts, the hovercraft moves forward and above the city, I look out of the window, down towards the buildings and see the Handlers firing at Sean and the other guys. My heart starts ramming itself against my rib cage as I hover above them, trying to figure out what I should do.

My eyes widen when I see a bullet enter Sean's leg. "Sean!" I scream before lowering the hovercraft right on top of the Handlers, they dive out of the way and avoid getting crushed flat. "Get in!" I scream at the five of them as I throw open the door. Jake and Kyle take either of Sean's arms and start dragging him towards the hovercraft. I look behind them as one Handler gets up and pulls out a gun and points it right on their backs. That gun isn't meant to stun or tranquilize, it's meant to kill.

"Behind you!" I scream snatching the gun from Silv's hand and aiming it at the Handler, I know that if I want too I can shoot him to kill. I aim at his feet and press the trigger, the scream that comes from the Handler lets me know that I've hit my target. "Get him in!" I say helping Jake and Kyle bring Sean inside the hovercraft.

Once they are all inside I shut the doors and hear the bullets hitting the bulletproof surface of the hovercraft. I raise us high above the city and press the camouflage button that I've never noticed before. I don't know what it does, but it must do something. I drive it forward, on the highest speed that it will go, and soon the Old City is far behind us.

"Are you okay?" I ask turning to look at Sean.

"Not really." He says through gritted teeth. I look at Jake and he nods at me before taking the wheel. I walk to Sean and look down at his leg. The bullet entered his mid thigh, there's blood oozing down his dark green pants.

"Jake, keep going until you hit the valley," I say.

"Sure thing." He says.

"We'll get to Doc soon." I place my hand on his forehead and look down into his eyes. "I don't know what to do!" I say totally losing it. Tears start to appear, but before they can escape my eyes I blink them away.

"It's just a bullet wound to the thigh, he'll live," Silv says. He shoves me to the left and looks down at Sean's leg. "Here." I watch as he grabs a knife from his back pocket and starts digging into Sean's leg.

"Oh God," I say before clenching my jaw tight so I don't scream. Sean takes a hold of my hand and I squeeze it into mine, soon Silv has a bloody bullet in his hands.

"There, now all you have to do is stitch it." Silv walks off and cleans his knife off on his shirt.

"He's pleasant." Sean murmurs.

"Sean_."

He looks up at me and smiles. "I'm okay Larina."

"Why did you stay behind? You could have died, don't ever tell me to run again."

“They could have shot you.” He says with a laugh in his voice, like I’m being ridiculous.

“They didn’t, they shot you.”

“And you shot one of them.” I look down at the floor and nod. “You saved us.” I look back at him and let a small smile cross my lips.

“I couldn’t just watch,” I whisper. Sean slowly sits up and groans as he puts pressure on his leg. “You shouldn’t_.” I stop talking as he cups my cheeks in his hands.

“I_.”

“We’re in the valley,” Jake calls out. I look over at him and sigh.

“I’ll take it from here,” I say. Raph showed me, a few days ago, where they hide the hovercraft. It’s inside the same cave as the Hideout but you have to go above the mountain instead of into it.

I pilot us above the mountain and see the hole directly bellow us. “Hold on,” I say.

“You do know how to drive this thing right?” Silv asks, only to receive a hand to the back of the head by Kyle.

“She saved our lives twice now, stop being such a jerk!” I find myself smiling at their exchange.

“I know how to fly it,” I say. Just to play with Silv, I let go of the lever and the hovercraft pummels to the ground.

“Holy_.” Silv starts to say. I take the lever into my hand and laugh as I softly ease us down into the landing pad.

“Got it.” I grin as I look back at them after I’ve turned the craft off.

“Funny.” Silv murmurs.

“Let’s get Sean to the hospital wing,” I say. I open the side door and watch as the four of them look around the place. Once we step out of the hovercraft with Sean being helped by Jake and Kyle, Raph runs over.

“You took the Craft?!” Raph demands.

“We found four recruits,” Sean says.

“He got shot, we need to take him to Doc.” I push past Raph.

He stops me with a single question. “Where’s Claire?” My eyes widen and I turn to look at Sean and his eyes meet mine.

“We forgot her at the Old City,” I say.

“What?!” Raph asks his eyes widening and his mouth turning up into a smile. For a split second I do feel bad about leaving her behind, then I remember that she tried to get me killed and I move on from the guilt.

“Sorry, Raph,” I say.

“Get Sean to Doc, I’ll go get her. When I come back we are going to have a good talk Peaches.” Raph says getting inside the hovercraft. I bite my lip and start to lead Jake and Kyle into the Hideout.

“And boys?” Raph calls out. Silv, Jake, Steve and Kyle stop and turn to face him. “Welcome to the Rebellion.” I roll my eyes and keep walking. He really likes saying that.

I lead the boys through the main lobby and down the steps to Doc’s office, when he sees Sean he sighs loudly. “Can’t you people go one day without getting hurt?” He asks.

“I had to go save her Doc,” Sean says.

“I’m pretty sure she’s the one who saved us,” Jake says smiling at me.

“We met some Handlers when we went looking for new people,” I explain looking over at Doc. His eyes flies to mine and he furrows his eyebrows.

“How many?”

“Three.”

“Where at?”

“The first city from Sector 7B,” I answer.

“Did they follow you?”

“No, one got shot and the other two I almost crushed with the hovercraft.”

“Good girl.” I let out a laugh and watch him work with Sean. After a few minutes of sitting there, the door is thrown open and standing there is Raph’s second in command.

“Boys, follow me and I’ll show you to your rooms.” He says crossing his arm over his chest.

“Who’s that?” Silv asks turning to look at me.

“That’s Raphael’s second in command,” I explain.

“You can call me Lu, now hurry it up. We can braid each others hair and get to know each other better some other time.” Lu says as he turns to walk away. The four guys follow him out of the door and I see Jake turning back to look at me, only he gets yelled at by Lu and quickly walks away.

“You’re a brave one Larina Matthews,” Doc says as he stitches Sean up.

“How so?” I ask.

“Sean told me what happened in the city.” I turn my attention to Sean and smile. “He’s all done, you can stay in here the night and I’ll check up on you tomorrow. Have a goodnight, Clarkson.” Doc nods his head at me and then leaves.

“I never thanked you for coming to save me.”

“Some save that turned out to be.”

“You came, that’s what matters.” I look down at my hands that are clasped together before standing up. “Goodnight Sean, rest okay?” I turn and walk to the door.

“Larina.” He says looking up at me.

“Yes?” I stop with my hand to the door knob and turn around to look at him.

“Come here please.” I nod and close the door before walking back to him. I watch him sit up with his back to the bed’s frame and smile at me. “I’ve wanted to tell you this for a while. Before we even got out of the Society.”

I sit down on the bed, with my legs to the side and look at him and wait. “I guess I’ve always felt the way I did and I thought for sure that you would have been my selection.” A smile forms on my face at the same time that a blush does. “Larina I_.” Before he can finish I lean forward and hug him. My eyes close and I let out a soft sigh.

“I was so scared when I saw you get shot, I don’t want you getting hurt,” I whisper when I pull back. I look down for a second before he places his finger to my chin and makes me look up at him.

"I love you." He looks me straight in the eyes as he says this and my heart actually stops beating.

"Sean I_." He grins and hugs me to him. "God Sean, you can't just assume that I was going to say it back!" I say as he crushes me against his chest. I look up at him and he plants a kiss on my cheek.

"Were you not?"

"I was."

"There you have it." I laugh and shake my head.

"You're crazy," I say, resting my head on his chest.

"But_."

"But I love you anyway," I whisper.

"Ha!" He kisses the top of my head and I let out a soft laugh. "I'll always be here for you Larina, and I'll always come and try to save you, even if it fails."

"That's reassuring." I joke.

"I'll do my best to keep you safe." I look up at him and see how serious he is.

"I know you will but don't go dying because of me."

"I make no promises." He smiles and hugs me again.

As I sit there in his arms I do feel safe and I'm glad to know how he truly feels about me and that he knows how I feel about him. It's one last thing I need to worry about. Though little did I know what other concerns lay ahead.

12

Raph's Plan

Three months later

Sean and I are eating dinner when Lu walks over and places her hand on our shoulders. "Raph wants to talk to you in the strategy room."

I look over at Sean as he looks over at me and nods. We both stand up and follow Lu to the strategy room, as we walk behind him I wonder, for the millionth time, what he's hiding behind that mask that he always wears. The strategy room is deep underground, it's a room filled with monitors and a large round table that is surrounded by chairs.

Once Sean and I get there, Raph stands up and looks at us. "Thanks, Lu," Raph says smiling at him.

"No problem Sir." Lu nods and walks out of the room. I turn to Raph and raise an eyebrow.

"What's going on Raph?" Sean asks the question that I was about to ask.

"You've been here for almost a year Sean and Larina has been here for more than three months, I trust both of you." He looks at us and walks over with a file in his hands, he sets it down on the table in front of us and nods at it. I pick it up and open it, my eyes widen as I stare inside.

Inside the folder is a detailed map of the entire Center. My eyes shoot up to Raph's and he smiles. "That time has come Larina." I hand the folder to Sean and ease myself into a chair.

“This plan is called ‘The Red Sky’ I want to send in our soldiers to invade and conquer the Center, once we do the Society is good as done for.” He sits down on a chair next to me and Sean stands behind my chair with his hand on the back of it. “However, I need someone on the inside to turn the security systems off so that when we are approaching we will go unnoticed.”

“How are you going to get someone_.” I start.

“I need two people who know the Society and can be in the Center because they are trusted by it.” I look back at Sean and he shrugs.

“Raph, turning off security systems and all is great but once you get in there you won’t stand a chance. Everyone at the Center is a Handler, Doctor, and Eraser, there are no citizens, meaning they are all armed and ready to fight to protect the Leader that lives there.” Sean says taking a chair and sitting in between Raph and me.

“I’m well aware how prepared they are for this, but not if all their security systems are off and we take them by surprise.” Sean’s eyes widen and I stare at Raph. He’s crazy!

“And then what? Once you’re at the Center, what will you do? They will be armed no matter_.”

Raph cuts me off. “Peaches, the element of surprise will help us a lot, and with all their security and monitors turned off, they won’t be able to call for help. So now all I need is two people that can pass off as a Handler and an Eraser to do the job.” He grins at us and I sigh loudly. He means us, doesn’t he?

“I’ll do it Raph,” I say. Sean turns and looks at me and shakes his head.

“Me too, if Larina goes so do I.” Raph nods at us and stands up.

“Good, I’ll go get everything you’ll need. Lu is waiting right outside, he’ll give you the tattoos.”

“Wait...What?!” I ask shooting up out of the chair.

“Tattoos, you need the Medal of Service to be seen as a trusted member of the Society, the only problem we have is this, Sean was filed as erased nine months ago.” Sean bites down at his lower lip. “And I’m assuming Larina, that you are marked as wanted for erasing.”

“Yeah,” I say nodding my head.

“So you can’t exactly go as yourselves.”

“So what do you suggest Raph?” Sean asks.

“Go get your tattoo’s, when you are done, report to Doc.” Raph nods and leaves the room. “They are all yours Lu.” He says placing a hand on his shoulder.

“Don’t touch me, Minkus!” Lu snaps before turning to us. “Let’s go.”

We follow him down the hallway and into a room that I’ve never been in before. “What is this place?” I ask.

“My office, who’s first?” He asks. I look over at him and see the large needle in his hands that he will use to give us the tattoos.

“Are you qualified to do this?” I ask.

“Yes, now sit down.” He points at the chair in the middle of the room and Sean places a hand on my shoulder. “Lover-boy first huh?” Lu asks giving a laugh. I watch as Sean sits down and Lu starts to give him the tattoo over the scar that has healed over.

“So what’s with the mask?” I ask as I walk over to watch Lu, quite gently draw out the fire encased in the thick circle.

“I don’t want anyone to know what I look like.”

“Why not?”

“Security measures.”

“Does anyone know what you look like?”

“Yes, Raph and Doc does.” He finishes the tattoo and wipes Sean’s wrist with a moist towel. “Alright Larina, your turn.” He looks up at me as I sit down on the chair. “You can hold her hand if you want,” Lu says to Sean as he takes my wrist into his hand. Sean takes a hold of my right hand and I smile up at him.

“So how about you Larina?” Lu asks.

“What about me?”

“Tell me about yourself, like your family.” Lu starts drawing out the tattoo and I cringe as the stinging pain comes.

“Um, I’m the only child. No one is allowed to have more than one kid.” Lu nods and stops as he watches me talk. “My mom and dad got the Medal of Service and they work at the Center now.”

“They must be so proud,” Lu says coolly.

“I don’t think they know,” I whisper looking down at my hands.

“So you never wanted to have siblings?” Lu asks.

“I never thought about it.”

“Huh.”

"How about you Lu? Do you have any brothers or sisters?" I look up at him and smile.

"Yeah, one sister. Well then there's Raph but he's not really my brother. His parents just raised me as their own."

"Oh, what happened to your real parents?" I ask.

"Don't know." He clears his throat and wipes my wrist. "Okay all done, I'm guessing you can get to Doc by yourself?"

"Yes, thanks." Sean nods at Lu and we head for the door.

"Good luck Larina," Lu calls out.

"Thanks, Lu, you too." I nod my head and leave with Sean.

"Didn't think he'd be friendly," I say.

"Yeah, he seems sort of like a jerk doesn't he?"

"I think he's had a rough life." I murmur.

Sean and I walk to the elevator and take it to the hospital wing. When we get there, Doc is waiting for us. "Going to the Center huh?" He asks grinning.

"I guess so Doc," Sean says smiling.

"Well, you can't go looking like that, follow me." We follow him down the hallway and into a room that is behind double white doors. My eyes widen as I stare at the machines and different gadgets within the room.

"What is this place?" I ask.

"This is my invention room, I've made all of these machines. Some work, others don't. Now let's see, where did I put that thing?!" He starts walking across the room and looking from machine to the next, Sean and I follow close after him.

"What's that?" Sean asks pointing to a huge gun looking thing.

"It's a laser," Doc says.

"What does it do?"

"Shoot things." He grins up at us and rolls out a large machine that looks a lot like a monitor attached to some sort of printer.

"Alright, this is my Mask." He says. I look at the machine and don't see a mask in it. "It makes masks." He explains.

"Doc, we don't need masks. We need something to disguise ourselves with." Sean says.

"Zip it Clarkson, Larina if you could step forward please," Doc says. I do so and he turns on the machine that gives a soft hum, I watch as a blue light scans my face. "Very good, Sean now you." He says. Sean steps forward and the machine scans his face too. "Very good, now watch this."

We step forward and look into the monitor of the machine, in its screen appears Sean's and my face. "Alright so we just need a few changes, let's see…" Doc starts typing what seems to be random numbers into the monitor and I watch as my face slowly morphs into a new person. Then he does the same thing to Sean's face. "Okay, now to print it out." Doc presses a large, red button and I watch as a laser shoots out of the machine and starts to form the faces that we see on the screen.

"Doc, this is amazing!" I say as I watch the girl I'll pretend to be, come to alive.

"I know." He winks at me and picks up the finished mask. "See this machine, also scans your face measurements. Meaning this mask should fit you like a glove." Doc places the mask over my face and it fits my face perfectly. "Your turn Clarkson." Doc removes Sean's mask from the stand and places it over Sean's face. Doc steps back and looks at the both of us with his arms crossed, he nods his head in approval and smiles. "Looks good, no one will even know it's you guys." He says. Doc leads us to a mirror and we stare at it, my eyes widens and I reach my hand up to touch it.

"It feels so real," I whisper.

"Yes, that's the thing, Larina. It has to look and feel as real as it can."

"Thanks, Doc," Sean says turning away from the mirror and nodding his head.

"Of course. Alright, that's all I can do for you. Give me back the masks and I'll make a few more tweaks, you can pick them up before you go."

"Thank you, Doc," I call out as Sean and I leave. "I think this just might work!" I say grinning at him.

"I think so too." He smiles down at me and messes my hair up. Sean and I walk to the floor with the quarters in it and stop in front of my door.

"Get some sleep, I'm sure Raph is going to put us through a lot before we head to the Center."

"Yeah." I nod. "Sleep well, Sean."

"You too Larina." He slowly pulls me to him and embraces me. "We'll do great." He whispers against my hair. I look up at him and study his face, he's worried.

"We will Sean." I take his hands into mine and squeeze them. "Good night."

"Good night." I step back and turn to open my door. "I love you."

"I love you too," I say turning to look at him. He winks at me before walking to his door, I roll my eyes at him and enter my room. "We'll be fine," I whisper as I press my back to the door.

In the morning, the first thing I do when I wake up is groan when I see Lu sitting on the edge of my bed, again. "What do you want?" I snap.

"Came to call you to training."

"What training?"

"Simulation training, Raph set up a whole simulation for you and your boyfriend." He stands up and nods his head at me.

"You can try knocking you know," I call out as he's leaving.

"Now, why would I do that?" He lets a loud laugh that sounds like a bark before leaving my room. I roll my eyes at him and start to get changed into some black pants and a white t-shirt.

I'm putting my hair up into a bun when Sean walks out of his room. "Did you receive a nice wake-up call too?" He asks grinning.

"Yes from Lu."

"From Lu?" His eyes narrow at me. "I got one from Claire."

"Yikes, you had it worse." I tease as I start to walk down the hall.

“Haha funny.” Sean catches up to me and we walk together to the training floor. In the large room, build for training, is now a simulation machine much like the ones in the Headquarters. “Where did you get this from?” Sean calls out to Raph.

“Had Doc make it, looks good huh?”

“Looks great Raph, how does he even know how to build one of these?” I ask.

“Peaches, that time when you saw me stealing the hovercraft from your Sector, wasn’t the first time I stole something. I go into you Sector pretty often, sometimes I steal things, other times I steal information. Like the blueprint for one of these.” Raph grins at me and opens the door.

“Nice,” Sean says.

“Step on in love birds.” He points to the machine and Sean and I step inside it together.

“Cozy?” Raph jokes. “Oh! I almost forgot, put these on. It will allow me to talk to you while you are in the simulation.” Raph hands Sean and I ear pieces. I watch as he closes the door. “Good luck guys!” He calls out and then everything turns extremely bright and I have to squeeze my eyes shut. I feel Sean take a hold of my hand right as I lose myself to the simulation.

I open my eyes several seconds later and feel the wind in my hair as the monorail drives onward. “We’re on the monorail?” I ask looking over at Sean. Only, Sean’s not there. “Sean?” I call out.

“Bad news Peaches.” I hear Raph say in my ears.

“What?” I ask not knowing if he can hear me or not. The monorail starts to move rather roughly and I feel it hits a few bumps along the rails. I hold onto the side of the open door and wait for Raph's response. "Well, the monorail is broken. You're going to have to jump."

"What?!" I demand, looking outside the monorail, where the floor is speeding past me.

"It's that or crash."

"Darn it Raph! Where's Sean?"

"Center."

"Why is he already at the Center?"

"Larina, we sent him earlier than you remember? You're supposed to meet him there."

"Oh." I rack my brain trying to remember what Raph is saying, but no memory of it comes.

"You need to jump now Peaches."

"But_."

"Larina do it!" He screams. My ears start to ring and I face the outside of the monorail. "It's going to crash!" He shouts sounding frustrated. I press my lips together, squeeze my eyes shut and jump. I feel the floor give away from me and then comes the impact. As I land, I start to roll across the ground and place my hands out to stop myself. I slowly sit up, with raw and cut up hands and look at the monorail as it crashes straight into a mountain. "You alive?"

"Shut up Raph." I snap. I slowly get up and look down at my bloody hands.

"Sorry for asking, the Center is a straight shot from there good luck."

I start walking straight like Raph said and soon I see the entrance of the Center, the force field around the whole thing is very obvious, but again it's not meant to be hidden. As I approach the entrance a Handler stops me. "Name." He says looking me over, mostly at my damaged hands.

"Uh_."

"Lora Johnson," Raph says.

"Lora Johnson," I repeat.

"Oh yes, welcome Miss Lora. What in God's name happened to you?"

"The monorail was going to crash, so I had to jump." His eyes widen and he types a code into a keypad and the iron gates open. "Go right in Miss Lora, your husband is waiting for you."

"Thanks," I say nodding my head. I walk through the iron gates and just as I do, I'm surrounded by Handlers. "Hello?" I say, cocking my head.

"Larina Matthews, you are wanted for erasement due to your crimes against the Society." The eldest Handler says.

"I'm not_."

"You are Larina Matthews." One of the Handlers approach me and rip the mask off my face and at once two of them take my arms in their hands. "Won't Emma Jones be so happy? Silly girl, you fell right into our trap."

With that, I hear a loud noise indicating the end of the simulation. When I step out, Raph looks up at me from the monitor. I glare at him and shove past him as I storm out of the room.

"What happened?" I hear Sean ask right as I leave.

"Larina!" Raph shouts after me. I don't stop walking, I keep going feeling the anger building inside of me.

"Matthews, stop right now!" I stop cold in my tracks and whirl around to face Lu head on.

"Don't get involved, this has nothing to do with you!" I shout.

"It has to do with all of us!" He snaps at me.

"Get out of my face."

"Go back and talk to Raph, he's your superior." I shove him hard as he says it and glare at his mask.

"No, he's your superior." I look at Raph as he walks over.

"We need to go over every possible scenario. You did awful Peaches!" I sigh loudly and bow my head. I did do awful, I got hurt and not only that, I got caught.

"What did you want me to do?"

"What I want you to do is get back in that simulation machine and practice every possible outcome," Raph says straightening out his shoulders.

"Raph_." I sigh loudly and nod. "Fine." I start walking back when Lu takes my wrist into his hand. I look up to where I assume his eyes are at.

"You shove me again and I will personally pound you to the ground." He hisses at me.

"Whatever." I yank my arm from his hand and walk back into the simulation room.

Sean walks over to me. "You okay?"

“Yeah, let’s get this done with.” Sean nods and we step back inside the simulation machine. “No ear piece,” I say as I set them down on the floor, Sean follows my lead.

“Good luck Peaches,” Raph says as he closes the door of the machine.

“You’re going to need it.” I hear Lu say right as I go under.

13

To the Center

A week later

"Do you need help?" I open my eyes and staring down at me is the girl that looks just like me. She has on a white hospital gown on, and her hair is down and around her shoulders. I slowly sit up and look around, all around me are buildings crashing to the floor and people screaming.

"What happened?" I ask her.

"The Rebel's won." She gives me a grin and holds out her hand to me.

"Is this… The Center?"

"Yup!" She lets out a laugh that seems familiar and I take her extended hand. She pulls me off the metal table I had just been in, and I look back to it. That was an erasing room.

"Wait!" I say, yanking my hand from her's. She turns her eyes to me and cocks her head in confusion. "Where's Sean, Raph, and all the others?!"

"They got erased." She says without a single hint of emotion in her voice.

"They_." I feel the color drain from my face as I stare at her. "They, got erased?"

"Yeah."

“Then how could the Rebels have won?”

“Well, Raph killed Emma Jones. After he did that he was taken away along with Sean and the others. For some reason, no one came to erase you.” She smiles at me.

“So, the Rebellion has fallen as well? There’s no one to lead it?”

“Of course there is!” I stare at her and wait for her to tell me who this person is. All she does is take a black mask that is laying on the floor and place it over her face. I open my mouth to speak, but everything starts to turn black and I feel myself fall over.

“Larina?!” My eyes shoot open when I hear Sean’s voice. I gasp out for air and look around at the white walls that surround us. I cling to Sean’s shoulder as I try to remember where we are. Then it hits me, we are in the simulation machine. “Are you okay?” Sean looks down at me with worried, hazel eyes and I nod.

“That was a weird one,” I say with a laugh as I release his shoulders.

“I was going to get erased on that one.” He says.

I look up at him and furrow my eyebrows. On my simulation, he did get erased. I look towards the door of the machine as it opens, standing there is Raph. Sean and I step out of the machine and I look up at Raph.

“How did you know about the girl?” I ask.

“What girl?”

“The girl from the simulation.” Raph cocks his head and looks at Sean.

"Raph, she had a different simulation than I did," Sean explains. Raph turns to look at me and cocks his head. "She said, it was a weird one."

"Peaches?"

"I woke up and the Center had fallen all around me, you guys had gotten erased. There were people screaming and_." I cover my ears hearing them even now. "There was this girl when I woke up from the metal table and she looked like me, she said that the Rebels had won but that you guys died. Then she put on this black mask that looks exactly like_." I look around the room and see Lu on the back of it, looking at some files.

"Sup." He calls out as he catches me staring at him.

"It looked like Lu's mask." I finish to Raph.

"Peaches, in this simulation you all got caught and you guys were about to be erased." I narrow my eyes as I stare at him.

"Then why did I_."

"You were dreaming," Raph says.

"You mean I fell asleep?"

"Yes." I blush at that and shake my head, that's embarrassing. "I've been working you guys hard, look get some sleep okay? Tomorrow is a big day." He places a hand on my shoulder and nods his head.

Tomorrow is a huge day, Sean and I are heading to the Center. "Have a goodnight Peaches," Raph calls out as Sean and I leave.

I look up at Sean and he smiles at me as he takes my hand in his. "You're okay right?"

"Yeah I'm fine, I guess I am just tired."

"Well we've had multiple simulations every day for the past week, it will tire you out. Not to mention all the training." I nod and soon we arrive in front of my door. "Good night Larina, sleep well okay?"

"You too Sean." I smile up at him and throw my arms around his waist as I hug him and close my eyes. "Do you think we'll be able to do it?" I ask.

"Of course we will. We'll be together, and we'll look out for one another." He nods and makes me look up at him. "Get some sleep okay?" He plants a kiss on my forehead and steps back.

"You too," I say with a smile. He grins, before turning away and walking into his room.

"Out Claire!" He snaps. I look across the hall and see Claire walk out of his room with a sunken look to her face. "Night Larina!" He calls out before closing the door and locking it.

"What are you looking at?" Claire asks as I look back at her.

"I wish Raph would have left you at the Old City," I say.

"What?" She snaps at me, her eyes growing wide.

"You heard me." With that, I slam my door shut and throw the bolt. All night, I dream of the girl that looks like me and wonder what she means.

I wake up in the morning with a knock on my door. I slowly get out of bed and walk to the door and open it. "Yes?" I say to Lu.

"Raph asked me to give you this." Lu holds out an Eraser's uniform and the mask that Doc made for me.

“Thanks.” I take them from him and start to close the door.

“Larina.” Lu stops the door with his foot and I wait. “Listen, Raph is too proud. It could be that his plan fails, but he’d never call for help. I don’t want anyone to die, it’s wishful thinking, but I don’t. Take this.” He hands me a small, black device with a single red button on it. “If anything goes wrong; meaning, if you get caught and are about to die, push this button and it will call me and send me your location. I will come as fast as I can and get you out alright?”

“Why?” I ask looking up at him.

“Look, you’re a pain in the neck but I still have to protect the Rebellion.”

“Oh, okay thanks, Lu.”

“No problem.” He nods and turns around and leaves down the hall. I close the door and undress and start to dress in the Eraser’s uniform. A white shirt, pants and a lab coat. As I look up in the mirror, I frown, I’m an Eraser once more. I sigh loudly and tell myself that it's all pretend and that I won’t have to Erase anyone. Hopefully. As I’m putting my hair up in an official Eraser bun, I start to wonder where Raph even got these clothes and decide that I probably don’t want to know the answer to that.

When a knock sounds I look towards the door and say: “Come in!” The door opens and I smile at Sean.

“Never thought I’d see you as an Eraser again.” He whispers.

“Never thought I’d see you as a Handler.” I look him up and down in his black Handler uniform and body armor. He actually looks great. I turn back to the mirror and finish the bun.

"Don't forget the mask." He says tossing me the mask. I catch it in both hands.

"Thanks." I slip the mask over my face and look into the mirror, if I didn't know what I look like, I'd never guess it was a mask. I can't even see the marks that tell me where the mask ends and where it's really me.

"Lora Johnson," Sean says walking behind me and looking into the mirror. He has his mask on too.

"Mike Johnson," I say with a smile.

"We look awful."

"Speak for yourself! I'm rocking this nose!" I say joking about the large nose on the face of the mask. Sean starts laughing and doubles over at it. "Was it really that funny?"

"Yes, because your real nose is so normal and cute." I feel myself flush behind the mask and feel grateful for it being there.

"Right, get out so I can finish up."

"Well hurry up, Raph wants to go over our story for the millionth time this week."

"Seriously?"

"Yup, bye beautiful." He teases as he leaves.

"Bye handsome." I joke back. I hear him laugh as he walks down the hall.

Once I've finished changing I meet up with Raph and Sean in the cafeteria. "About time Larina," Raph says.

"She's a girl, they are required to take a long time getting ready," Sean says only to receive a slap on the arm.

“Not funny.” I sit down next to Raph and he grins at me.

“Tell me the story you are going to tell Emma Jones.” I look to Sean and he sticks his tongue out at me.

“We are husband and wife, our names are Lora and Mike Johnson and we are loyal subjects to the Society. We are both twenty-two years old and I’ve been Eraser since I was twenty and he has been a Handler since he was twenty.”

“Very good, that about covers it.” Raph stands up and pulls me to him in a hug. “Be careful out there alright Peaches?”

“Be careful in here,” I say hugging him back. He chuckles and messes my hair up.

“It was nice working with you, Sean,” Raph says once we’ve pulled away. He extends his hand out to Sean, which Sean takes and grins.

“You do know, we’re not going to die right?”

“You never know.”

“That’s reassuring.” I murmur. Raph laughs and tries hard to stop laughing and fails. “We’re going,” I say taking Sean’s hand in mine.

“Good luck you two,” Raph calls out as we leave the cafeteria.

Once Sean and I pass through the steel hallway that leads to the entrance of the Hideout, and step out into the tunnel Sean squeezes my hand. “This is it! Are you ready?”

“As I’ll ever be.” I murmur.

“Good, let's go.” He winks at me and we start to jog. We jog out of the valley that holds the Hideout, before leaving the many mountains behind us as we run across the opened fields. I don’t say anything to Sean, but running out here with the sun high above us makes me feel very exposed and uncomfortable. What if the Handlers decide to look around the Old City, where they saw Rebels hiding in?

After nearly two hours of running, walking, resting, talking and panting we arrive at the Old City. “Just keep your eyes opened, and I got your back,” Sean says nodding his head at me, he pulls out his gun and I follow suit and start to walk through the city. It seems that my steps are extra loud as we walk through the broken streets and over leaves that have begun to fall out of the trees.

We pass the library and Sean chuckles to himself, most likely remembering all that happened that day. “Keep going,” I say. We have to get to Sector 7B before the monorail arrives at the station. If we get there too late, the whole plan will be delayed. Sean and I keep going and soon exit the Old City without any incident.

Then comes the hard part, walking through the plains that sit in front of the Old City and that lead straight to Sector 7B. Anyone looking out from the iron gate at the border of the Sector, will surely see us and think something is up.

Sean and I move quickly, trying to stay to the right of the iron gate the whole time so that if someone happens to look out, they won’t spot us unless they look very hard. After miles of walking, we arrive at the looming iron gate and I look inside of the Sector that used to be my home what seems like forever ago. “Miss it?” Sean asks as he starts scaling up it.

"No, of course not." I follow after him, I'm much more clumsy. However, soon we are over and down the fence looking like any regular Handler and Eraser. "Let's go," I say taking off towards the monorail station that sits in front of the Headquarters.

"We're in luck, here it comes!" Sean points at the speeding monorail.

"Oh! Almost missed it!" We both tense up and turn around when we hear a very familiar voice. Standing five feet from us is Sherrie Maxwell. Oh, God. As if on cue, my hands become clammy and my mouth drops open. I regain myself with a nudge from Sean with his elbow.

"Head Handler Maxwell," Sean says nodding his head.

"Ah hello Mr. Johnson, how are you this fine afternoon?" She asks smiling at him.

"Just fine." He says. I stare at him and he slowly shakes his head at me. How does she know that his name is Mike?

"And you Mrs. Johnson?"

"I'm great and yourself Head Handler?" I muster.

"Just fine, going to the Center and the both of you?"

"Us too," Sean says smiling.

"Oh, that's right! You both received the Medal of Service, I'm sure you will love your new assignments and the Center is lucky to have the both of you." She nods at us and passes us as she boards the monorail.

"Sean_."

"Not now Larina." He whispers. We board the monorail and sit as close to the door as possible, and as far from Sherrie as possible as well. “I think that Lora and Mike Johnson are real Society citizens.” He whispers leaning into me.

“So, what do you think happened to them?” I look into Sean’s eyes and he shrugs. I shudder at the mere possibility of what might have happened to them and look out of the window as the monorail leaves the station.

“Mind if I sit here?” Sherrie asks walking towards us. What’s wrong with her seat? Why can’t she stay there?

“Of course not,” Sean says.

“Wonderful.” She sits herself down across from us and smiles. “So are you both excited to be able to work at the Center?”

“Very, it’s such a privilege!” I say with a fake smile.

“It indeed is. Mr. Johnson, I’m sure you will become Head Handler in no time.” Sherrie says.

“I’m sure you will darling,” I say placing my hand on his. He throws me a: “Don’t push it.” Look which I chose to ignore.

“And you Miss Lora, you are such a great Eraser! I’m sure you will soon become Head Eraser!” Sherrie grins and I smile back at her.

“Let’s hope so Head Handler Maxwell.”

“You know there was ever one girl that was able to erase as many people as you have. However, she turned into a complete fake.” Sherrie looks down at her hands and sighs.

“What happened to her?” I ask, knowing very well who this girl she is speaking of is.

“She got erased.” Of course, she would lie, how could she possibly say that someone escaped out of a Sector that she is in control of?

“Good thing,” Sean says. I throw him a glare which makes his let out a laugh.

“You two are so cute together! I knew when I selected you both for each other it was the right thing to do!” She selected? This, of course, shouldn’t surprise me one bit. Of course, the Selection is a fraud, just like everything else in this awful place.

“I knew at once as well,” Sean says taking my hand in his and planting a kiss on the top of it. My cheeks turn a bright color behind the mask and I fear that the glow from them will give us away.

“Me too,” I whisper resting my head on his shoulder.

“Well, I assume you two have lots to talk about. Enjoy your ride and good luck at the Center.” Sherrie says smiling as she stands up and walks back to her seat.

“Who knew someone who hates us, would wish us good luck?” Sean jokes.

I let out a soft laugh and close my eyes, he wraps his arm around my shoulder and I feel myself slowly drift off to sleep.

“Larina.” I hear a soft voice whisper against my cheek. I stir in my sleep and hear a soft laugh. “Get up Larina, we’re here.” I shoot up when I hear that and look out at the dark world outside. “Good evening.” I look at Sean and smile.

“Hi, we’re here?” I ask, looking out the window. My eyes widen as I stare at the Center. A place surrounded by other Sectors, filled with buildings meant for training and houses only for those who earned to be here, and of course the source of all the wrong that goes on in all of the Society. My mind wonders to my parents, and I find myself wondering if we'll run into them while we are here.

"Yes, let's get going." Sean takes my hand in his and pulls me up to my feet. I follow closely after him as we exit the monorail and it's station. The Headquarter of the Center, which also happens to be Emma Jones' home, is a straight shot from the station. We walk towards the tall and dark building. There aren't any people at all on the streets, it's past curfew.

Once we arrive at the front doors of the Headquarters, two Handlers stops us. "Good evening, how can I help you both?" An older Handler asks.

"We've been transferred from Sector 7B," Sean says.

"Oh, you are the Johnson's?" He asks.

"We are," I say nodding my head.

"Welcome to the Center Mr. and Mrs. Johnson, come in please." The Handler opens the door and after giving the younger Handler a look, he leads us through the Headquarters.

I'm amazed at how luxurious this place is, it looks more like a mansion on the inside than a Headquarters. "I'm sure you want to speak to Mrs. Jones, however, she is asleep. You'll have to do that first thing in the morning."

Sean and I exchange looks and then nod at the Handler. "I'll show you both to your room."

Sean and I follow the Handler up the giant staircase, for a few floors up and down a hallway that is lined with doors. He opens the door and Sean and I stare inside the room. For one thing, the room is huge, there's a large window on the left side that leads to a balcony and a bathroom that is on the right side of the room. Luckily there are two beds in the room, two small beds, but two beds the same. "Do you prefer a room with only one bed?" The Handler asks turning to look at us.

"No!" We both say at the same time.

"Alright then, this will be your room for now. Welcome to the Center."

14

Emma Jones

In the morning, Sean and I are woken up by a knock on the door. "One second!" I call out as the both of us hurry to put on our masks. The good thing about being at the Center is one thing, there are no cameras at all in it. Everything is so top secret and classified that Emma Jones doesn't want any footage of what happens inside.

"That's quite alright Mrs. Johnson, once you've finished changing just go to Emma Jones' office." I look to Sean, who has his mask half on.

"Okay thank you."

"It's the last door on the second floor of the Headquarters. It's the big double doors, there's no way to miss it." The guy says.

"Thanks," Sean calls out. When I look back at him he has his mask completely on. "We need to get changed, I'll go in the bathroom." He takes the Handler uniform from the closet, that had already been prepared for "Our" arrival and enters the bathroom before closing the door.

I quickly change into the Eraser uniform and pull my hair out of my face in a ponytail. Soon, Sean walks out of the bathroom all suited up and we leave the room and head down the stairs and towards Emma Jones' office. "We'll be fine." I keep repeating in my head over and over again.

"Ready?" Sean asks once we've arrived in front of the massive, dark wood doors. I only nod and watch as he reaches out and knocks on the door.

“Who is it?” Comes a voice full of authority.

“Leader Jones, this is Mike Johnson and Lora Johnson. We transferred from_.” Sean gets cut off when the doors are thrown open and standing there is Emma Jones herself. I stare at her and press my lips together, feeling an uncertainty inside of me.

Emma Jones has dark hair, and equally dark eyes on pale skin. She’s rather tall and slim even though she is fit. Her eyes take us in with such power that I lower mine from her own. “You are the Johnson's?” She asks.

“Yes Ma’am,” Sean says bowing his head.

“Rather young aren’t you?”

“We’re twenty-two, Ma’am.” I keep quiet as Sean and Emma Jones talk.

“Great, why don’t the both of you come in and we can talk in private, yes?” We both nod in unison and enter her large office that holds a window right behind her desk that is so large that it goes from the ceiling to the floor. There is a closet to the right side of her desk and many filing cabinets spread all about it. “Have a seat Mr. and Mrs. Johnson.” Emma sits on her large, black chair behind her desk and rests her chin in her slender hands as she watches us closely.

Everything inside of me is screaming that something is going to go wrong, that she will see past our masks. Literally. “How was your travel from 7B?” She asks leaning back on her chair and watching us just as closely.

“It was wonderful, the monorail has always been a very comfortable way of transportation,” Sean says smiling.

“I agree, I don’t ride on it often, but I do agree with you, Mr. Johnson.” She turns her dark eyes to me and I feel my posture stiffen at once. "And you Mrs. Johnson? How are you this fine morning?"

"Wonderful Leader Jones, it's always been a dream of mine to get the chance to be transferred to the Center."

"Hm, yes. Only the best of the best are sent here and according to your Head Handler, you two are it."

"Thank you, Ma'am." Sean and I say together.

She smiles at the two of us and shakes her head slightly. "You two certainly are a great match aren't you?"

"We are Ma'am." Sean takes my hand in his and squeezes it.

"Hm." Emma pushes her chair from her desk and stands up. My heart jumps to my throat as I watch her, thinking she's on to our disguises. However, she simply walks over to a small table with a coffee maker, sugar and cream and grabs her a cup. "Would either of you like some coffee?"

"No thank you." We say at the same time. I then watch her stir sugar into that cup a gazillion times, before she returns to her desk.

"Sherrie Maxwell has informed me of your very high performance as citizens of the Society, that makes me very happy to hear. Now you are aware of what it is done here at the Center?"

"Yes Ma'am," Sean says.

"Very good, Mr. Johnson you will be training here in the Headquarters and Mrs. Johnson you will train at the Erasing Facility and also in the Institution here at the Center." My stomach lurches forward and I feel like I might throw up. Back in the Erasing Facility?! "As you know no one is actually sent to the Institution nor is anyone erased here at the Center, you are simply going to be training there, so you can be the best Eraser you can become. Once your training is complete you will go back to a Sector selected for you, and become Head Handler and Head Eraser." I feel a sense of relief take over my insides as she informs me that I won't be doing any erasing at the Center.

"That will be all for today, Mr. and Mrs. Johnson. Go ahead and make your way to the dining hall, you will find it in the cafeteria building right next door. Do enjoy your breakfast." She stands up then, indicating the end of our conversation.

"Thank you, Ma'am," Sean says. I don't say anything, I'm so lost in thought that I only snap out of it with a nudge from Sean.

"Yes, thank you, Leader Jones." I nod my head and follow Sean out of the door.

"Your trainers will meet you at the dining hall to talk to you about your schedules. Best of luck, close the door on your way out." With that, she turns back to her monitor and we leave her office.

"We did it," Sean whispers as we walk down the hall.

"The whole time I was expecting her to reach over and yank our masks right off!" I admit.

"Me too." Sean and I exchange a look before bursting out in laughter.

We make our way out of the Headquarters and walk across the street towards the Cafeteria. The first thing, or rather, the first people I see when I step into the dining room, are my parents. My eyes start to water and I take a step in their direction when Sean places a hand on my shoulder.

"Larina, no."

"But_." He takes my face into his hands and I look up into his eyes.

"I know you miss them and love them, but they are loyal to the Society. Plus they don't know that it's you Larina, the mask remember?" My heart sinks and I lower my eyes to the floor.

"I remember."

"Let's get something to eat alright?" I only nod. I follow Sean into the line of people that are waiting to get their food. Deep inside there's an ache as I look back towards my parents who are sitting at a table, talking and looking really somber.

"Next." I look back to the kitchen worker as she calls Sean and me up. We get our food, which is some sort of chicken with a small salad, and head towards a table that is as far from my parents as possible.

"I'm really sorry Larina," Sean whispers reaching across the table and taking my hand in his.

"I'm fine."

"Hi, there!" My heart stops beating when I look up and see that standing behind Sean, are my parents. They are looking right at us.

"Hello Ma'am," Sean says nodding his head at mom. "Sir." He says turning to dad.

"Hi," I whisper, feeling my heart slowly regain its pace.

"You are the Johnson couple right?" Dad asks sitting down right beside Sean.

"Yes, that's us," Sean says smiling. I watch my parents, behind their smiles and words, is a thick sadness that they can't disguise. Especially not from me.

"I'm Clef Matthews and this is Geo, my wife. We are going to be the one's training you." My eyes widen and I turn to look at Sean whose eyes are just as wide.

"That's great Mr. Matthews," Sean says.

"Handler Matthews will do."

"I'll be training you, sweetie, what's your name?" Mom turns her dark eyes to me and my heart drops to the pit of my stomach. I miss them both so much, it's been so long!

"Lar_." I stop when Sean throws me a look. "Lora," I say. Mom watches me closely and cocks her head. "Everything alright?" I ask.

"Yes, you remind me of my daughter." I press my lips together and stare at the table.

"I do?"

"Yes, she's a_."

"Geo!" Dad snaps which makes Sean, mom and I look up at him. "She got erased," Dad says.

My mouth drops open as I stare at them. They were told that I was erased.

"How come?" I ask.

"She fell in love," Mom says with a bitter tone in her voice.

"She was caught kissing a man who wasn't her selected," Dad says. Mom clenches her jaw and turns back to me. "Handler Johnson, why don't you get your food and we can go talk about your schedule?" Dad says placing a hand on Sean's shoulder.

"Yes, sir." I watch as they both get up and leave the table. I slowly turn back to mom.

"She was a great young lady, I_." Mom places her hands on her face and I hear her try to control her breathing. "I didn't want to come here and leave her behind, she was so young. I knew she liked that Handler, but I never thought she would_." Not being able to stand it anymore I throw my arms around mom and start to cry into her shoulders.

"I'm so sorry!" I say pulling back and looking into her eyes. Her eyes narrow for a split second before she hugs me back.

"You have no idea how much I need this Mrs. Johnson" She whispers. We quickly pull apart though, we are after all, in the Center. "Let's go back to the Institution shall we?" I nod and leave my food, untouched at the table.

"Do you mind if I ask you something mo_. Doctor Matthews?" I cringe at my slip up.

"No, go ahead."

"How did you get to train an Eraser if you are a Doctor at the Institution?"

"Good question, we were short on Erasers and I had no one to train so Leader Jones thought I would do just fine teaching the Erasers."

"I think she's right," I say with a smile.

"Your parents must be so proud of you!" She says as we leave the building and head towards the tall, white Institution building.

“No,” I whisper.

“No?”

“Er, they miss me is all I meant to say.”

“Oh, I see. I understand the feeling. You’re probably my daughter’s age aren't you?”

“I’m twenty-two.” I lie.

“You’re a little older, she’d be almost twenty.”

“Oh, she was so young.” I feel bad about lying to mom but, I don’t have any other choice at the moment.

“Yes, she was. Let’s get going.” I hadn’t noticed but we stopped walking. I follow after her into the Institution.

The Center’s Institution is a lot like the one back in Sector 7B. “You can step into my office, Mrs. Johnson.” Mom opens the second door in the main hallway and I step inside it. I look around the large office, before turning back to look at her.

“Wow.”

“It’s nice isn’t it?”

“Yeah.”

“Alright Mrs. Johnson, I already have your schedule right here.” She hands me a folder and I open it. Inside the folder is at least fifty pages of what my schedule will be. Page after page of meetings, training and a whole lot of time.

“That’s a lot,” I say.

“It sure is, you will begin after lunch today alright? Come back then.” Mom opens the door to her office and

I head to it. "You'll be back in a Sector before you know it, Mrs. Johnson."

"Thank you, Ma'am." She nods and turns away from me and towards the monitor in her desk. I close the door and walk out of the Institution, where Sean is walking towards me. "Hi_.Whoa!" He takes my wrist in his hand and starts dragging me behind the Institution. "What's wrong?" I ask.

"Your parents are training us." He says.

"I know."

"We can't let them find out who we are Larina."

"I know that too."

"I think your dad suspects something."

"What? How can he already suspect something, Sean?"

"He's perspective, I don't know Larina!" He runs his hand through his face and lets out a loud sigh. "I worked under him for a year back in Sector 7B. He always knew when something was off."

"So what do we do?"

"There's nothing we can do, just be careful around your mom alright?" He looks me in the eye and I nod. "Remember what we are here for."

"I know, I remember."

"Good, I have to go over this ridiculous schedule." He murmurs. I let out a soft laugh and show him my schedule. "Gee, yours is worst!" He grins and I look up at him with a smile stamped on my face. We both jump from where we are standing when we hear a loud voice shouting out orders.

“Get into your quarters at once, this is a drill!”

“I guess we should_.”

Sean nods and offers me his hand, which I take and we both make our way to the Headquarters. “Hurry it up, people!” The man shouts out.

“Who is that guy anyway?” I whisper to Sean.

“That’s Timothy Ryan, he’s Emma Jones’ second in command.” A young man says as he walks quickly with us towards the Headquarters.

“Oh,” I say.

“I’m Jon Michaels.” He says smiling at me.

“Lora.” I nod.

“And I’m Mike Johnson, her husband,” Sean says pulling me to him. I roll my eyes at him and Jon stares at the two of us.

“Nice to meet the both of you.” He smiles and winks at me before walking into the Headquarters. I press my lips together and look up at Sean.

“What was that?” He asks.

“I think he winked at me,” I say with a laugh in my voice.

“What is it about your huge nose that people think it’s so attractive?” He jokes as he leads me towards our room.

“I don’t know, they just can’t help themselves.” I joke along. “Seriously Sean, he was just being nice.”

“If he was just being nice he wouldn’t have winked at you.”

"Maybe he had something in his eye?"

"Right." Sean closes the door to our room and I watch as he walks over to his bed and sits down on it. "So, when do you start your training?"

"My mom said after lunch."

"Hm."

"How about you?"

"Your dad said the same thing." I walk over to him and sit down beside him.

"What do you think we'll have to do?" I whisper as I look over at him.

"Your dad said something about a simulation." My heart stops beating and my mouth parts. "We just have to do our best to do as a loyal citizen would do."

"Sean_."

"We'll be fine." He whispers squeezing my hands. Will we?

After lunch, mom walks over to me with a lot of files in her hands. "Are you ready Mrs. Johnson?" She asks.

"I'm ready," I whisper throwing a look back at Sean, who is being approached by dad. Sean discreetly nods at me before standing up and walking out of the Cafeteria with dad.

"Follow me," Mom says. She turns around and walks the way that she came, out of the Cafeteria and across the street to the Institution. "You will go through a simulation, it's a very complex simulation that you aren't used to." I nod and try to keep up with her as she walks on and leaves me to trail behind her.

When we enter the Institution she goes straight up a flight of stairs and into the only room on the floor. Mom turns back to me and looks me over. “Close the door please.”

I do as I’m told and step deeper into the room, and watch as she starts switching on the simulation machine. “In this Simulation, you will be very well aware that you are in a simulation. Do as you would normally do when you are erasing someone.” She turns to me after pressing her hands to the scanner on the machine’s door. “Alright, in you go.”

I press my lips together and step inside the machine. The minute the door closes, my heart clenches inside me and I tell myself over and over that I’ll do fine, I’ll know it’s just a simulation. “Ready Mrs. Johnson?” I hear mom ask.

“Ready.”

“Very well, good luck.” With that, the machine turns on and I feel myself being swept away into its brightness. I squeeze my eyes shut and feel the world around me spin, when I open my eyes I’m in an erasing room. My eyes go directly to the girl who is sitting on the chair. Oh no. Even though there’s a metal cuff around her mouth and she’s looking down at the floor, I know it’s the girl that looks like me.

Why does she keep appearing everywhere? Especially now that I’m being watched by my own mother? “This is a simulation Larina, it’s not real. Erase her.” I say to myself. I take a step towards the girl and her head shoots up, she looks at me with scared eyes.

Her eyes grow to the size of golf balls when I walk to the cabinet where the death serum is at. My eyes wonder to the sleep serum, and I feel my hands reach for it. I stop just in time and take the death serum into my shaky hands.

I slowly turn to the girl and her eyes go from me to the death serum and back again, my entire body starts to shake when she shakes her head over and over again, pleading with me, with her eyes. I press my lips together as I suck the serum up into the syringe and walk to her. I have to do this, I can't have anyone suspecting that I'm not loyal to the Society, I can't be the reason the Rebels fail.

When I look at the girl, I see that the metal cuff isn't in her mouth anymore. "Please don't!" The girl screams as I approach her. I feel the tears sting at my eyes and I clench my jaw tightly to keep from screaming.

"Who are you?!" I demand as I stop right in front of her. She doesn't answer me, she just stares into my eyes. "Just do it, Larina." I hear myself say in my head. I step to the side and hold the syringe firmly in one hand and look at the girl's neck.

"Don't kill me!"

"I'm erasing you," I say looking into her eyes.

"You don't believe that!" She shouts. I have to shut her up before she gives me up. I quickly inject the serum into her neck and watch as she goes limp. I drop the syringe onto the floor and see it break into a gazillion pieces of glass.

My heart stops beating as I see the life leave her eyes. Oh my God, my hands fly to my mouth and I quickly drop them and roll the metal table over to the girl, I have to finish this strong. I have to_.

Before I can finish the erasing, I hear a loud noise, before looking around and seeing that I'm in the simulation machine once more. Mom ended the simulation early, that can't be good. I reach for the door and jump back as the door is thrown open, I look at mom who's staring back at me with her hands to her mouth and her eyes filled with water.

"M_.Doctor Matthews?" I ask.

"How do you know about her?" She asks her voice shaky from the tears.

"Her?" I ask.

"The girl you were erasing, that's my daughter." So the girl is me?

"I_. I knew Larina before she was erased." I lie.

"That wasn't Larina! That was Luisa." My eyes narrow and I cock my head as I stare at mom.

"Luisa?" I watch mom fall to the floor in a heap of tears and misery. My lips begin to quiver as I watch her. "Who is Luisa? I thought your daughter was Larina Matthews." I slowly crouch next to her and she looks up at me.

"Larina had a twin sister when she was born, we had to have her erased." My eyes widen and I feel myself lose balance, I place my hands on the floor to keep myself up.

"What?"

"Larina was a twin. When we saw two of them, we were so sad because we knew that we wouldn't be able to keep them. Sherrie chose to erase Luisa, she was the older baby."

"Larina, had a sister?" I ask looking into mom's eyes. I had a sister? I was a twin? She got…erased. I feel a deep pain in my heart and I slowly sit down on the floor beside mom.

"Yes." I look to mom and I feel tears fall onto the floor.

“Oh my God.” My hands fly to my mouth and I start to cry right then and there. The tears slide down my face, behind and over the mask and I shake my head in complete disbelief. Oh my God! I shoot up and run out of the room, and out of the Institution. I don’t stop running until I’ve reached my room in the Headquarters.

Once I’m there, I throw the door closed and walk numbly to my bed and slowly lower myself into it. I can’t believe all this time I had a sister.

Sean walks in hours later looking exhausted. He doesn’t even notice me sitting on my bed with my back to the bed’s frame and my knees up to my chest. “Your dad is very tiring.” He murmurs as he falls onto his bed on his back. I slowly turn to look at him and nod. “How was your day?” I sigh softly and rest my head on my knees and close my eyes. “Larina?” I hear him shift on the bed to a sitting position and I can picture him staring at me with a worried expression on his face. “Hey, what’s wrong?” I hear him get off his bed and walk over to me. The right side of my bed lowers as he sits down beside me and wraps his arm around my shoulder. “Larina?”

I raise my head and look at him, before wiping my face with my hands. “Um, I found out that I had a twin sister. She was erased at birth.”

Sean’s eyes narrow in confusion before his eyes widen. “Serious?”

“Yeah, remember the simulation we did together that I fell asleep back at the Hideout?”

“Yes.” He nods.

“The girl that was with me, was her I guess. I kept seeing her throughout this year. In dreams, in simulations, in everything and I always knew she wasn’t me. Today my mom stopped the simulation after I erased Luisa, that was her name."

"You erased_."

"I thought she was me, I couldn't be the reason for the Rebels to fail Sean! So I did what I had to do, I erased my own sister, that I didn't even know I had! When I came out of that machine, my mom was in tears. She fell to the floor and told me all about how I'm a twin and how Sherrie chose to erase Luisa and keep me around."

"Larina, I'm so sorry." He holds me closer to him and I let out a sigh.

"I wonder what it would have been like to have her around. I wonder what she would have been like."

"I'm sure she would have been a great person, like you." I let myself smile as I look up at him. "What can I do to make you feel better?"

"Nothing really." I sit up straight and wipe the last of the tears from my face and turn to look at him. I'm decided that I can't let personal things get in the way of what we are supposed to do. "So, tell me what happened during your training."

"Larina, we don't have to_."

"I need my thoughts to be somewhere else. I never knew her, I wish I had but I didn't and I can't let that get in the way of the mission. I can't cry anymore, mom must be wondering why I cared so much." I lower my eyes to the covers and bite on my lower lip. "I wonder if she suspects."

"I don't know." Sean leans the back of his head against the bed frame and sighs. "The training was a lot of physical stuff. Running, climbing and maneuvering. Your dad sure is fit for a man his age!" Sean lets out a laugh and I smile as I lean my back against the bed frame alongside him.

"He was always very dedicated as a Handler."

"Yeah." Sean nods and looks at me. "I didn't have to do a simulation, tomorrow he said I'd have to show him my hovercraft and hover board skills."

"Oh." I never stayed long enough at my training to figure out what tomorrow will bring.

"And there's one more thing, they are holding some sort of party tomorrow night. Suppose to be very formal, I think it's for Emma Jones' wedding anniversary and we are invited."

"Ugh, really?"

"Yes, and by invited, I mean we have to go."

"Got it." I lean my head against his shoulder and he wraps me in a comforting hug.

"Are you okay Larina?"

"No, but I will be." He smiles softly at me and leans down before planting a kiss on my cheek. I close my eyes and take his hand into mine.

"You will be, I'm here for you okay?" He says when he pulls back. I open my eyes and look back into his, there's something so comforting about those hazel eyes of his.

"Thanks, Sean."

"Anytime." He grins and hugs me tighter. "I love you."

"I love you too."

“Excuse me, Mr. And Mrs. Johnson?” We jump away from each other when Timothy Ryan barges into our room.

“Yes?” Sean asks. I look at him and see a hint of a pink shade in his cheeks, which makes me smile.

“Just here to let you know that your clothing for the anniversary party tomorrow will be delivered in the morning, the party starts at seven sharp and ends at ten p.m.” Wow, a party past curfew?

“Thank you, sir,” Sean says.

“Uh huh, have a good night.” Timothy nods at us and leaves the room. Sean and I exchange looks and I smile.

“That was embarrassing!” We both say at the same time before we both double over laughing.

15

The Unaffected

I look in the mirror as I braid my hair up and then coil it above my head in a complicated looking bun. The wedding anniversary for Emma Jones and her husband, whoever that is, starts in an hour. Sean is getting ready in the bathroom as I get ready in the bedroom. I step back and look myself over in the mirror to make sure everything is right. I nod and smile, this dress is so fancy.

I turn a little and make sure the corset is done up right, it is. The dress code for the anniversary is black and white. The dress that was sent this morning, that I have on is gorgeous. The bodice is white, and the sleeves fall over my shoulders exposing them. The skirt part of the dress is black and flows down to the floor covering even my feet. It's also quite long on the back of the skirt so there's a tail dragging behind me as I walk. I twirl around like a little girl and giggle at myself.

"Can I come in?" Sean calls out from the bathroom door.

"Yeah," I call out. I turn back to the mirror and smooth out the invisible wrinkles on the bodice. I turn to look at him and his eyes widen. "You look very handsome," I say. His hair is fixed, for a change, he has a white button-down shirt and black dress pants. His tie is hanging around his neck, though not done up yet.

"You look gorgeous." He says walking to me and looking me over.

"Thank you." I feel myself flush red before I look down at the floor. "Uh, we have to hurry. The party is going to start soon you know." I turn back to the mirror and put on the earrings that were sent along with the dress.

"Larina?" Sean whispers from behind me. The hair on my arms stands at its end at hearing him so close.

"Y…yeah?" I turn around and look at him.

"Any idea how to do this tie thing?" I let out a laugh as I see that he managed to somehow tie a knot on the tie.

"Yes." I walk over to him and I carefully undo the knot. I take the tie from around his neck and smooth it out before reaching over and draping it around the back of his neck. "My mom thought me how to do this when I was little," I say as I fix his tie. I let the tie drop over his chest and smooth it down. "And there you go. All done." I look up at him and smile, it fades when I see him staring at me with a serious look on his face. "What's wrong?"

"Nothing, you just look beautiful is all."

I press my lips together as I try to contain a smile and fail. "You already said that."

"I'll probably be saying it a lot more."

"You don't have too, I got it. I'm gorgeous." I joke.

"Yes, you are." He takes my hand into his and plants a kiss there. I turn a deep scarlet color when a small noise comes out of my mouth in the form of an "Awww." Sean, of course, thinks it's hilarious and starts laughing at me.

"Let's go you goof!" I say.

"Mask!" Sean calls out, throwing me my mask. Phew, I almost forgot about that thing! I quickly put it on and look at him for approval, when I look back at him I see that he already has his mask on.

“Okay?” I ask.

“Yep, let’s go.” He leads me out of the door with a hand to the small of my back. “It’s a shame you have to hide who you really are Larina, you look amazing.” I’m only able to glance quickly at him before turning away in embarrassment.

We walk down the hallway, down the stairs to the main level of the Headquarters and finally into the main hall where they are holding the party. I stop at the doorway, making Sean bump into me, as I stare around the room. They decorated the main hall so it would like like we are outside, staring up at stars. Whoever decorated this place, did an amazing job! There’s small, twinkling lights hung up on the ceiling and around the walls. “This is so beautiful,” I say as I take a step forward.

“Johnsons! Over here!” Dad calls out from across the room. Sean offers me his hand, which I take, and we walk together over to my parents.

“Mrs. Johnson! You look beautiful!” Dad says smiling.

“Thank you, Handler Matthews,” I say nodding my head. I can’t help but notice how close mom is watching me, I guess she has a reason too, with the way I acted and all.

“Mrs. Matthews you look lovely, doesn’t she Mike?” I ask looking at Sean.

“You certainly do,” Sean says smiling at mom.

“Thank you.” She says coolly. I bite my lower lip and dad notices the tension in the air.

“Handler Johnson, why don’t we go and talk about how you did today?” Dad places a hand on Sean’s shoulder, before walking off, forcing Sean after him.

“You really do look_.” I start.

“Come with me,” Mom says. Before I can say anything, she leads me to the side of the room next to the food that has been laid out on top of a large, rectangular table.

“Yes, Mrs_.”

“Larina, I know it’s you.” My mouth starts to part but I quickly regain myself.

“Pardon?”

“Stop lying to your mother!” Her face goes from angry to happy in seconds. “A mother always knows!” She takes my face into her hands and I look down at her. “What is this? A mask?” She pulls at the cheeks of the mask and I brush her hands off.

“Mom!” I throw my arms around her and she hugs me back. “I’ve missed you so much,” I whisper.

“I’m so happy you’re alive! When Sherrie called and said you’ve been erased_.” She shakes her head and I reach over and wipe the tears from her eyes.

“Where have you been hiding Larina? How did you get away?”

“I ran away before they could catch me, I’ll have to tell you everything later. Right now it’s not the best time.”

“Good point.” She smiles at me and lets me go as she looks me over. “I’m guessing that Mike is that Handler you’re in love with right?”

“Yes…Ow!” I hold my arm in my hand after she slaps me playfully.

“That’s for scaring me half to death and for trying to fool your mother!”

"Does dad know?"

"I don't hide anything from your father, Larina."

"Mom, I had a twin?" Her face sinks and she presses her lips together.

"We have a lot to talk about, don't we?" I nod. "Right now it's not a good time though, enjoy the party sweetie. We'll talk another time." Mom places a hand to my cheek and I smile.

That's when dad and Sean walk back over to where mom and I are standing. By the look on Sean's face, I can tell that he had an interesting conversation with dad, and it had nothing to do with how he did as a Handler today. Sean stands beside me, looking stiff and worried. I give him a look with a single question in mind. "Are you okay?" He only nods and turns to my parents.

"It's really nice to see the both of you again." He whispers.

"You to son," Dad says nodding. "Keep her safe." Dad drapes an arm around mom's shoulders and smiles at me. "How are you kiddo?" I press my lips together and quickly hug him.

"I missed you," I whisper.

"I missed you too." He pats my head and pulls back as he looks at me. "Look at that nose." I let out a laugh and Sean joins in.

"Go have fun, be careful," Mom says. Sean and I nod before we walk away, we don't get very far before Emma Jones takes a microphone and starts to speak through it.

"Thank you all so much for joining Keith and myself for our twentieth wedding anniversary!" There isn't one sound in the room as she talks. "I love you, honey." She says waving to a man in the crowd. He waves back and I give a small smile at that. "Please enjoy the party." With that short speech, Emma steps down from the stage and walks to her husband. I watch them talk, he says something to her, she smiles and nods her head before they start to slowly dance to the music.

"Almost too peaceful." I hear someone from behind me say. I feel a cold shiver run down my back, I turn around to figure out who it was, but it could have been anyone.

"You okay?" Sean asks leaning down to whisper in my ear.

"I'm fine."

"Want to dance?" I smile up at him and nod my head. He offers me his hand, which I take and we start to sway back and forth to the soft sound of the classical music being played. Every now and again I see Emma Jones dancing with her husband. She might be the cause of all the awful things that go on in the Society, but she seems to love her husband very much. I turn back to Sean and he grins at me as he spins me around, the spin ends with two sounds. One is my laughter and other is someone's scream.

Sean and I both turn to the sound of the scream and my eyes widen when I see Keith Jones lying on the floor dead, in front of Emma.

My mouth parts as I stare at her staring down at her husband. My hands fly to my mouth as people start to scream and panic, throughout the whole thing though, I never once see Emma shed a tear, scream or even act surprised. She must be in complete shock. "Let's get out of here!" Sean scoops me up in his arms and quickly races out of the main hall and up the stairs and finally into our room where he locks the door once we are inside.

"Someone killed him," I whisper, slowly easing myself onto the floor. My hands go back to my mouth as I sit there surrounded by the black skirt of the dress.

"Someone did," Sean whispers sitting down next to me.

"Do you think it was a_." I look up and Sean's eyes meet mine. The way he's looking at me tells me all I need to know. He thinks it was a Rebel too.

"What if it wasn't one of us?" I ask looking down at the floor. What if it was someone who just hated Keith or Emma?

"Larina, they'll catch whoever it was." I look up at him again and my mouth starts to quiver in fear. "We're safe here." I bow my head and clasps my hands together. "Hey," I look up slowly and he takes my face in his hand. "I'll keep you safe." With that, he pulls me to him and we stay there hugging each other until our doors are thrown open and an older Handler is standing there.

"Emma Jones is requesting everyone back at the main hall." He says.

"But_." Sean starts. The Handler throws Sean a silencing glare, before leaving and slamming the door shut behind him.

"Come on Sean," I whisper, taking his hand in mine.

We slowly start to walk back to the main hall, the whole time I think someone is going to jump out and attack us. As we're descending the staircase I stop when I hear hushed voices from below us. Sean stops to listen in with me.

"What are you going to tell them?" It's Timothy Ryan.

"That they did it, hide the gun. It never happened." Emma responds. My eyes widen and I look up to Sean,

Sean takes my hand and his and we fly up the stairs and round the corner before pressing our backs to it. I have a feeling we weren't supposed to have heard that. Timothy Ryan killed Emma's husband, under her orders!

I watch as Sean pokes his head out and sighs before turning to me and nodding. "Let's go." We walk down the stairs and head straight into the main hall. Mom and dad are looking around frantically, they soon find us and quickly walk over. "Are you kids alright?" Mom asks checking us over.

"Yes," I whisper.

"Where did you go?" Dad asks

"Uh," Sean runs his hand through his fixed hair, messing it all up again. "I went on 'save Larina mode' and took her up to the room." My cheeks get a slight pink color to them as I look up at him. I let out a small laugh despite the circumstances. Mom, dad, and Sean all turn to me. "What?" Sean asks.

"Nothing, it's just funny that you have a 'save Larina mode'" He rolls his eyes at me before turning to my parents.

"Thank you, Sean," Dad says placing a hand on Sean's shoulder.

"You're welcome sir." Sean nods. Our conversation is cut short when Emma Jones takes the microphone into her hands and taps on it to get everyone's attention.

"This is not to leave this room." She says as she glares down at all of us, her white dress is splattered in_. I think I'm going to be sick. I take a step back and hold my stomach in my hands as I look up at her. "Tonight was supposed to be a happy day, a day to celebrate twenty years of a happy marriage!" I look at Sean and he slowly shakes his head. “However someone thought that it was a good time to end it, and we know who it was.”

Everyone is silent as they listen to her, I don’t think anyone is even breathing as they wait to find out who murdered Keith Jones.

“There’s a small group known as the Unaffected. They live far from here, hidden in the mountains past all of our Sectors. They have their own city that they call ‘Valley’ They have everything in that city, everything but the Society. We’ve tried, peacefully, to welcome them into our Society and they refused. They threw us out and attacked our man as they left. The deed tonight was caused by these, horrendous people.” My eyes widen as I stare at her. A group of people that aren’t part of the Society?!

“I will avenge my dear Keith’s death and we will attack these people and take over their city and they will no longer be a threat to any of us. They don’t have our system, they are disorderly and savage. They can cause our own precious system to go up in chaos and_.” She lets out a bitter laugh that sends a cold chill down my spine. “We can’t have that!” Emma Jones look down at the audience as people start to clap. Sean and I remain still and in complete shock as we stare up at her. “Although they live far from here and their masses are significantly smaller than ours, it's a large enough number that can cause problems, as they have shown tonight. Rest assured loyal citizens of the Society, we will attack them and anyone who gets in our way!”

People send Emma Jones off with a huge round of applause and as I stand there in the middle of it all, my thoughts are drowned by all the noise. I look down at my feet and my mouth widens along with my eyes. “You may all return to your quarters, have a good night.” With that Emma Jones leaves the room and Timothy Ryan follows close after her.

Everyone starts to leave the main hall and soon standing there are just my parents, Sean and I. “Have good night kids.” Dad says nodding at us and leading mom away before we have time to say anything.

I look up at Sean and he shakes his head. “In the bedroom.” With that, we walk quickly back to our room and lock the door behind us.

I ease myself down on the edge of my bed and fold my hands on top of my lap. “The Unaffected Sean?” I ask looking up at him. He looks over at me from where he’s standing in front of the door. “We have to tell Raph, they could help him!”

“We need to stop that attack on them.”

“How would we even do that Sean?” He walks over to me, takes my hands in his and stands me up.

“We are going to have to sabotage that attack.”

“Once Raph invades, they won’t be able to_.”

“Who knows when Jones is planning on attacking them? We need to act now.”

“Okay, how do you think we do it even?”

“We need to find out when they are planning to do it. I’m guessing the plans for the attack are all in Emma Jones’ office.”

My eyes widen as I stare at him. “You mean_?”

“Yes, we are going to have to sneak into her office, find the plans and shut them down.”

“Oh boy.”

“We can do it.” He says smiling at me.

“We can do it,” I reassure myself.

In the morning I’m woken up by a lot of shouting. I jump out of bed, and the first thing I notice is that Sean isn’t here. I put my mask on and race out of the room, my heart is pounding as I race down the stairs. I feel a deep sense of relief when I reach the main floor of the Headquarters and see Sean along with many other Handlers training outside, and making tons of noises including, screaming.

I sigh loudly and rest against the door frame as I watch him climb up a building strapped to a harness. “They are loud aren’t they?” Jon Michaels asks as he walks over to me. All the sudden I feel self-conscious about what I’m wearing. My pajamas.

“Yeah, they woke me up,” I say with a smile.

“Nice pajamas.” He says grinning. His dark eyes look deep into my own and I press my lips together as I take a step back.

“I have to go change and get ready for the day, it was good seeing you, Handler Michaels.” I nod my head and jog back towards the stairs.

“Have a great day Lora!” He calls out. I keep going and not until I’m inside my room that I realize he didn’t call me Mrs. Johnson, he called me by my fake first name.

Ten minutes later, I’m down the stairs meeting mom for our ‘Training.’ “Let’s go, there’s a lot we have to do today.” She says by which she means, we have a lot to talk about. I follow her into the Erasing Facility and my heart stops when I see Jon Michaels inside the room. What is he doing here? I look over at mom as she stares at him.

“Timothy told me you need help today?” He asks. Mom looks at me with an annoyed look that no one can tell it's there besides dad and I, before turning to look at him.

"Yes, we need a subject to erase." I let out a small smile as his eyes widen.

"What?" He asks.

"Of course, we're using the sleep serum and not cremating anyone." He looks over at me and I stare back. What is it with this guy anyway?

"We understand if you don't want to do it, Handler Michaels. We can get Mike to help us, Doctor Matthews." I say turning to look at mom.

"No, I'll do it!" Jon says nodding his head in determination.

"Great, have a seat," Mom says. Jon does so and mom turns to me. "Proceed Mrs. Johnson."

I walk over to the cabinet, take the sleep serum into my hands, suck it into the syringe and walk over to Jon. "Ready?" I ask. He nods and closes his eyes as he sits on the chair as straight as a ruler. I inject the serum into his neck and he's out within seconds.

"Great now we can talk," Mom says rolling Jon into a closet. She closes the door and turns to me. "First where have you been this whole time?"

"I ran to an abandoned city, Sean found me and brought me to the Rebels." Mom's eyes widen and I watch her normally olive colored skin turn pale.

"Rebels?"

"Yes."

"And why are you here at the Center Larina?"

“Sean and I came here to turn off the security systems so that the Rebels can invade.”

“Dear God.” Mom sits down and hides her face in her hands.

“Mom, you can’t think that the Society is a good thing. Right?” I walk over to her and kneel down in front of her chair. “Mom?”

“They took your sister from me, they made your father and I leave you behind, and they told me that you were dead. I don’t think that the Society is a good thing Larina, but what can we do?”

“That’s what Sean and I are doing, we’re going to disable the security systems and then the Rebels will attack, we’ll take the Society down and have a place where people can be free to do what they want.”

“There’s no way to take down the Society Larina.” Mom looks me in the eyes and takes my hand into hers. “The Society is powerful, they have weapons, not to mention all the loyal Handlers and citizens. They won’t stand by and watch. Larina, going against the Society is a suicide mission. You and Sean are going to get caught and_.”

I sigh softly and shake my head. “I can’t convince you to join us, but can I trust you not to say anything? Not even to dad?”

“I won’t say a word.” I nod and stand up. “Larina think about this, you could_.”

“Mom! They killed your daughter, they took my sister. They want me dead, I’ve thought about it for the last year! I don’t want to be a part of this awful place and I’m going to do my part to make sure that they fall.” I walk away and throw open the door.

“Larina!” Mom calls out. I stop but don’t turn around to face her. “I love you, sweetie, be careful.” I nod and walk out of the room and close the door quietly behind me.

I hug myself as I walk back to where Sean is training with the other Handlers, I pass them, but don’t get very far before Sean runs over.

“Hey.” He places a hand on my shoulder and I look up at him. He pants a little and lets out a slow breath before asking. “Everything okay?”

“Yeah, Training ended early today.”

“You sure?”

“We’ll talk later.” I look up at him and he nods. I watch him jog back to the other Handlers and dad, of course, calls him out.

“Give me three laps Johnson!”

16

Memory Reader?

"Larina, wake up." I open my eyes and look up to see Sean staring down at me.

"What's wrong?" I ask, still half asleep.

"I want to show you something."

"It's_." I look at the clock on the wall. "Three in the morning Sean!"

"I can't show it to you when everyone is awake, come on." He tugs on my hand and I slowly sit up and sigh as I stand up and face him.

"Okay, what?"

"Follow me." He walks out of our room and I follow after him. The hallway of the Headquarters is dead quiet, there's not one person awake, no one is crazy enough to be awake at this time of night. No one but my crazy boyfriend and I anyway. Sean leads us up another flight of stairs to a floor that contains doors after doors with scanners in each one.

I find that I wake up at once after seeing all those locked doors. "What is this place?" I whisper as I follow after him.

"All the classified things that Emma Jones doesn't want citizens knowing about." Sean pulls out a rubber glove from his pocket and places it over his hand. I raise an eyebrow at him and he smiles. "It's your dad's glove. I sort of stole it, it has his hand print in it. He's allowed into any of these rooms because he is training to be a Head Handler." Sean places his gloved hand over the scanner, I watch the light over it, go from red to green. "And that's how you trick the system." Sean winks at me before entering the room, I follow after him rolling my eyes and thinking that he has too much energy for it being three in the morning. Sean closes the door after I've entered and flips on the light switch. I look around the room and my eyes go straight to the only thing in the room. A giant monitor looking thing that is attached to a Dream Catcher. "A Dream Catcher?" I ask.

"No."

"Sean, that's a Dream Catcher."

"That's what the Society wants you to think it is, you see it's also a Memory Reader." My eyes furrow as I stare at him. "It reads the Memory that the person had that day, they say it's only a Dream Catcher, but there are people's memories in here as well ." Sean smiles at me as he turns the machine on. "And the best part? They keep every single citizen of the Society's memory in this bad boy. All you have to do is type in a name, watch." I watch Sean type in his own name. "Sean Clarkson."

The machine gives away a soft humming sound before millions of pictures are displayed on the monitor. "So let's say I wanted to see a specific memory I'd type in something like_." I watch him type in. "Kiss." My eyes widen as the picture enlarges onto the monitor and shoots to the middle of the room and starts to play. I remember that day all too well, it's the first time Sean and I kissed. My cheeks flush as I watch it happen, and I find myself lowering my eyes.

"Pretty cool huh?"

"You couldn't have picked a different memory?"

"It's one of my favorites." He says grinning at me. I let out a soft laugh and look at the machine. "Anything you'd like to know?"

“Luisa Matthews.” I say.

“I don’t think they have erased at birth memories here.” He says.

“Then I want to see my mom’s.” I step forward and type in mom’s name. It shows a bunch of pictures and I narrow it down to one when I type in “Child’s birth” However when I try to play it, it doesn’t let me because it says the memory has been forgotten.

“I wanted to see my sister,” I whisper.

“There’s one more person you can try,” Sean says to me. He steps beside me and types in Sherrie Maxwell’s name. He narrows it down to birth and then types in my name. “There it is, the day you were born.” He says. I click on it and watch the memory that is displayed in the room.

Sherrie must have been there for nearly the whole thing because the memory starts with her walking inside the room where my parents are waiting. “I’m sorry Mr. And Mrs. Matthews but one of your children will have to be erased. We cannot have twins in the Society.”

Mom starts to cry as dad holds her and nods at Sherrie. “I will bring you the baby that will remain with you once everything checks out. Please rest Mrs. Matthews, you’ve had a rough day.” With that Sherrie leaves the room and walks down a long, white hallway into another room that holds two cribs. One has my name in it, the other has my sister’s.

I reach out and take Sean’s hand in mine as I think that I will see Luisa being erased. That’s not exactly what happens. My eyes widen as I watch Sherrie place a single word in front of my crib. “Erase.”

“You’re not strong enough little one, your sister has a better chance,” Sherrie says looking down at me. She smiles and I watch as she turns away from me and towards Luisa. "You will go to your parents soon enough, so no fussing alright?" Sherrie nods her head and leaves the room. My baby self, starts to cry, and then the memory ends and I'm left staring at nothing at all.

"Larina?" Sean whispers.

I press my lips together and look over at him. "It was supposed to have been me. I was supposed to have been erased."

"But you weren't."

"No I wasn't, but I was the one that was supposed to have been though. Luisa should have been here and_."

"You both should have been here Larina."

"What do you think happened?"

"Someone messed up?" He asks.

"Not exactly." We both spin around and face dad. He's standing at the door watching the both of us. He doesn't seem to be feeling anything as he stares back at us. "You forgot your masks." He tosses us our masks and we catch them. "Follow me." With that, he leaves the room and Sean and I scramble to put our masks on and follow him out of the room, down the stairs and into mom's and dad's room that happen to be in the Headquarters as well.

Mom looks up from reading a book when we enter. "What are you kids doing up at this time at night?" She asks shutting her book and standing up from the bed. I want to ask her the same thing.

"I found these two on my rounds, sneaking up to the classified rooms," Dad says sitting down on a chair next to a dresser.

“Larina?” Mom asks looking at me.

“We were at the Memory Reader room, I know it’s not only a Dream Catcher.” Mom and dad exchange looks before turning to the both of us. “I was the one who was supposed to have been erased, not Luisa. What happened?”

“That is none of your business, and you shouldn’t be poking around in things that don't concern you.” Dad says standing up and glaring at Sean and I. “What are you even doing here Larina? You and your boyfriend here were both supposed to have been erased.”

“Clef!” Mom shouts throwing a silencing glare at him.

“This is your doing isn’t it Clarkson? Taking my daughter from the Society?” Dad faces Sean head on and I hate to say that Sean doesn’t back down.

“I’m not doing anything of the sort, sir, she is her own person and she chose to leave this awful place herself. It was that or die.”

“Hadn’t she broken the law, there wouldn’t have been that problem.”

“Dad! Don’t you care at all about anything?! They erased your daughter, they were going to erase me!”

“We are citizens of the Society Larina Matthews, and I’m very glad that you are alive. However_.” He looks at Sean and then back at me. “I want to know what is it that you are doing here.”

“They are looking for answers Clef, Larina has the right to know.”

“We have the right to obey the law!” Sean clenches his teeth as he stares at Dad. It never crossed my mind that dad might choose the Society over his family. I'm actually afraid that he'll give us up to Emma Jones.

"You are being very unreasonable!" Mom says.

"And you are being influenced by rebels and I will be no part of it!" With that dad storms out, slamming the door after him.

"Mom, is dad going to tell Emma who we really are?"

"No, he wouldn't be the cause of his own daughter's death." Mom sits down on the bed and places her hand on her forehead. "Larina sweetie, I know you want answers. I just wish that you wouldn't be so reckless in trying to find them."

"Mom_."

"Your father switched the signs." She says shutting me up at once. My hands fly to my mouth and I feel Sean softly hug me from behind. "He sneaked into the room and switched the signs. You're right, you were the one who was supposed to be erased."

"Why would he do that?" Sean asks the question I'm not able to ask.

"Luisa was different from birth. You see all the babies are injected with a medicine and they either cry or are quiet. As you both know, you aren't supposed to cry. Luisa did." Mom looks at me and a look of sadness crosses her face. "And you have always been different Larina, it's just that you were so frail when you were born, so little." She holds out her arms as if she's holding a baby and slowly lowers her hands on top of her lap. "You didn't have the energy to cry, your father thought that because Luisa cried she'd be a problem to the Society, so he switched the signs and you were spared." Tears start to appear but I quickly blink them away, refusing to cry about this. Dad chose the Society over his family then, I have no doubt he'd do it again, that is if he hasn't already.

"How can you_."

"Your father has always been very loyal to the Society since he was a child. One of you had to be erased, he just made sure that Luisa was the one to be erased because he didn't want to eventually lose both of you."

"And now look what happened, maybe he should have let her live."

"Don't say that." Mom and Sean say at the same time.

"It's his fault that she died, he's a_."

"Watch it, Larina," Dad says walking back into the room. I glare at him and shake my head.

"How could you be so cruel?"

"Cruel? You should know all the facts before you assume things."

"I know the facts."

"No, you don't." He sits down next to mom and takes her hand into his and squeezes it. "I should have told you this long ago my dear, I didn't want to cause you more pain than you were already suffering. I don't expect you to forgive me, but I did what I thought was best for all of us."

"You did what you thought was best for the Society," I say, I feel Sean tense up from behind me. I don't back down though, I stare into dad's eyes and dare him to contradict me.

"I took Luisa away from here, I brought her to an abandoned city where I found a couple, they had a boy that was three at the time. I asked them to take care of her for us. " My eyes widen and I let out a gasp at the same time that Sean does. "Geo, Luisa was never erased. I don't know if she's still alive or if she's okay but she was never erased here at the Society. I couldn't watch one of our daughters be killed."

Both my hands fly to my mouth as I stare at my parents hugging and telling each other that they are sorry. "I'm so sorry dad, I didn't_."

"Of course you didn't, no one did and no one will. This doesn't leave this room." Dad looks at Sean and Sean nods. "It was the one time I'd disobey the Society, I won't do it again. Get to bed." With that Sean and I are pretty much kicked out of my parents' room, without any further explanation about Luisa.

"She could be alive," I say looking up at Sean. We return to our rooms and I'm not surprised at all that I dream about Luisa that night.

A week later

"Come on Johnson, your wife is watching, you don't want to disappoint her do you?" Jon asks pointing his shock gun at Sean. I watch Jon press the trigger three times and each time Sean dodges the shots with ease and in the end, he rounds Jon and takes the gun from him.

"I never disappoint her," Sean says and my eyes widen when he presses the trigger and shocks Jon.

"Gun Johnson," Dad calls out.

Mom never makes me train, we've talked about it and she knows I never erased anyone, nor will I practice doing so. Our "Training." always ends earlier than usual, so I get to watch Sean in his training. Dad isn't so easy on him. I watch dad whack the back of Sean's head with the handle of the gun. "Go sit down." Sean grins as he walks over to me and sits extremely close.

"Hi." He says placing a kiss on my cheek.

"Hi," I say.

"I'm about to kill your boyfriend." He murmurs motioning his head to Jon.

"Don't do that, and he's not my boyfriend. Don't be stupid, you're my_." His smile makes me stop short. "Shut up." I murmur looking down at my hands.

"I'm your_?"

"Boyfriend Sean, you're my boyfriend."

"There it is." He throws his arms around me and kisses me right on the cheek, again. I stick my tongue out at him and he lets out a chuckle before messing my hair up. "Goofball." He whispers bringing me closer to him.

"Johnson get your butt over here," Dad shouts. I roll my eyes and watch Sean walk back over to where dad is standing.

"Yes, sir?"

"Men, sometimes being a Handler involves getting physical. You need to be prepared for anything." Dad looks around the yard at all the Handlers watching him. "Johnson you are going to be a good for nothing Handler that broke the law by kissing someone that isn't your selected." I shake my head and let out a soft sigh.

"That's specific," Sean says.

"Quiet." Dad gives Sean a stern look, before turning his attention back to the other Handlers. "Who wants to volunteer to take Johnson down?" It's not surprising that Jon shoots his hand up. "Alright, Jon you're up." Jon walks over and stands in front of Sean, next to dad.

"Bring him down Jon." Dad walks off the center of the yard and sits next to me. "What do you think kiddo?"

"That was an extremely specific example, dad." He grins at me and nods his head to Sean and Jon.

"They need their training, here put this on. It'll let you hear them better." Dad hands me an earpiece and I place it in my right ear. Everything is blocked out from my hearing besides Sean and Jon and what I hear makes me worry for Jon's safety.

"Let's say who wins gets Lora?" Jon says. I can see Sean's face turn bright red with anger from where I'm sitting and that's pretty far.

"Let's say if I win I pound your face and if I lose I do the same. Leave her out of this." Sean snaps throwing a punch. Jon dodges it and I hear him laugh rather bitterly.

"You're not that good of a fighter are you Johnson? What's the matter, afraid to not be good en_." My eyes widen when Sean punches the air out of Jon's gut.

"Dad?" I ask.

"Yes, sweetie?"

"What if they kill each other?"

"I wouldn't mind it."

"Dad!"

"Stop worrying Larina, I'll make sure they don't totally kill each other."

“Thank you.” I look back at Sean and Jon and my eyes widen when I see that they are both on the floor. Sean is on top of Jon punching at his face. “Uh, dad?”

“Yes?”

“Dad!”

“It’s good for them!” I groan and throw the ear piece at dad and storm to Sean and Jon. “Break it up!” I shout. I pull Sean off of Jon and he laughs before capturing me in a surprising kiss. “Are you hurt?” I ask checking his face. He has a couple bruises forming, but Jon looks worse. “You okay Handler Michaels?” I ask.

“I might need a kiss.” He says sitting up and wiping the blood from his lips.

I look at Sean who is about to throttle Jon again. “Let's get you cleaned up,” I say helping Jon up.

“Clean him up?!” Sean snaps.

“He’s bleeding.”

“How about me?”

“You’re not bleeding.” I point out. Jon throws a triumphant look at Sean before I lead him away. “Let’s get you to the hospital alright?” I say.

“Thanks, Lora.”

“You really should call me Mrs. Johnson or Eraser Johnson you know.”

“Eh.” Jon shrugs at that and we walk across the street and towards the hospital. “I don’t think I need to see a Doctor, just get cleaned up.”

“I suppose so.” I press my lips together and have him sit down on the bench in front of the hospital. “I’ll be back, I'm going to go get some wipes or something." I nod my head and enter the hospital.

"Good afternoon Eraser Johnson!" A Doctor calls out as I enter.

"Afternoon," I call out. "Could I get some wipes please?" I ask the secretary at the front desk.

"Of course Mrs. Johnson." She bows her head and hurries away.

"What happened? Someone get hurt?" The Doctor asks.

"Yeah," I say. The secretary returns and hands me a few wipes. "Thank you very much." I nod my head and turn to leave.

"Have a good day Mrs. Johnson!" The secretary calls out.

"You too!" I call back as I exit the hospital. "Alright Handler Michaels, let's get you cleaned up." I sit beside him and softly dab at the cut on his lip. "You and Mike should really stop being at each others throats." I point out as I set the bloody wipe aside and get another one.

"It was just practice."

"Right," I say sarcastically.

"I just don't like the guy."

"I do."

"Well, he's your husband." He points out.

"Exactly, he's my husband." Jon looks into my eyes with his dark brown ones and I look back. "Handler Michaels, I'm flattered that you have feelings for me, but I'm married to Mike and I love him. There's really no point in fighting over_." I get interrupted when he kisses me full on the mouth. I shove him away and stand up fast and wipe my mouth. “That was a mistake,” I say glaring at him.

“Was it?” He stands up and grins at me.

“Yes, it was!” I slap him across the face before throwing all the wipes at his face and storming off. I see Sean at once and walk to him.

“Get that wimp cleaned up did you?”

“He kissed me.”

“He’s dead!” I watch Sean storm off and as much as I want to see him pound Jon to the ground, I can’t let him do that. He could get into trouble.

“Sean don’t! Remember why we’re here.” I hurry up to catch up to him.

“But he_.”

“I slapped him, it’s fine.”

“Can I kill him when we leave this place?” He asks shoving his hands into his pocket as he turns to face me.

“Sure.” Sean smiles and reaches over and wipes my mouth with his thumb.

“I really don’t like that guy.”

“The feeling is mutual, he doesn’t like you much either.”

“Good.” Sean offers me his hand and I take it. “Let’s go make a plan, we need to stop that attack.” Sean looks down at me and I nod. “Maybe I can change the coordinates and make it so the attack is at Jon’s quarters.”

I let out a laugh and we start walking towards the Headquarters. "Are you finished with your training?" I ask with a laugh in my voice.

"Nope."

My eyes widen. "Isn't_."

"I'll deal with your dad later. I'm not here to train anyway."

"Good point." We enter the Headquarters and head straight for our room and close the door. "Alright, what's the plan?"

17

Infiltration

I look at the clock on the wall as it strikes midnight. I'm just waiting for Sean to change so we can carry out our plan of shutting down the attack on the Unaffected. I stand up and start to pace in front of the mirror, feeling my stomach tie itself into a knot of butterflies and worry.

I catch a glimpse of myself and sigh softly letting my worries out with the breath. My hair is up in a loose bun, I have on black clothing for camouflaging reasons and dark boots. I turn to the bathroom door when Sean walks out.

"Ready?" He asks putting the mask on over his face.

"As I'll ever be," I whisper, putting my mask over my face as well. Sean opens the door to the room and pokes his head out to make sure there aren't any Handlers doing their rounds up here. When it's clear to move on, he turns to me and nods. We leave the room and walk down the hallway and towards the staircase. We stand at the top of the staircase and look around to make sure the coast is clear. Everything is pitch black, there isn't one light on_. Except for that Handler's flashlight! The Handler is at the bottom of the stair scouting down there. I grab Sean by the back of his shirt and pull him behind the wall before the Handler can spot us.

My heart starts ramming itself against my rib cage as I wait, I look across the hallway, where the flashlight's beam is slowly making it's way to the right side of the Headquarters and soon is completely gone. "Okay, I think we're good," I say looking at Sean. He nods and we make our way quickly, but quietly, down the stairs. We quickly round the corner where the stairs meets the second floor and head straight for Emma Jones' office. Sean and I both stop cold in our tracks when we see that standing, or rather slouching, right outside her door is two Handlers keeping guard, they are both asleep. I recognize one of them at once, Jon.

I look to Sean to see what we should do, turn back or_. I guess we're going back because he's walking out of the hallway. I follow him and when we are out of earshot I ask: "What do we do?"

"There's another way to get up to her office." He says.

"And that is?" He grins, which has me worrying, before he heads down the stairs to the main floor and towards the entrance of the Headquarters. "Sean what are you_." The night's cold air hits me hard, it's freezing out here! I wrap my arms around myself and follow closely after Sean. He heads left and stops just below a window. At once, I know what his plan is.

"I'll go in first, then you come up okay?" He says. The window is about ten feet from the ground, meaning we're going to have scale up the wall.

I watch Sean scale up the wall with ease, I don't know how he's climbing up that wall. It's completely smooth! Soon he's at the window, when he goes to open it he smiles as it opens right up. "Alright, Larina your turn." He says looking down at me.

I bite down at my lower lip as I stare up at the window that is a whole five feet taller than I am. I exhale and start to slowly climb up the wall. I reach up for the next crack on the wall and grab on to it just as my foot slips and I let out a gasp as I dangle there for a second. I have to remind myself that the worst thing that can happen if I fall from here is a sprained ankle. I'm literally a foot from the ground. "Come on Larina, you can do it," I tell myself. I place my feet flat against the wall and pull myself up with my arms and start to climb up without any incident.

I finally reach the window, after what seems like forever and pull myself inside and land on the floor on my knees. “Ow.” I murmur.

“Good job,” Sean whispers helping me up to my feet. “Alright let’s get this done, quickly.” I nod my head and walk over to the monitor in Emma Jones’ desk. I sit down on her chair and turn the monitor on, the blue light illuminates my face as I stare at the screen. A single word stares back at me, taunting us for our stupidity. “Password.”

“Sean,” I say.

“What?”

“There’s a password on her monitor.” He walks over and stares at the screen. “What should I do?”

“I don’t know, type something in.” He reaches for the keypad but I stop him.

“No! I’m sure the Leader of the Society has a lot of classified things in her monitor, if we get the wrong password, I’m sure an alarm will sound or something like that.”

“You’re probably right, meaning we have to find out what the password is.”

“You look in the filing cabinets, I’ll search her desk,” I say.

“Okay.” He nods and walks over to the filing cabinets. I start rummaging through the drawers that are on her desk. There’s a lot of paperwork and names of people, but I don’t see anything that could possibly be the password.

"Anything?" I ask looking over at Sean once I've gone over every drawer.

"Not yet." He says as he continues his search. I walk over to the large closet and throw open the doors. I press my lips together. Coats and shoes, besides that there's nothing in the closet. I close the door and head back to the desk and place my hands on my hips as I try to figure something out.

I look around the desk and something catches my eyes, a small piece of paper is sticking out from under the keypad. I take the keypad into my hands and flip it over and read the paper.

"I love you Em. Love, Keith." I get a deep sadness inside me, thinking about how she had him killed while he truly did love her. I'm about to set the keypad back down when I see something written in the keypad itself. I cock my head and peer at it, but I can't make it out. Whatever is written, was done in invisible ink.

"Sean look at this" I whisper. Sean looks over at me and sets down a pile of papers before walking over to me and looking at the keypad. "It's written in invisible ink," I say.

"Let's find out what it says." He says. He grabs a dark marker from a drawer in her desk and runs the dark marker over the back of the keypad where the hidden words are at. Once he's done, he wipes the thick line he made and smiles as the dark marker sticks to the invisible ink making the words readable. "There you go." He says smiling.

I read the words and I'm happy to see that it's the password to her monitor. I set the keypad down and type in the password. "O7JONES"

"Why seven?" Sean asks as the monitor accepts the password and lets me in.

“She’s the seventh leader.” I point out.

“Aren’t you smart?” Sean asks.

“Yes.” I grin as I look for the right file in her computer. On the top right corner, there’s a folder that was opened just a few hours ago. I go to it and my eyes widen when a countdown appears on the screen. “Six days, seven hours, two minutes and three seconds.”

“You think that’s it?” Sean asks. I point at the top of the screen where it says: “Attack on the Unaffected.” Sean runs his hand through his hair and smiles sheepishly. “Guess so huh?”

“Yup, I just have to turn this thing off and delete any data she might have about the Unaffected.” He stands behind me, peering over my shoulder and making me very nervous. “Sean!” I turn my head sharply to him and he raises an eyebrow. “Go keep watch, I can’t focus with you watching.”

“Why? Do I distract you?” He grins and steps closer to me.

“No you don’t, now go.” I can’t suppress the smile as it escapes my lips and takes over my whole face.

“Not at all,” Sean says as he walks over to the door of the office and places his ear to it. With him no longer standing over me, I’m able to shut down the countdown.

After a few minutes, Sean whispers: “Larina!” I look up at him and wait. “Someone is coming in!” My eyes widen and I quickly close all the files I’ve been messing with and shut down the monitor. “Closet,” Sean says dragging me in behind him. He enters the closet and pulls me inside, before closing the door and softly shoving me deeper into the closet.

"Sean, the marker!" I say. From the slits on the door of the closet, I can see the marker right in front of the monitor. "We forgot the_." Sean places a hand over my mouth when someone opens the door and steps inside. Right when they do, Sean takes a step back and stands right beside me. I look out through the slits and my hands fly to my mouth as I get a glimpse of the window. We left it open!

"You aren't supposed to be going in there, Michaels!" The Handler who was "Guarding" the door says.

"I thought I heard voices," Jon says stepping deeper into the room.

"Who would be inside Emma Jones' office?" I look at Sean and he takes my hand in his and squeezes it, before bringing me to him. I can hear his heart beat against my ear and it tells me a lot. He's just as nervous about being found as I am.

"I don't know, but I heard voices."

"You were sleeping, it could have been in your dream."

"Yeah, I guess_." Jon stops talking and walks over to the opened window. I press my lips together and wait for him to put two and two together. "You think Emma Jones left this opened?" He asks.

"I'm sure she did, now let's get out of here before someone catches us!" The other Handler walks out of the room and luckily Jon starts to follow him. I let out a quick breath and take it back just as quick when Jon turns and stares right at the closet.

"Sean?" I whisper.

"Get back," Sean says. I start walking deeper into the closet and Sean follows me, soon we are behind the thick coats that belong to Emma Jones. I feel the back of the wall with my hands and press my back against it.

"Jon, what are you doing?"

"I heard something coming from the closet," Jon says. I look up at Sean and he stares down at me. I have no idea what we are going to do, if Jon opens the door he's going to find us in here! I press myself harder against the wall and feel something poke me in the back. I touch it with my hands and pull at it. It's a door! I open the door and step through the hidden door and pull Sean in after me.

Once we are both inside the secret room, I close the door quietly and throw the bolt. It's pitch black in the room that we've just entered and all I can hear is the sound of my own heart beating. I stop breathing altogether when I hear the closet door open. "Jon there's no one here, let's go!" The Handler snaps at him.

"Weird, I thought for sure there was someone here," Jon whispers.

"I think you need to sleep, man." With that Jon closes the closet door and only when I hear the door to the office close, do I breath again. Which is good, because I'm pretty sure I've started turning blue from the lack of oxygen.

"Good job finding this place Larina!" Sean hugs me quickly and I can hear his heart beating just as fast as mine.

"We were almost done for!" I say looking up at him in the darkness.

"Let's get this done with and get out of here!" Sean opens the door and we step out of the room, and as much as I want to find out what's in the room, we need to finish what we came here for.

We walk out of the closet and into the office and I look around quickly. "Let's wipe the marker off this thing," I say.

"How?"

"She keeps water in there," I say pointing to the small table that I watched Emma Jones making coffee at. I turn on the monitor, type in the password and go into the monitor's files and documents. I type in Unaffected and my eyes widen as I see all the information and data that she has about them. I highlight it all and press delete.

"Are you sure you want to delete 243 files?"

"Yes," I whisper as I press the button. I watch as all the files are deleted completely. I quickly search attacks and do the same thing with those files. Soon there's nothing in the monitor about the Unaffected. "Done," I say. Sean hands me a wet rag and I take the keypad in my hands and carefully wipe away all the black marker from the password.

I smile as the words slowly disappear, I place the marker back into the drawer and turn to look at Sean. "All done?" He asks.

"All done."

"Good, let's get the hell out of here." He leads me to the window and I carefully scale down the wall and land on both of my feet for a change. Sean climbs out of the window and closes it after him before scaling down the wall and landing next to me. "We did it!" He says grinning.

"We did, now let's get to bed, I'm exhausted!"

"Agreed." Sean and I walk towards the entrance of the Headquarters and slowly open the door. We close it behind us and quietly make our way towards the stairs.

“Stop right there!” Jon shouts.

“Oh no,” I say.

“Larina?” Sean whispers.

“Yeah?” I whisper back.

“Take your mask off,” Sean instructs. I do so and watch him do the same. He throws our masks into a vase and turns to face Jon head on.

“Who are you two? What are you doing here?”

“I’ve been waiting to do this for a while,” Sean says before punching Jon hard on the face. Of course, once he does that, he has to keep punching Jon until he’s passed out on the floor.

“Was that really necessary?” I ask when Sean delivers a final blow to Jon’s side.

“Completely,” Sean says smiling at me.

“Who goes there?!” The Handler who was watching the door with Jon asks. It only takes one look at the passed out Jon for the Handler to realize we are a threat, and by we I mean Sean, but I’m placed in that category by association.

Sean then has to take out this Handler as well, the Handler gives several blows to Sean that makes him stumble a few times. This guy won’t go down, no matter how hard Sean hits him, and Sean is starting to get hurt as well. I look around trying to find a way to help him when my eyes land on the vase we threw our masks in.

I sneak away from Sean and the Handler and pick up the vase in my hands. While the Handler is busy pounding Sean’s face I sneak up behind him and send the vase smashing onto his head. My eyes widen as the vase shatters on the guy's head and he is sent to the floor, I'm satisfied to see that he's knocked out.

"Sorry," I whisper before turning to Sean. "Are you okay?"

"Fine." He moans as he slowly gets up off of the floor. "Let's get out of here." I nod we start making our way up the stairs.

When we are half way up, I remember about our masks and run down the stairs and pick them up. That's when Jon starts to wake up. "Go," I say to Sean, before turning back to Jon and kicking him back to dreamland. "Night night," I say as I run up the stairs and run alongside Sean to our room.

"That was close," Sean whispers as he closes the door behind us.

"Too close," I whisper. I look at him and frown as I see the bruises forming on his jaw and cheeks. He's bleeding from his lip. It reminds me of the day that I was supposed to have erased him, he was a beat up then too. "Let's clean you up," I say, cupping his cheek with my hands. "Poor baby, you're so brave." I hug him quickly and he hugs me back and gives a soft chuckle.

"Maybe I should get hurt more often."

"No, you shouldn't." I help him over to the bed and have him sit down. "How are your ribs?" I ask, knowing that the Handler kicked him a few times in them.

"Bruised." He moans before falling over on the bed and closing his eyes. I pout, feeling bad for him and walk to the bathroom and wet a towel before walking back to sit next to where he's laying down.

I softly dab at his lips and clean him up as he lays there staring up at me with those eyes of his that have me catching my breath even now. "Better?" I ask.

"Much better, thanks, Larina."

"Of course, rest okay? You need it." I stroke his hair and lean down, before placing a kiss on his forehead. I stand up and walk to the bathroom and throw the bloody towel into the trash chute.

When I walk back into the room, I see that Sean has fallen asleep. I smile softly at him and take an extra cover from the closet and place it on him. "Goodnight Sean," I whisper before getting in my bed and covering myself. I must really be exhausted because I fall asleep right away.

The minute I close my eyes, I wish that I can open them again. However, I'm not that lucky. With my eyes closed, I dream and this isn't a happy dream either.

"You are responsible for everything that is about to happen Larina Matthews." Emma Jones says. I shake my head and try to break free from the restraints that hold me on the chair. From where I'm sitting I can see everyone that I care about dying. One after the other they go limp after they are erased. Mom, dad, Raphael, and Luisa. Sean isn't so lucky, he isn't just erased. He's beaten until he's bloody and once that's over he collapses on the floor and moans something I can't understand.

He becomes a blur as tears start spilling out of my eyes and over my cheeks. "Stop! Please stop!" I scream. That's when Jon walks into the room and places a gun right to Sean's head.

Right as he pulls the trigger I shoot out of bed and gasp for air as I look around in the dark room. "Larina? Are you okay?" Sean asks looking over at me.

I sigh softly and lay back against my pillow and stare at the ceiling. “Bad dream,” I whisper. Deep inside I fear that what I just saw, will be what really happens to everyone I care about. That one by one, I’ll lose them all.

18

Security Off

Sean and I stare at each other as all the residents of the Center, enter the town hall for a mandatory meeting. We woke up this morning with Timothy Ryan yelling at the entrance of the Headquarters that everyone is to attend a meeting at the town hall, anyone who doesn't attend will be kicked out of the Center immediately.

Once everyone has entered the assembly hall and has taken their seats, Emma Jones steps up to the stage and stares down at all of us. Sean reaches over and takes my hand in his.

"Last night, someone hacked our system." She says. My heart drops to the pit of my stomach. "They broke into the Headquarters and into my office and shut down a very important plan we had." She starts pacing in front of the stage, and even from the back of the room I can see that her face is boiling red with rage. "They deleted a lot of important information from my monitor, in turn deleting all the information from the other monitors as well. They attacked two loyal Handlers and got away."

Everyone starts murmuring all at once and from the corner of my eyes, I can see mom and dad staring at me. "Rest assured, we will find these people who hacked us and they will be erased. Until then, everyone will have supervision around the clock by someone I chose for you." Emma Jones stares down at the audience, waiting for anyone to say anything that will trigger her. "That will be all, your supervisor will be at your quarters tonight. Have a good day." With that, she walks off the stage and leaves the assembly hall.

Mom and dad approach Sean and me, almost immediately. I stand up and Sean slowly does too, he's still in pain from fighting last night. "Are you okay Handler Johnson?" Dad asks staring at Sean.

"Yes, sir."

"You seem to be hurt." Dad looks over at me and raises an eyebrow, expecting me to spill the beans. Not going to happen.

"I'm totally fine sir." Sean nods his head and places an arm around my shoulder. He stares straight into dad's eyes and dad smiles.

"You'll do fine in training today then, won't you?"

"Always do sir."

"Then let's get going." Dad nods his head towards the exit of the town hall and I look at Sean and frown. He nods at me and follows dad out of the building.

"It was you, wasn't it sweetie?" Mom whispers.

"Let's go train mom." I walk to the entrance of the town hall and she follows me all the way to the Erasing Facility. I pull my hair out of my face and face mom.

"Larina_."

"You know it was Sean and me, we had to stop the attack on those people."

"You mean the people that killed Keith Jones?" Her eyes widen as she stares down at me.

"They didn't kill Keith Jones mom, I overheard Emma Jones talking to Timothy Ryan. She had him killed."

"What?!"

“I heard them talking.”

“That’s awful!” Mom starts pacing and then turns to me. “Why would she do that?”

“I don’t know.” I press my lips together and look at the floor. “But he loved her.”

“Mrs. Johnson?” I look at the door when someone barges in.

“Yes?” I ask.

“It’s your husband.” My eyes widen and I quickly follow the Handler to where Sean is at. I get there in time to see Jon deliver a blow to Sean’s head, Sean falls to the floor and doesn’t get up.

“What’s going on?!” I demand, throwing dad a look, as I walk to Jon and shove him away from Sean. I kneel next to where Sean is passed out and place his head on my lap.

“It was you two, wasn’t it?! You hacked the system!” Jon shouts.

“What are you talking about Michaels?” Dad demands.

“They are the ones who_.” I look up and my glare meets Jon’s.

“That’s quite an accusation, Michaels, if I were you I’d shut my big mouth unless you have proof.” Jon looks at dad and then back at me.

“I’ll prove it then!” He steps towards me and that’s when dad loses it and sends Jon flying across the yard with a single punch.

“Do not touch that girl. Simms, take him to Emma Jones.” Dad orders one of the Handlers. Simms nods and escorts Jon out of the yard and towards the Headquarters.

"Sean, what happened?" I whisper cupping his cheeks in my hands. He moans something before his eyes open.

"All I asked was what happened to his face." He says with a chuckle.

"You idiot," I say.

"Guess I deserved that."

"Are you okay?"

"He let me have it." Sean slowly leans up and whispers in my ear. "Guess we're even now." He laughs before laying back down and coughing.

"Let's get you to the hospital, son," Dad says. He takes Sean into his arms and throws him over his shoulder without a care in the world, before walking off. I start to follow when dad throws me a look. "Go to your quarters, I'll let you know when you can come over."

"But_!"

"NOW!" Dad turns from me and jogs off with Sean over his shoulder like he weighs nothing at all. I sigh softly and walk back to the Headquarters, the minute I step in, I stop in my tracks as I see a very familiar face going up the stairs and turning down the hall towards Emma Jones' office. Claire? I hear the door close after her and I quickly walk up the stairs and run towards the door where I hear her talking to someone inside.

What is she doing here?! Did Raph send her? I press my ear to the door so I can listen in. I quickly pull out my phone and press the record button, wanting to record everything she's saying in case I happen to miss something.

“Alright Ryan what do you want?”

“Aren’t you all grown up Claire Jones? Mommy must me so proud.” Wait, Claire Jones? As in Emma Jones’ daughter?! Holy_.

“Yes she is, what do you want?” Claire repeats. My eyes widen as I realize that Raph was right not to trust her. She’s the Leader of the Society’s daughter!

“As you know daddy died last week.”

“So?” Wow, that family has issues.

“Your mom asked me to take him out and I did.”

“Great one last person to worry about, how do we take her out?” My eyes drop to the floor as I realize that Timothy Ryan isn’t as loyal to Emma Jones as he appears to be. Not only that, her own daughter is plotting against her. Like mother, like daughter I guess.

“There’s a huge dinner, ball thing tonight, all the Head Handlers are coming, I’m thinking we add a little something extra to her wine,” Timothy says.

My hands fly to my mouth as I stand there. I can’t believe what I’m_. Just then, my phone starts to ring. Oh no! I pull it out and right as I turn it off, I see that it was Raph calling me, it’s time to shut the security off.

“What was that?” Claire asks. My head shoots up and my eyes widen, before I bolt down the hall and run up the stairs and into my room before she even gets a chance to think about opening the door. I close the door to the room behind me and lean my back against it as I sit there gasping for air and not believing what I just heard.

I pull out my phone and call Raph back. “When I call you, you’re supposed to answer!” He snaps.

“Miss you too Raph.”

“Hi peaches, how’s it going?”

“Um fine? I just figured out Claire is Emma Jones’ daughter, besides that everything is good. Oh, and Sean is in the hospital. You know what? Things aren’t all that great actually!”

“Why is Sean in the hospital?!”

“He got beat up.” I hear Raph start to laugh and I tap my feet on the floor waiting for him to stop.

“Wait, did you say Claire is Emma Jones’ daughter?!”

“Yes!”

“I knew it!”

“Yeah, you were right, congratulations. Anyway, what do you want?”

“I need you to turn off the securities tonight. We are on our way now and we should be there first thing in the morning.”

“What already?!”

“Yes, is that a problem?”

“No, it’s just that Sean is in the_.”

“You’ll have to do it Peaches. When you turn it off, call me.”

“Okay, I’ll do it.”

“Good girl, see you in the morning.”

“See you.” The phone goes dead and I stand there staring at the phone.

At around noon, I receive a box that contains a gorgeous orange dress inside. I guess I'm supposed to attend this dinner thing that is going on? Great, how am I going to attend the dinner and turn the security system off?!

I get ready for the dinner and get dressed in the orange dress that is shaped much like a flower. It goes all the way to my ankles and it has sleeves that reach my elbow. I let my hair down and place the mask over my face and nod at myself in the mirror. Before I go to the dinner, I'm going to go check on Sean and tell him what's going on. As I open the door to leave the room, I see a man standing there, he has to be at least six feet tall. He's super big, and by big I mean huge! "How can I help you?"

"I'm your supervisor." Dang it! I completely forgot about that!

"Great," I say.

"Where are you off to?" He asks. I pass him on the door and start to walk towards the stairs.

"Going to go visit my husband, he's in the hospital," I say. The man nods and follows after me without another word. How am I going to tell Sean what's happening with this guy following me everywhere?! I exit the Headquarters and walk towards the hospital. Once I get to the hospital I turn to the man and smile. "I know you're doing your job and all, but is there any chance you could let me talk to my husband alone?"

"I suppose so." He murmurs nodding his head.

"Thanks." He nods and proceeds to follow me through the hospital and only stops when we arrive in front of the room Sean is in. "I'll be in there," I say nodding.

"I'll be out here." He nods and leans his back against the wall and stares at me.

"Okay then." I nod and walk inside the room and see dad sitting there. "Hi," I say closing the door behind me.

"Hey sweetie," Dad says.

"Hi Larina," Sean says smiling at me from the bed.

"You okay?"

"Minor concussion," Dad says.

"How hard did that idiot hit you?!" I walk over and sit down on the edge of the bed and take Sean's hand into mine.

"Pretty hard." Sean laughs and smiles up at me. "What are you doing dressed up like that?" Sean asks.

"There's a huge dinner tonight, I'm attending."

"I want to go with you." He starts to sit up but dad places a hand on his shoulder.

"Not a chance son, you're in no shape to attend anything. You stay here and rest, I'll be at the dinner and I'll make sure that I have my 'save Larina mode' on." Sean laughs and nods at dad.

"Thanks, sir."

"Uh huh, I have to go get ready and make sure your mother is ready as well," Dad says turning to me. I nod at him and turn to look at Sean. "Get better soon Clarkson." Dad nods at Sean before leaving the room.

"Your dad is okay," Sean says taking my hands into his.

I shrug, I'm not really sure how to feel about my dad lately. “Raph called me today, he said the security has to be shut down today so he can get here in the morning.”

Sean’s eyes widen as he stares back at me. “What, seriously?”

“Yeah.”

“But_.”

“I’ll have to do it, I mean it can’t be that hard right?” Sean raises an eyebrow at me and I sigh loudly before hanging my head. “Okay so it’ll be hard, but I can do it. I mean you’re in no shape to help me.”

“Larina, I don’t think you should go alone.”

“It’s going to be fine Sean! I’ll come get you as soon as Raph arrives.”

“I’m not sitting in this blasted hospital while you do everything.” He goes to sit up but I place a hand on his chest to stop him.

“Yes you are, you need to get better. Tomorrow is going to be a big day.” I nod and cup his cheek with my hand. “I love you, get better. Okay?”

“Larina_.” He starts.

“Sean_,” I say mimicking his tone. He glares at me and sighs before giving in.

“Don’t get caught.”

“I won’t.”

“And don’t kiss anyone.”

I roll my eyes and shake my head. “You and ruining my plans.” I joke.

"Haha funny," He gives me an annoyed look. "Be careful."

"I will be."

I stand up and give him a big smile before walking out of the room. My bear, er...supervisor walks over to me. "All done and ready to go?" He asks.

"Yes." I nod and we both exit the hospital room and head towards the Headquarters. The minute we get there, my eyes widen as I see every Head Handler from each Sector shaking hands with Timothy Ryan. If only they knew...

"Hello Mrs. Johnson!" Sherrie Maxwell says walking over.

"Hello Head Handler Maxwell." I nod at her and take a step to leave, but she has other plans.

"How have you been?"

"I've been great and you how have you been Ma'am?"

"Just fine! Excited for tonight."

"As am I, if you would excuse me." I nod my head and head towards the main hall where the ball will be held at. There are people prepping for the ball and dinner, I walk inside and the supervisor follows after me. I have to find a way to get this guy off my back, that's when I see mom and dad. I walk straight towards them and stop right in front of dad.

"Handler Matthews, I feel rather uncomfortable with this guy following me everywhere I go. I can't even change without him being there." I say.

"Oh?" Dad looks up at the huge guy and I see right away that I'm not getting any help from him.

“Yes, anything that can be done?” I ask clenching my teeth together and giving dad a death glare.

“You can pretend he’s not there.” Dad grins and wraps an arm around mom. She shakes her head with a smile on her face as she stares back at me.

“Thanks for nothing.” I murmur.

“Anytime!” Dad calls out as I turn to leave.

“I know it’s hard to have someone towing after you Mrs. Johnson, but it is for the safety of all of the citizens of the Society.”

“I know.” I murmur.

“Good, now where exactly are we going?”

“Up to my room until it’s time for the dinner and ball.”

“Good idea.” So I walk to my room with this giant following me. Once I get there I close the door on his face and throw the bolt.

“Sorry big guy, but I don’t feel comfortable with you inside my room when my husband isn’t in here.”

“Understandable Mrs. Johnson. My name is Phillip though.”

“Nice to meet you, Phillip.” I murmur. I stand in the middle of the room, trying to figure out how I’ll get rid of Phillip and turn the security off. My eyes widen and a smile crosses my face as a plan hits me right on the head. I walk over to the bathroom and crouch down before opening the cabinet under the sink and pulling out a shock gun from inside it. Sean hid it in there, for emergencies. This is it. I pull the hem of my dress up to my knees and tuck the gun inside the knee high boots I have on. Can’t take over a whole government in high heels! However, with the dress being so long, no one can tell that I have boots on. Now when the time is right, I'll be able to get rid of Phillip. I walk over to the dresser in the room and grab a pair of rubber gloves and a roll of large tape from one of the drawers. "This should do," I say. I look to the door and smile to myself.

Two hours later, Phillip and I walk into the main hall where everything is fixed for the large dinner to be held in honor of all the "Great" Head Handlers.

As I walk forward and take my seat, I see that Emma Jones isn't here yet. However, there is a lovely red wine sitting in front of her chair at the head of the table. I press my lips together and find Claire at once. She's pretty noticeable from here, she has on the shortest and most revealing dress in the entire place.

"Mrs. Johnson?" Phillip asks.

"Yes?"

"I need to use the restroom."

Oh for crying out loud! "Just go, you don't have to ask for my permission, you have to be twice my age."

"Hmph." He murmurs as he storms off and leaves me there. Once he's gone, I look around the large room to make sure no one is watching me, before I walk over to Emma Jones' seat. I need to get rid of that wine before Emma Jones drinks it. No, not because I like her or anything like that, but because it would cause too much commotion if the Leader of the Society would drop dead and the Rebels don't need everyone in this place on guard.

"Hey!" I freeze up when Claire storms over to me as I have the glass of wine in my hands.

"Yes?" I quickly turn and "Trip" on the leg of the chair and send the wine all over her hair, face, and dress. "Oh my goodness! I am so sorry, let me help you." I take a white napkin and start rubbing at her shocked face. "There you go!" I smile and slowly set the napkin and glass down. "Have a good night Miss Jones."

"You clumsy idiot."

"I hope you choke on that." I murmur before I walk away.

"What?!" I hear her hiss, I don't turn to face her though. I keep walking until I stop right in front of Emma Jones herself.

"Leader Jones!" I say my eyes widening.

"Lora, what just happened over there with my daughter?"

"I tripped and I spilled the wine on her, I feel awful!" I say.

"Accidents do happen. However, why were you with my glass in your hand?" Her cold blue eyes stare down into mine and I know that the only way to not get busted, is, to tell the truth.

"I was going to throw it out," I whisper.

"Why?"

"I heard someone saying they were going to put something extra in your wine tonight." I lower my eyes and quickly look back to her to see her expression. She's standing completely straight and staring down at me. I have her full attention.

"Who was this person Lora?"

"It was Timothy Ryan," I whisper. Her eyes widen and she looks around the room until she sees him from across the room.

“I see, thank you very much, Lora. Your service won’t be forgotten.”

“Of course ma’am.” I nod my head and excuse myself, I have to get up to that security room before Phillip returns from the_. Too late, he’s already rounding the corner.

“Where are you heading to Mrs. Johnson?” He asks.

“I uh, need to go get something from my room.” I lie.

“Okay.” He nods and I take a step forward and he does the same. I sigh softly and make my way towards the staircase, I go up one step above the floor my room is at when Phillip stops me. “Your room is on that floor_.” I spin around and lift my leg to deliver a kick to the side of Phillip’s head. It contacts quite nicely and I watch him start to fall backward. I gasp and quickly grab a hold of his tie and feel myself start to slide from the steps as his weight starts pulling me down. He needs to go down now! “What are you_?” He starts to say once he’s recovered from the kick to the head. I pull out the shock gun and press the trigger three times. He goes limp and I struggle to hold him up. I pull him down a hallway and drag him into an opened room, where I shove him inside a closet. I kneel down next to him and grab the bottom of my skirt and rip it around my knees. I take the ripped up dress piece and tie it around his mouth so he won’t yell for help once he’s awake.

“Alright now give me that big hand of yours.” I take his hand in mine and pull out the tape from my pocket. I unwind the tape and press it softly against his hand, I peel it back and smile at the perfect hand print that is stuck to the tape. I then carefully place the tape to the rubber glove and stand up.

“Goodnight big guy,” I say as I softly close the closet door on him. I jog out of the room and make my way up to the classified rooms. It takes me three minutes to find the security room and once I find it, I place the rubber glove against the scanner on the door. I press my lips together as I watch the light stay red for what seems like hours before the door gives a soft beeping sound and the light turns green. "Yes!" I exclaim. My eyes widen and I clap my hands over my mouth and hurry inside the room.

I close the door behind me and lock it, before turning to look at all the monitors in the room. There are so many different buttons and levers… I walk over to the main monitor and see all the different types of security measures they've placed in the Center. I turn away from the monitors and go to the levers. This is it, I have to turn off all the security systems and the force field. I press my lips together as I stare at all of the levers, buttons, and monitors, feeling really overwhelmed.

I take a lever into my hand that is conveniently labeled "Force field" and flip it off. My whole insides become mush as I feel the entire place start to shake as the force field is lowered into the ground. I hold my breath, my hand still onto the lever and wait for the shaking to stop. Soon it does and I look towards the door, waiting for someone to pound on the door and demand an explanation.

Luckily, no one seems to suspects anything out of the ordinary. They must think it's an earthquake or something of the sort.

I walk over to the monitors and starts switching them all off, one after the other I turn the monitors off. I walk to a desk and throw open a drawer to find some scissors inside. I grab them and walk back to the monitors, I kneel down next to the cords and cut them all. I'm not taking a chance pressing the wrong button, I'm ruining everything instead.

Once everything is done, I stand up and freeze, when I feel someone directly behind me. "You know, it took a while for me to realize why you look so familiar." I spin around and face Claire.

"I knew all along you weren't trustworthy!" I say glaring at her.

"And I knew all along that I hated you, Larina." She grabs at the mask on my face and tears it off of me. "Hi." She waves and I glare at her.

"Give me that back and get out," I say.

She starts laughing and shakes her head like I'm being ridiculous. "Or what?" She pouts as she stares at me.

"Or I'll tell your mom that you were plotting against her." I fold my arms over my chest and smile at her with a "Gotcha." look on my face.

"Puh-lease Larina, do you think my mom is going to choose you, a rebel, instead of her own daughter?"

"No, you're right she'll choose you." I nod my head and look at the floor pretending to be defeated. "Oh, wait!" I shoot my head up and smile as my eyes meet her's, I pull out my phone and wave it in front of her face. "I got a recording of you talking to Timothy Ryan, that could possibly persuade her to be on my side." I wrinkle my nose as I grin at her.

That's when she launches herself at me and sends us both to the floor. "Get off of me!" I snap as roll over, sending her off me and onto the floor, before kneeling down on her arms. "If I so dream of you ruining this for the rebels, I will show this to your mom and you can be erased for all I care!" I snap slapping her on the face with the phone on my hand. She groans at the pain before grabbing at my hair. "OW!!!" I scream. I take a hold of her hair and she starts to scream as well. "Shut up!" I shout pressing my hands hard over her mouth. She murmurs something and I get up and dust myself off. "You can't win this one, Claire!" I say glaring down at her.

"Yes I_." It's really time for her shut up. I pull out the shock gun and press the trigger five times. She goes limp and I smile.

"No, you can't." I open my phone and call Raph. It rings three times before he answers. "Everything is shut down." I look down at the passed out Claire.

"Great job Peaches!"

"Oh and I took Claire Jones down."

"You took someone down?"

"She was threatening to ruin your plan!" I lean down and take the mask she ripped off me into my hands.

"Well good job Peaches."

"So what should I do with her?"

"Give her to Doc."

My eyes widen as I stare straight ahead. "What?"

"Doc, you know Doc Larina!"

"I know Doc, but how am I supposed to_."

"Isn't he there with you? I sent him in so he could be your supervisor. He has a mask on too, we added fake muscles under his shirt. He looks pretty ridiculous, he's going by the name Phillip." My mouth drops as I listen to Raph.

"Raph! He didn't tell me that it was him! I thought he was really Phillip!"

"Huh, why are you so worried?"

"Because I kicked him into next Tuesday and shoved him into a closet!" I snap.

"Holy_." Raph interrupts himself with an unending laugh.

"Raph!"

"Well what do you want me to do? Go wake him up! Good job Peaches, see you in the morning." Raph gives a last laugh before hanging up. I quickly leave the security room, I have to go get poor Doc!

I rush down the hallway, down the stairs, and enter the room I left Doc in. The minute I enter, I stop cold in my tracks and a deep blush settles in my cheeks. "Doc, I'm so sorry. I didn't_."

He takes off the mask and places his glasses over his eyes. "You have quite a kick, Matthews."

"I'm so_."

"I know you're sorry, did you get the security turned off?"

"Yes sir!"

"Good girl."

"Raph told me that you would take care of Claire?" I ask. Doc raises an eyebrow looking confused, so I quickly explain what I'm talking about.

"Alright, take me to her. I'll deal with that and you make sure that you are ready for tomorrow, it's going to be a big day." I nod and turn around to lead him to the security room. I stop once out of the room and turn to look at him.

"Sorry again," I say smiling sheepishly at him.

"It's fine Larina! Seriously, Raph taught you well. You can defend yourself." He nods and smiles.

"But, why didn't you tell me it was you?"

"More convincing if you didn't know."

"Good point." I nod my head and walk up the stairs and straight into the security room and look down at Claire. "You got this then Doc?" I ask.

"You know it."

19

Red Sky

The sky glows an eerie red color as the sun peeks over the horizon and the Rebels march on towards the city. No one knows that they are coming of course, but I know what the red glow in the sky means the minute I see it. It's Raph's signal that he's coming and once he gets here, all hell is going to break loose.

I walk out of my bedroom after I take the device Lu gave to me into my pocket, and make my way to the hospital with my head down, trying not to draw any attention to myself. By now everyone knows the security has been compromised and that all the monitors have been ruined, and everywhere I walk I hear the same word over and over again. "Unaffected"

I throw open the door of the room Sean is staying at and see that he's buttoning up his shirt when I walk in. "Hi." He says smiling at me.

"Did you see it?"

"Yup, what is everyone saying?"

"They don't know what to think about the red glow on the sky, but they think the security being destroyed was the Unaffected doing."

"Good, the last suspicion we have the better." He nods and walks to me. "So what happened last night?"

I look up at him and am about to tell him all about Phillip being Doc and Claire being Jones' daughter when someone throws the door to the hospital room open. We look over at the new person who is second in command to Emma Jones, dad.

“We need all Handlers out there Clarkson, I don’t care if they are your friends. They are going down.” My eyes meet dad’s and he sharply turns away from me and walks out of the room.

“What do we do? They saw them.” I say turning to look at Sean.

“Call Raph.” I pull out my phone and dial Raph’s phone number. I hold it out to Sean and he takes the phone from me. “Raph_.” Sean goes silent and nods as his face takes on a serious expression.

“But_.”

I jump backward as Raph starts screaming from the other line. “Stay there, don’t get caught. We’ll meet up soon enough!” With that, he hangs up and I look at Sean.

“What do we do?” I ask.

“Stay in the city and don’t get caught.” He walks past me and towards the door. “Coming?” He calls out. I sigh and follow after him, with butterflies invading my stomach.

The minute Sean and I step out of the hospital my eyes widen as I stare at the scene in front of me, the rebels have already entered the city. I can easily tell them apart from the Handlers, they are the ones falling to the floor. “Sean what do we_.”

“Keep your head down and follow me.” Sean takes my hand into his and drags me behind the hospital, he takes me down an alleyway and leads me straight into the Headquarters.

“Sean_.” I start.

“Stay in here and stay safe.” He turns to leave.

“What?!” I demand.

“Just stay here!” He snaps turning around to face me.

“I’m not_Ah!” My eyes widen as I look up at him after he takes my shoulders into his hands and holds me there.

“This isn’t looking good Larina, just stay here!” He backs me up until I’m behind the double doors and closes them. “Stay there!” He shouts as he runs outside towards the chaos.

Yeah right, like I’m going to stay in here! I wait for him to get out of view, before throwing open the door and racing outside. I dodge fighting people and firing bullets. This is insane! After several minutes of running and looking around, I find Raph, fighting a Handler next to the hospital.

“Raph!” I say.

“Oh hey, Peaches.” He grins at me and receives a punch to the face.

“Hi, what’s the plan?”

“You’re looking at it.” He kicks at the Handler and the poor guy goes flying backward. “One sec,” Raph says holding up at finger at me and walking over to the Handler. My eyes widen when Raph kills him on the spot. “Where have you been hiding?”

“Sean told me to stay in the Headquarters,” I say.

“Awww, here take this.” He hands me a handgun and I take it from him. “Here’s the plan, no one knows you’re a Rebel yet. So, go inside the Headquarters and find Emma Jones.”

“Then do what?” I look up into his eyes and wait for the answer I’m scared to receive.

“Don’t look so worried, I want her alive. For now.”

“So find Emma Jones and then_?”

“Then take her somewhere safe, I’m assuming she trusts you by now? Behind you!” He shouts. I turn around and see a man running towards me, a knife in his hand. I shoot him in the leg and watch him fall over. Raph turns to me and smiles.

“Sorry,” I whisper to the guy. “She trusts me, I saved her life yesterday,” I say turning to look at Raph.

“Seriously?” I nod and he shakes his head. “Take her somewhere safe, press this button and I’ll come within five minutes.” He hands me a small device. “If I don’t come, it means I’m dead. Then you finish her off, got it?”

“Got it.” I nod and take off running.

“Hey, Peaches!” Raph shouts. I turn around and wait. “I’ve missed you.” I smile and roll my eyes as I turn away from him and run towards the Headquarters. As I’m running I see mom looking around at the horror unfolding before her. I take a step forward and see dad running towards me.

“Take your mother and get inside, now!” He shouts shoving me towards mom. Mom turns to look at me with big, scared eyes. “Go inside with Larina,” Dad says to Mom before he turns to leave.

“What about you Clef?!” Mom shouts running after him.

“I’m going to stay out here and fight, get inside Geo!” He steps back and looks down at mom.

"But_." She stops talking when he captures her in a kiss.

"I love you, go inside, please. I don't want to lose you." He cups her cheek in his hands and kisses the tip of her nose before running off.

"Let's go, mom," I say, taking her hand into mine and dragging her after me.

"Is this your friends' doing?" She asks as we race towards the Headquarters.

"Yes," I whisper.

"Eraser Johnson, Doctor Matthews get inside!" A Handler shouts as he passes mom and I. I nod at her and we enter the Headquarters. The minute I enter a shiver runs down my spine. It's so dark and quiet in here, I have to find Emma Jones and get mom to a safe place. I walk towards Emma Jones' office with mom towing after me. I knock on the door once, but no one answers, so I slowly open the door and scream when a bullet whizzes past my head. I quickly turn to look at mom to make sure she's okay, once I see that she is, I turn back towards the door.

"Leader Jones it's Lora and Doctor Matthews!" I shout.

"Eraser Johnson!" Emma Jones runs towards the door and opens it. "Did I hit you?"

"You missed us by a hair," I say.

"Good, come in." I step inside and pull mom in behind me. Emma Jones closes the door after us and looks over at mom and me.

"Ma'am we need to get you somewhere safe, it's looking really bad out there."

"Follow me." She nods and walks towards the closet, the minute she opens it, I know where she's taking us. The hidden room at the back of the closet. "I had a bunker placed inside here, for such an occasion." She says. She turns to us and smiles. "You both are welcome to come in." I let mom go in first and then I get inside the room and shut the door after us.

The minute the door closes I hear a loud noise coming from above us. Mom covers her ears and sinks to the floor. Emma Jones tries to comfort mom by sitting beside her and telling her how the Rebels will fall. I pull out the device that Raph gave me and push the button, now all I have to do is wait for Raph to get here.

"Do you think my husband is alive?" Mom asks looking at Emma Jones.

I look down at her and press my lips together. "Clef is a good Handler Geo, he's probably fine. He's my second in command now. I chose him for a reason." That seems to calm mom's worries. Emma Jones looks up at me and catches me off guard by her question. "And where's Mike?"

"He's out there," I whisper. Worry floods my insides as I stare down into her blue eyes, time is ticking away and soon Raph will barge in and take her down.

"He's such a brave young man." Emma Jones says.

"Yes, he is," Mom says looking up at me with a worried look.

I slowly ease myself besides mom and she takes my hand into hers. "They'll be fine." She whispers. I only nod and look down at the device in my hands.

More then five minutes go by, but there is no sign of Raph. Where is he?! He was supposed to have come by now! His words play back in my head. “If I don’t come, it means I’m dead. Then you finish her off, got it?”

Raph didn’t come, does that mean he’s dead? I slowly stand up and both mom and Emma Jones looks up at me. “Did you hear something?” Emma Jones asks when I pull out the gun.

“No.” I rip the mask from my face and her eyes widen as she shoots up to her feet. “My name is Larina Matthews, I’m with the Rebellion and your time as the Leader has come to an end.” I put my finger to the trigger and just as I’m about to push it, mom jumps to her feet.

“Larina Matthews! I forbid you to shoot this woman!” She shouts. I look at mom and shake my head.

“Mom, stay out of this.”

“Mom?! She’s your daughter?!” Emma Jones throws a look at mom and I sigh. I aim the gun at Emma Jones once again and mom snaps at me one more time.

“Mom seriously I_.” Just then the doors are thrown open to the bunker and standing there are Raph, Silv, Jake, and Sean.

“Sorry, I’m late,” Raph says entering the room with a gun pointed at Emma Jones.

“Oh my God!” Mom screams. I for one, am glad to see the four of them for several reasons. Reason one: They are alive. Reason two: I don’t have to kill anyone!!!

I lower my gun and the minute I do, a gun is pointed right at me, by none other than Emma Jones herself. I tense up at once and look over at mom, I’m pretty sure she’s going to watch her daughter die.

“Drop the gun, Jones,” Sean says pointing his gun at her. I look over at him and see that he has blood running down his arm. His eyes meet mine and I see that he’s scared, I’m scared too.

“How about I don’t?” I see the minute that Emma Jones presses the trigger, I see when mom knocks her over sending the bullet not into my head, but my stomach. I scream and fall to the floor, right as I hit the floor someone else screams and falls directly beside me. I groan and I ease myself up and look at the fallen person. Emma Jones lays dead in front of me. I scream and scoot backward until my back hits the wall, I wrap my arms around my stomach, where the bullet entered and stay there staring at her.

“Larina?!” Sean crouches down beside me and takes my face into his hands.

“I’m fine,” I say looking into his eyes.

“Liar.”

“You’re bleeding too.”

“We’re all bleeding! We’re all hurt, let’s get the hell out of here before someone finds out that Sean killed Jones!” Raph snaps. I look up at him and my eyes widen when I see several Handlers standing in the hallway.

“Round them up, boys.” The eldest Handler says. He walks into the room and watches as the other Handlers march in and take each of us by the arm, holding guns to our heads. “Doctor Matthews, you’re safe now.” The Handler says walking over to mom.

“Please, that’s my daughter,” Mom says reaching out to me as I’m dragged away.

The last thing I hear as the door closes behind me hurts more than the wound on my stomach. “I’m sorry Doctor

Matthews, we have orders from your husband. All Rebels are to be erased."

I'm doubled over as I'm lead to the Erasing Facility along with Sean, Jake, Silv, and Raph. "We lost." I hear Jake say as we are lead into the room.

The Handler leading me inside shoves me and I trip and am sent to the floor, where I land on my stomach. I scream and hold myself into a ball on the floor. The pain from the wound is spreading all over my body, the pain from my own dad ordering my death is all over my heart. Everything inside me seems to hurt, and I don't know how I remember it, but I do. I pull out the device Lu gave me and press the button, before tucking it away inside my pocket. He said to push the button in case things went bad, well they did.

"Larina," Sean whispers sitting beside me and holding me to him. "I'm so sorry." He scoops me up in his arms and wraps me in an embrace.

"Raph, what do we do?" Jake asks. I look up at Raph and wait for him to say something. "Raph?"

"I don't know." Raph slumps to the floor and covers his face with his hands. I sit there in Sean's arms looking over at Raph and wondering how this all happened, and all at once three words come to me. "It's dad's fault." If dad wasn't the new Leader, if he wasn't so loyal to the Society, if he didn't choose it over his own family, the Rebels could have won.

Sean killed Emma Jones, this should have all come to an end. I never thought about dad being the cause of our downfall. Poor mom.

We all look towards the door when an Eraser enters the room. "Alright Rebels, how does it feel to lose?" She grins at us and walks over to the chair. "Every time someone rises against the Society, they fail. There is no overthrowing the Society, you can't win and that's why every last one of your Rebel friends is going to die." She turns to us with a syringe in her hand that is filled with the death serum. "So, who's first?" None of us expects anyone to volunteer, but when Jake does, my eyes widens. "I'll go first." He whispers.

"Jake no!" I shout. Sean helps me up and I walk to him. "Don't do this!" I say.

"Miss Larina, I was supposed to have been erased months ago. You gave me more time and I'm so grateful to you." Jake takes my face into his hands. "Let me give you more time." He leans in and plants a soft kiss on my cheek.

"Jake_." I start. The Eraser grabs a hold of Jake and sits him down on the chair before restraining him, which is unnecessary. Jake isn't even putting up a fight, he's just sitting there, waiting to be killed. I approach the Eraser and am about to launch myself at her when she turns sharply to me with a gun in her hand.

"I'll make sure you go first, girl." She says.

"NO!" Sean screams. He pulls me back and the Eraser laughs.

"How cute, you can only save her for so long Rebel scum." She turns her attention to Jake and inches the needle closer to his neck. "You broke the law, you left the Society and you killed the Leader and because of that, you will all die!" With that, she stabs Jake in the neck with the needle and my scream carries out across the room as I stare at him going limp.

"Jake?" I whisper, but he's gone. Dead.

Sean takes me into his arms. I stare at the Eraser as she goes on with the erasing, cremating, and finally turning to Raph so she can kill him next. “Raph, no,” I whisper as he sits down on the chair.

“Don’t worry Peaches.” He says.

“Oh, I’d worry if I were you.” The Eraser says with a laugh.

Just then someone barges into the room and shoots the Eraser three times before looking at the four of us.

“Lu!”

20

Escape?

"Yeah, I'm happy to see you guys too. Good thing you called me Larina, things couldn't be worse." Lu says as he walks over to Raph and undoes his restraints.

"Thanks, Lu."

"No problem." Lu nods and turns to look at Sean, Silv, and I. "We need to get going, if we stay here we'll end up like all the others." Lu heads for the door and stops when Raph asks him a question.

"The others? Is everyone_."

"Everyone attacked the Sectors Raph, they were all caught. I escaped Sector 25C and came here as soon as I got Larina's call, you were lucky I was only one Sector over." I stare at Lu as he tells Raph that all the other Rebels were caught, they are all going to be erased.

"How did you call Lu?" Raph asks turning to look at me.

I ignore him and ask: "Can we save them?"

"Not without dying, and you look like you're getting there." Lu walks over to me and lifts my shirt up, which makes me blush. "We have to take that bullet out of there later. For now, let's just bandage you up and stop the bleeding." Lu quickly wraps my stomach with some bandages and lets my shirt drop. "That should do it, for now, alright she can't walk without slowing us down so_." Lu scans the room and his eyes lands on Silv. "You carry her."

Silv only nods and walks over to me, right as he's about to take me into his arms, Sean steps up. "I can carry her."

"Not a chance lover boy, your arm is badly injured, you'll slow us down carrying her."

"But_."

"No buts about it Sean, let's get going!" Raph says. He follows Lu out of the room and Silv scoops me up in his arms and I look up into his gray eyes.

"Thanks, Silv."

"Had to return the favor at some point, I guess." He murmurs. I look over at Sean, who doesn't look too happy with my current situation.

"Let's go!" Raph shouts, poking his head back in the door. Silv jogs out of the room, with me in his arms and Sean follows after us, holding the back.

We sneak down the hallway, and I close my eyes as we pass doors with screaming people inside it. This has to be harder for Raph, he must recognize all those screams. "Come on Raph," Lu says turning back and seeing how Raph is about to emotionally lose it. Raph starts to slow down and Silv passes him so that we are right behind Lu.

"Alright here's the thing, we can't go back to the base. Anyone know where we can go?"

"I know a place," Sean says running up to Lu.

"Alright, type in the coordinates there." Lu hands Sean a small pad and Sean starts to typing in the coordinates of the place.

"Where are you thinking Clarkson?" Silv asks.

“The Unaffected,” Sean says. Lu, Raph, and Silv all stare at Sean with a confused look on their faces. “We’ll talk about it when we are out of here!”

“He’s right, we don’t have time to sit around and talk. We need to get out of the Center.” Lu says. We round a corner and I see the entrance of the Facility.

“How do we get out?” I ask.

“The monorail station.” He says.

“What?!” My eyes widen as I stare at him.

“Just focus on staying alive, let me deal with the whole getting us out of here thing alright?!” Lu snaps at me before slowly walking out of the building. Sean smiles softly at me and nods for Silv to go next. We walk out of the building, and from here I can see a group of Rebels being led into the Headquarters.

“Raph can’t we_.” I start.

“Shut up.” Silv whispers. I clamp my mouth shut and hang my head as Silv follows Lu down an alleyway.

“Alright, so how do we get out of here without being spotted?” Raph asks shoving his hands deep into his pockets. Silv sets me down on the floor and nods at me before walking over to Raph and Lu.

I zone out as Silv, Sean, Raph and Lu talk about a plan. My vision is getting blurry and I find myself grabbing at my stomach a few times before Sean looks over at me. I watch him walk over and crouch down in front of me before taking my face into his hands. “Larina?” He asks.

“So what’s the plan?” I ask, ignoring the worried look on his face.

“Are you okay?”

"My stomach is hurting, but I'm fine."

"Can't we get the bullet out now Lu?" Sean asks looking over at Lu.

"No." With that Lu goes back to talking to Raph, at the end of the conversation the plan is that we might lose someone. Someone has to run out and grab the Handlers' attention so that the rest of us can run to the station.

"That's an awful plan," I say.

"It has to be done though," Lu says. He straightens up and nods at Raph before taking a step out of the alley.

"Lu!" Raph shouts. Lu stops and turns to look at Raph. "Don't die."

"Thanks." Lu murmurs before running out of the alley and straight towards some Handlers. I watch him pull out two guns and shoot them in the air.

"Hey, there's one!" A Handler shouts. Three Handler starts pursuing Lu.

"That's our cue, let's go!" Raph says.

Right as we are about to leave the alley, someone sneaks up on us. Raph pulls out a gun and the person quickly removes the mask that is over his face. I watch Raph lower the gun and look over at me. "Mom?!" I ask. She walks over to me, in Silv's arms and hugs me which makes Silv really uncomfortable.

"My baby, you're hurt." She says looking down at the blood that has seeped through my white shirt.

"I'm okay mom really."

"Mrs. Matthews, we really have to go," Sean says walking over to mom. "If we don't, we'll get caught."

“I’m so glad you’re alive sweetie,” Mom says completely ignoring Sean.

“Mom_.”

“Follow me, I’ll get you to the station.” She nods and heads out of the alley. We all exchange looks and hesitantly follow after mom who is walking straight towards the station like nothing is going on.

“Doctor Matthews, you caught all of those?” A Handler shouts out.

“Yes, taking them to the next Sector over, this one is already too full.” She calls out.

“Do you need back up ma’am?”

I watch mom pull out a gun and shake her head. “I got it, thank you.” The Handler nods and walks on to pursue other Rebels.

“Thank you, Mrs. Matthews,” Raph says. We all stop in our tracks when we hear a scream coming from behind us. I look and see Lu, fighting off the three Handlers, my eyes widen as two of the Handlers take each of Lu’s arms and the other rips the mask of his face. My mouth drops as a dark cascade of long hair falls down, over and around Lu’s shoulder. Wait… Lu is a girl?! The Handlers come to a complete halt at seeing that the “Guy” they had been fighting is a girl.

“A friend of yours?” Mom asks.

“Yes,” I say not believing what I’m seeing. I watch mom walk over and shout at the three Handlers.

“I’ll take it from here thank you.” Mom snaps glaring at the three Handlers and daring them to overstep her, after all, she is the wife of the Leader.

“Doctor Matthews, we_.” One Handler starts to say.

"The Center is filled with Rebels being erased, I'll take them to the next Sector over. If you have a problem with that, you can go speak to my husband." I can see the color drain from the Handler's face and for some reason, the color drains out of mom's face as she looks at Lu.

"No need Ma'am." The Handler nods and leads the other Handlers away. I watch Lu look over at mom and for a split second I think she's going to shoot mom, She doesn't. She simply stands there in complete shock as mom throws her arms around her and starts to cry. Lu's arms are at her sides as she stands there, wondering why my mom is hugging her.

"I guess you'd find out soon enough." I hear Raph murmur. Mom steps back and takes Lu's face into her hands and kisses her cheeks. I press my lips together feeling really confused, only when mom and Lu walk over I understand why mom is acting the way she is.

Lu is Luisa my twin sister. My eyes meet Lu's and she nods over at me. "Larina this is_." Mom starts.

"We've met," I say.

"You've_."

"Only I always thought she was a guy." I turn and glare at my sister. "Why didn't you tell me you were my sister?!" I demand.

"Because it didn't matter." She coils her long hair in a sloppy bun above her head and boards the monorail. I look after her and turn to Raph.

"She told me not to bring it up, Peaches."

"I can't believe this," I say.

“I’m so happy, both my babies are alive!” Mom says. I look over at mom and shake my head, I’m speechless. Completely speechless.

We all stop talking when dad’s voice sounds over the speakers at the monorail station. “Attention all residents of the Center.” He says. I exchange looks with Sean. “All Rebels have been caught and are being erased, they were not able to take the Society down. We continue to stand strong and undefeated as always. Let this be a sign to anyone who ever tries this little stunt again, no one will be spared. You cannot take us down!”

“We have to get out of here,” Raph says. He looks over at Silv, who starts to carry me inside the monorail.

“Wait!” I say. I turn to look at mom who is still standing outside looking up at us. “Mom, come with us,” I say.

“Oh honey, I love you and I’m so proud of you. But I can’t leave your father, I know that both my babies are okay and alive.”

“But mom he’s_.”

“He’s doing what he thinks is right.” Mom whispers.

“No he’s_.”

“Hate to break this up, but there are Handlers coming and the monorail is about to leave. Let’s go!” Lu shouts before she disappears inside the cart.

“She’s a lot like your father.” Mom whispers. Mom reaches over and takes my hand into hers. “Be safe sweetie.” She nods and takes a step back. “I love you, Larina.”

“I love you too mom.” I look down as Silv enters the monorail and sets me down on a seat. Sean takes the seat next to me and holds me to him.

As the monorail starts to move, I look out the window and watch mom become smaller and smaller and tears start to slide down my eyes.

“Get down, everyone. We’re going to be passing Sectors, at Sector 1A we get off.” Raph says.

Sean helps me down from the seat, and we sit on the floor between two seats. I stare at the ground, replaying everything that happened.

The Rebels invaded, they lost, we were caught, Jake died, Lu saved us, Lu is a girl, Lu is my sister, she never told me…

“Lover-boy,” Lu calls out walking over to Sean, before sitting down beside him.

“What?”

“When we get off the monorail, you lead us to this place of yours.” Sean nods. “You have the transmitter that I gave you?” She asks.

“Yes.”

“Good, hope you’re all comfy it’s going to be a long twelve-hour ride,” Lu says leaning the back of her head against the front of the seat. I watch her close her eyes and cross her left leg over her right one. “Stop staring at me.” She says with her eyes still closed. I drop my eyes to the floor and sigh. Well, at least she’s alive.

After three hours of riding on the monorail, the sun sinks down behind the mountains leaving the world in complete darkness. Everyone seems to be asleep, everyone but me.

I give a soft sigh and Lu's eyes open. She looks over at me and gives me a soft smile. "How are you holding up Larina?" She whispers.

"How do you think I'm holding up? We lost Lu, my… Our dad wanted to have me killed, he's the leader now and not only that, I'm still trying to figure out why you never told me you are my sister."

"I never told you because it wasn't important like I said."

"How is it not important Luisa? I never knew you existed, you probably never knew I existed and then I thought you were erased at birth."

"Well, I wasn't. Our lovely dad_." She throws me a sarcastic look, which makes me give away to a smile. "Brought me to the abandoned city, Raph's parents took me from him and raised me as their own."

"You grew up beside Raph then?" I ask.

"Yes, I did. Then his parents died and well, Raph became the leader and I became second in command."

"Wow."

"Yeah, how's your stomach?" She asks nodding down at my bandaged stomach. Sean removed the bullet from inside me, it hurt a lot and I had to bite my tongue so I wouldn't scream. Now the pain is just numb.

"Fine."

"Hm, well for all it's worth… I'm glad we got to meet." I reach over and squeeze her hand.

"Me too." I smile and she smiles back at me.

"Alright, I'm going to sleep. You should too Larina." I nod and turn away from her when she closes her eyes.

Sean told me that the place we're heading is the hidden city that belongs to the Unaffected. "The Valley" I never do end up going to sleep, I look up and out of the window at the sky, as we pass Sector after Sector.

At dawn, I sit up on the seat and look out at the end of Sector 1A. The sun starts to rise from behind the mountains, it illuminates the plains, fields and the entire world.

The light of the sun gives me hope that I thought I lost. Hope that things will be better. Better with the Unaffected.

Preview of The Unaffected

The Unaffected

Larissa Willits

This book was originally published in hardcover by Larissa Willits in 2017.

ISBN-13: 978-1545041253

ISBN-10: 1545041253

For J.H.

1

City among mountains

The sun has risen high up in the sky by the time that we get off the monorail at the station in Sector 1A. Luckily for us, the station is at the edge of the city and beyond that, the Society has no control of. Sector 1A is the last Sector that is under the Society, once we pass the border we take off running past the fields and up into the mountainous regions.

Luisa, my twin sister, I didn't know I had until a few hours ago, and Raph is leading us. Silv is holding the back, looking gloomier than usual. Sean is holding the transmitter that Luisa gave him and telling her and Raph which way to go. Then there's me, Larina Matthews. I'm silently trailing along thinking about all that has happened, I walk slowly and Silv has stepped a few times on my heel to remind me to pick up my pace. Well, it's hard to walk fast when you have a bullet wound on your stomach! Sure Sean removed the bullet, however, this thing needs some stitches!

We walk on towards the hidden city run by the Unaffected, leaving behind the Sectors that remain under the Society's control. Under my father's control.

After an hour of walking in a straight path through two huge mountains, Sean looks up from the transmitter. "Up that mountain." He says. I crane my neck up to see the top of the mountain he's pointing to, of course, it has to be the tallest mountain… "There should be a valley down at its base, and that's where their city should be."

"Hope you're right lover boy," Luisa says sighing a little as we start to hike up the tall mountain.

The sun is right over us, making us pretty visible even from far away. We could easily be spotted by any flying hover crafts that decide to pass by.

"Your transmitter is the one telling me which way to go." Sean points out. After that we go on in silence, the mountain starts to get steeper towards the middle of it.

"Let's stop here for a second," Raph says slumping down on a huge boulder. Luisa, Silv, Sean and I all sit down around the boulder and look behind us. I can see so much from up here.

"I think that two of us should go up this mountain and see if the city is really down there, and if it is, then we go down and explain everything to them," Raph says.

"That's a good idea," Sean says nodding.

"So_." Raph looks around and smiles softly at me. "Sean and I will go up and we'll come back to get you guys," Raph says standing up. Sean stands up as well and looks down at me.

"You'll be okay right?" He asks.

"Yeah." I nod and watch as Sean and Raph start to scale up the tall mountain, soon they are nothing but specks up in the distance.

"Can't believe we made it!" I say smiling as I try to lighten the mood.

"Almost," Lu says.

"If they let us in that is." Silv murmurs. Lu rolls her eyes at his negativity and turns back to me.

"How's the wound?"

"It's hurting again, but I don't think it's bleeding anymore, so that's good."

All the sudden I feel myself being dragged as Silv screams: "Get down!" Silv takes Lu's and my hands in his and drags us under the ledge of the mountain.

"What is it?" I ask peeking out from under the rocks that are hiding us.

"Hover board." He points at something and I see a single hover board riding straight for us. Whoever is in that thing, will easily see Sean and Raph.

"Larina, give me your gun," Lu says holding out her hand. I take the gun in my hands and hold it out to her, she takes it and stands up and aims it at the person in the hover board.

Five seconds later, she lowers the gun and grins back at Silv and I. "What are you doing?!" Silv demands, getting up to his feet.

"It's Doc!" She smiles widely and runs over to the edge of the mountain to meet him. I half walk, half run after her feeling glad that Doc made it!

Doc lands the hover board and throws his arms around Lu and I. "Hi kids." He says, messing our hair up.

"Doc! How did you get away?" I ask.

"Well, you asked me to take care of Claire, so I left the Center just in time for Raph to march in. Unfortunately, during all that commotion, Claire got away." I shrug, not really caring about what happens to her. "Raph asked me to head into 1A to help the Rebels that were invading there. By the time I got to 1A, everyone was taken captive, I tried to save some of them, but it was no use." Doc hangs his head and sighs softly. "Where are your boyfriends?"

"They are climbing up the mountain." I say at the same time that Lu says: "He's not my boyfriend!" I see a tint of red on her cheeks.

"Bet they could have used the hover board huh?" Doc asks. He places his hand up to his forehead to shield his eyes from the sun and nods. "Yup, they could have used the Hover board."

"I'll take it up to them, then I'll come back," Silv says walking over. Doc nods and hands the hover board to Silv. "Stay hidden," Silv says looking directly into my eyes.

"Okay," I say nodding. He nods and I watch as he hovers up to where Sean and Raph must be at.

"So tell me what happened," Doc says looking at Lu and I. We sit down on the hard floor of the mountain and Doc joins us. Lu tells him her part of the story, the marching towards the Sectors and having to save Raph, Sean, Silv and I. She leaves out the part where she met mom.

"And you Larina?"

"Everything started going downhill fast. Sean killed Jones and I was shot, he was shot, everyone was dying and then Lu came and saved us like she said."

"And you found out that she's your twin."

"There's that too," I say smiling over at her. "Our dad is the Leader of the Society now, he ordered all our deaths, including mine," I whisper.

"What are you going to do about it?" Doc asks, giving me a deep frown.

"I'm going to take him down." Lu looks over at me and presses her lips together. She opens her mouth to say something when Raph appears out of nowhere.

"They are there." He says panting a little as he doubles over in exhaustion.

"They are?!" I ask jumping up to my feet.

"They are, you won't believe it Peaches. It's amazing!" He says grinning at me.

"Let's go then!" I start for the mountain when Raph takes my shoulder in his hand.

"Hold it Peaches, your wound is starting to bleed again. You take the hover board and Lu, Doc and_." Raph stops and grins when he realizes Doc is here. "Doc you made it!"

"Sure did Minkus."

"That's great! Well, Larina go up on the hover board. We'll meet you up there, okay?"

"Are you sure?" I ask.

"Would you go already? Before I take it?" Lu asks, gently shoving me towards the mountain. I nod and jump up on the board.

"Thanks, Raph," I say nodding.

"Sure thing Peaches." He smiles and the board starts to slowly ascend. The higher I get, the more scared I feel. When I reach the very top of the mountains, my knees buckles and I feel myself getting dizzy.

"Over here!" Silv says waving me over to where he and Sean are at. I press forward, despite the fact that I'm starting to see two of everything. I never knew I was afraid of heights...

I feel myself lose my balance, my feet slips and I feel the hover board fly to the right and I'm left standing on air. I start to fall fast, and I squeeze my eyes shut. I hold my breath as the floor gets closer, but I never make contact with it. I look up into Sean's eyes as he stares down into mine after catching me.

"Oh my God." He murmurs. I look down and my eyes widen as I see that he caught me just in time, I was about to fall back down the mountain. There would have been no coming back from that. Sean takes one step back after the other until we are safely away from the edge of the mountain.

"You_." I start but stop when he brings me closer to him.

"You scared me!" He says letting out a slow breath.

"I scared me too," I say with a laugh.

"Great job, you broke the Hover board," Silv says nodding over to where the Hover board crashed against the floor. Sean throws Silv a glare and let me say something: if glares could kill.

"Are you okay?" Sean asks looking down at me.

"I'm fine thanks to you, are you okay?"

"I'm fine Larina, you're the one that just fell."

"Yeah but that was a_."

"Oh my God! You're both okay, you didn't die. Stop with the Lovey-dovey stuff already!" Silv barks at us. Sean and I exchange looks before we look back at Silv.

"I love you, Larina," Sean says clearly trying to annoy Silv.

“I love you too Seany woony.” Sean lets out a loud laugh, before setting me on my feet.

“Gross,” Silv says shaking his head.

“I think they’re cute,” Raph says walking over with Luisa and Doc. “You okay Peaches?”

‘She’s fine!” Silv shouts.

“Calm down dude,” Lu says throwing a small pebble at him. Silv rolls his eyes and looks down the mountain.

“So who’s going down there?” Silv asks shoving his hands into his pocket.

“Can you make it there without bleeding out?” Lu asks looking at my stomach, that has begun bleeding again.

“That’s why I want her down there fast,” Sean says picking me up in his arms again.

“Sean_.” Raph starts.

“I want to get her to a doctor.” He says.

“What am I? Chopped liver?” Doc asks crossing his arms over his chest.

“A Doctor with tools that can stitch her up,” Sean explains.

“Okay Sean, you get her down there and check things out. When you know we can go in, come get us.” Raph says.

“Okay.” Sean nods and starts heading down the mountain.

“Be careful lover boy!” Lu calls out.

“I will be!” Sean calls back. I smile and look down at the floor. For some reason, this side of the mountain has a little dirt path leading straight towards its base.

As we get closer to the base of the mountain, Sean stops and his eyes widen as does mine. In the Valley between the Mountains, stands a city as strong as any city run by the Society. Only this one resembles the Old City, minus all the vegetation taking over the buildings part.

There are houses, that all look different from one another, cars, that the Society no longer has. Trees! They have trees right inside the city, along with flowers and lakes! It’s so beautiful, but it’s all hidden at eye level, by a tall and dark wall made completely out of stone.

“Wow, look at that,” Sean says as we near the stone wall.

“I can walk now,” I say trying to get down from his arms.

“Stop it, you can walk after you’re stitched up. I don’t want you dying on me.”

“Sean, if I were going to die, I would have done it a while ago. I’ll tell you if I plan on it.”

“Fine.” He slowly sets me down and we walk alongside the huge wall, trying to locate an entrance. We walk about a hundred feet or so along the wall when someone steps in front of our path. The man stares down at us with a glare so harsh, I’m forced to look away.

“Who are you? What do you want?” He asks studying us closely.

“My name is Sean Clarkson, and this is Larina Matthews. We came from Sector 7B of the Society.” I throw him a look of disbelief. Why did he go and tell him where we came from?! I'm sure, these people don't want anyone from the Society anywhere near their city.

"You are Society spies?!" The man asks pulling out a huge gun. See?!

"No!" I shout. The man looks at me and raises his eyebrow. "Sir, we escaped there. We are with the Rebels, we tried to take the Society down and failed. We have six people in our party including us two."

"So what do you want from us?"

"We were hoping to speak to your Leader, we'd like to see if he would allow us to live here?" Sean asks.

"And why would we want you here?" The man asks slinging his gun over his shoulder.

"We stopped an attack that the Society planned in your city. Sean and I did." I say. The man narrows his eyes at me and looks me up and down.

"You're bleeding?" He asks.

"I got shot," I whisper.

"Fine, go get your friends." The man says looking at Sean. He then looks at me. "Come in, let's get you to the hospital."

I smile widely and nod my head. "Thank you so much sir!"

"Of course, as soon as you are stitched up you will go speak to President Mcaffee"

"President?" Sean asks.

"That's what we call our Leader." The man explains.

“Oh.” Sean and I say at the same time. “I’ll go get the others, go with him okay Larina?” Sean asks.

“Okay.” I nod and watch as he jogs away and up the mountain to get the others.

“Alright, you come with me.” The man says. I follow after him as he walks a few yards down the wall. He stops suddenly and looks at a small panel on the wall. He throws it open and punches in a code that I don’t quite catch and I watch as the wall rumbles before splitting down the middle and sliding to its sides, opening a large entrance to the city.

“How_.” I start.

“This is no ordinary wall. It’s covered by stone, but there are wires and electricity running along this whole place. The Valley is protected by this wall, it’s a huge circle really.” The man explains.

“That’s amazing!” I say.

“Yes, now let's get you to the hospital before you bleed out, alright? Then I have to go and take your friends to the President.” I nod and slowly follow after him as he walks into the city. I get lost in thought as I look around this place, several people stop what they are doing as we pass them. They all look at me, I must look so weird to them, dressed all in white and bleeding…

“Alright, get in.” I look back at the man and see him standing in front of a yellow car. “This is a taxi cab.” He explains. I nod and look inside at the guy who is driving it.

“Hello,” I say.

“Take her to the hospital will you Bob? She’s hurt.” The man says.

“No problem, hop in kiddo.” Bob, the driver says. I ease myself into the seat of the car and look around in it. It’s a lot like a giant box and it sure is less advanced than a hovercraft. “Ready to go kid?” He asks.

“Yes sir, I’m ready.” I nod and he drives off after the man that lead me into the city closes one of the four doors.

“How did you get hurt like that?” Bob asks.

“I got shot.” His eyes widen as he stares at me.

“Alright then.” I notice that he speeds up once I’ve told him that I’ve been shot, maybe he’s afraid that I will die? “We’re here, this is the hospital.” He says. I look out the tainted window and my eyes widen. Their hospital is a lot different than the ones at the Society. It’s a tall, rectangular, white building with a gazillion windows. There are red letters that spell out "Hospital" on top of the door. “Well don’t just sit around here, get inside will you?!” Bob says getting out of the car and opening the door for me.

“Sorry,” I say.

“No problem, I’ll walk you in.” I nod and follow after him up the stone path that leads to the main entrance. Bob opens the door, by hand, and leads me forward. The first thing I notice about the place is that it smells like nothing. Back in the Society, the hospitals smell like medicine and chemicals. “Stop gawking around!” Bob snaps pushing me towards the front desk.

“How can I help you?” The lady at the front desk asks. I look at her as she stares back at me. She has thick black hair, pale skin and oval glasses that covers her blue eyes. “Well?”

“She got shot,” Bob says.

"Oh dear!" The lady shoots up out of her seat and walks to me. "Let's get into a room right away." She proceeds to drag me down a hallway and into a room. "Lay down, I'll get a doctor to see you right away!"

I don't even have time to say thanks before she speeds off, leaving me standing in the middle of the room. I look towards the metal bed that has white covers in it and walk over to it. I ease myself down into it and hold my hands together as I wait there for the doctor to walk in.

"Hello, so I heard you've been shot?" I look up five minutes later at the blonde woman that has walked in, she reminds me a lot of Sherrie Maxwell.

"Yes, I have."

"Very odd. Let us take a look shall we?" She approaches me and lifts my shirt up. "You've removed the bullet?" She asks.

"My boyfriend did."

"Smart boyfriend." She smiles up at me and lets my shirt drop back into its place. "Alright, we'll get you stitched up and out of here in no time alright? What's your name sweetie?"

"Larina Matthews."

"Pretty name, I'm Doctor Shona." She holds out her hand to me and I take it. "It's nice to meet you Larina."

"You too Doctor Shona." I smile at her and she walks over to a desk at the far back of the room and brings back a stitching kit.

"It's going to pinch a little."

Thirty minutes later, I'm all stitched up and ready to leave the hospital to go meet the President. "You come back in a few weeks and we'll get the stitches out for you alright?" Doctor Shona says as she leads me to the door.

"Yes, ma'am." I smile at her and take a step out of the room, I stop though when I remember something. "Uh, where are my friends?"

"I believe they are at the House." I stare at her, wondering what "The House" is. "Oh, you're new here aren't you? It's the triangular building at the very end of the city, it's where President Mcaffee lives."

"Oh okay."

"It's pretty close from here, just a few blocks away." I nod and walk out of the hospital. When I step out, I'm met by Raph, Silv, Sean, and Lu.

"And she lives!" Lu says walking over to me and messing my hair up.

"Yeah, yeah," I say sticking my tongue out at her.

"How are you feeling?" Sean asks walking over.

"Okay, actually." I smile and look at my friends. "What do you guys think?"

"This place is weird." Silv, of course, has to be negative.

"It's incredible!" Raph says grinning at me.

"We need to go talk to the President," I say looking up at him.

"So we've heard, I expected as much though," Raph says.

"It's supposed to be a triangular building," I say as we start to walk away from the hospital.

"Think that's it?" Sean asks when we've walked for about ten minutes and are standing across the street from a giant, upside down, triangular building that is made entirely of glass.

"Think if we throw a rock at it, the whole thing will fall apart?" Lu asks, grinning. She bumps shoulders with me and walks over to stand beside Raph.

"Don't," Raph warns as he starts to cross the street. I follow after him, and Sean follows after me. Silv holds the back, he seems comfortable there.

I look up at the odd building and wonder what kind of person lives in a place like this. Unlike all the other buildings and the entire city itself, it's very futuristic looking. It sure stands out among a city that it's theme seems to be "Before the Society"

We enter the weird building and are at once met by two men who talk only to Raph. "You are the Rebels?" One of them asks him. Raph only nods.

"The President will see you in her office, follow us." The man leads us down a hallway and as I walk behind Lu and Raph, I look around me and find it strange that no matter where I look, I can see the city outside. There are many different rooms that aren't made out of glass of course, but all the outer walls are. "Knock and you may enter." The man says once we arrive in front of white, double doors.

Raph nods at the two man and knocks once before a woman's voice comes through the door. "Come in."

Raph opens the door and stops in the middle of the doorway. I look up at him and wonder what's wrong, then Luisa freezes as she stares upon the President and my heart stops beating, fearing the worst.

Then Raph speaks. "Sandra?"

Author's Note

My name is Lari, I'm originally from Brazil but now I live in the US with my family. I'm a writer and singer(When no one is listening) I'm inspired by the Society around us and the events surrounding our times. I've loved writing since I was twelve years old, when an Author came to give a speech at my school. He said anyone could become an Author and so after nine years and many many stories later, I decided to publish my first book!

I wrote The Society when I was sixteen and in high school. However, back then it was called "Experiment of the Government" Yeah that's a mouth full!

I brought that story back after five years, and made some adjustments and worked on it for a while until it became The Society that you just read!

I'm glad that I brought it back, because I truly love the story and I hope you did too.

Thanks for reading!

Love- Lari.

Made in the USA
Columbia, SC
06 July 2017